HUNTERLAND

HUNTERLAND

DANA CLAIRE

CamCat
Books

CamCat Publishing, LLC
Brentwood, Tennessee 37027
camcatpublishing.com

This is a work of fiction. Names, characters, places, and incidents are either products of the author's imagination or are used fictitiously.

Hardcover ISBN 9780744307344
Paperback ISBN 9780744307351
Large-Print Paperback ISBN 9780744307368
eBook ISBN 9780744307375
Audiobook ISBN 9780744307382

Library of Congress Control Number: 2022941967

Book and cover design by Maryann Appel

5   3   1   2   4

For my husband,
your support and unconditional love
gives me wings.

———

1

OLIVIA

Yet another teacher dead.

High-pitched screams and the blare of fire alarms echoed through the school's hallways. The student body stood paralyzed, crammed arm to arm in the main lobby, gaping at our athletic advisor's corpse suspended from the ceiling, the hefty rope used for climbing in gym class snaked around his broken neck. His cognac-colored shoes dangled several feet from my face. His open eyes, glassy and lifeless, stared at the wall. Bruises dotted his collarbone, and fragmented black-and-blue splotches spread up toward his chin.

Another hanging.

Jessica whimpered as she trembled in my arms. "Your dad, Liv. Call him."

I shook my head. I had no doubt he was already on his way, so I didn't even jump when my cell phone rang in my pocket. I swiped to answer.

"Livy, where are you? Where's Pepper?" my dad asked through the speaker. He tried to hide it, but I could hear the concern in his voice.

"School," I answered, pulling myself together with a calming breath and rubbing my amethyst stone resting inside my coat pocket.

Principal McKenna and several other teachers had come onto the scene, ushering all the students out the front and side doors. But I just stood there, with Jessica's arm looped through mine, her other hand holding my forearm in a death grip.

"Another teacher's dead, Dad. What the hell is going on? There's no way these are all suicides."

"Language, Livy. Language," he said, robotically, as if *now* was the perfect time to impart life lessons.

Three deaths.

The first death, Mr. Camber, our health teacher, had been deemed a suicide. The second, Mrs. Dreyfuss, our school nurse, was still under investigation. And now, here we were, back from winter break, ready for a fresh start, and . . . *this*. Mr. Kline. Why would anyone target the teachers of Falkville Falls High School?

"Ms. Davis, Ms. Packey, please exit the building," Principal McKenna said. The creases around her lips and eyes belied her calm, in-charge tone.

"I have to find Pepper." My voice finally caught up with my brain.

My sister was challenging, but she and Dad were all I had. I was four when Mom died giving birth to Pepper. Dad rarely talked about Mom, and my memories of her were fuzzy.

"All the students have been asked to exit the school. You can find her outside," Principal McKenna said through clenched jaws.

I'd almost forgotten I was on the phone until I heard my father's command. "Go outside. I'm one block away. I'll find Pepper." Directions given, he hung up.

Jessica hauled me by the elbow. "Come on, Liv. Let's look for her outside."

I slipped out of Jessica's grasp, zipped up my jacket, and shoved through the herd of students pushing out the front doors we'd entered minutes earlier. Falkville Falls High School hosted less than five hundred students, but with everyone crammed on the lawn, it resembled a rock-concert venue.

I played with my soothing stone, flipping it between my fingers, as I searched the crowd for Pepper. Amethyst was supposed to relieve stress and bring balance to my mind and body, but when it came to my little sister, no crystal or stone would help. I'd saged her room so many times, the strong earthy scent had been absorbed into the furniture.

I heaved a sigh of relief when I found her, glued to Dustin's towering frame. Once I'd woven my way through the crowd, I let my backpack drop to the snow-dusted ground at their feet.

"I got her," Dustin said, squeezing Pepper into his side.

I released the breath I had been holding and stopped rubbing my stone. What would I do without Dustin and Jessica?

He retrieved my bag while maintaining his grip on a wriggling Pepper. She grunted like a bull, but he didn't even break a sweat.

"You'll love this," Dustin continued. "Your adorable kid sister was smoking behind the dumpsters, where she, along with her felonious friends, Billy Lyons and crew, decided to deface the brick wall."

Pepper let out an irritable breath like a toddler.

Dustin raised his bushy brows while securing the bag strap back over my shoulder. "But don't worry. She's *extremely* intelligent; it's not like she left her tag so the cops know exactly who did it or anything."

Pepper used the outline of our mother's wedding band—a gorgeous series of white gold circlets, one for every letter of her name—as her signature. Other than her nose ring, it was the only jewelry Pepper wore. A regular rebel without a cause. Literally—without any cause whatsoever.

"Why, Pepper?" I demanded, not that I expected an answer. The girl was the queen of eye rolls and tight lips.

Ignoring me, she turned on Dustin. "Get off me, you oversized pain in the ass! Go find your own girl to grope." With a final yank, she tore her arm free and glared in my direction. "Seriously, your friends are as annoying as you are. Why can't you all leave me the hell alone?"

"We'll leave you alone when you start making better decisions." I folded my arms to keep my hands from shaking her. A lump formed in my throat, but I swallowed it down. "You continue getting in trouble like this, you're gonna end up in juvenile detention. Dad and I can't act as a shield for you forever."

"Sounds like a picnic compared to getting policed by you." She swung her backpack over her shoulder, hitting Dustin in the side. He didn't flinch.

"Does it?" I said, raising a brow. "We love you. We don't want you to end up in jail."

"Oh, please," she said, waving me off. "You wouldn't even miss me. Besides, making poor decisions is my strong suit. It's an art form I've perfected over the years."

"Not really something I'd be proud of," Jessica mumbled.

Pepper flipped her vibrant blue hair over her shoulder. I couldn't even remember the last time I'd seen her with her natural chestnut color—hair once just like our mother's. "I'm leaving this dumpster dive of a town the second I turn eighteen."

"Well, it's unfortunate you feel that way. I hope you end up changing—"

Sirens made me pivot midsentence. Fire trucks, police cars, and an ambulance barreled into the lot. Kids scattered like mice to get out of the way.

Most of the seniors hurried to their cars while buses arrived to take the underclassmen home. Dad stepped out of one of the police vehicles that pulled onto the grass. He jogged toward us without shutting off the engine.

Concern flooded his eyes as he raked them over Pepper and me.

"We're fine," I answered his unspoken question. "Mr. Kline, not so much."

I motioned to the school's main doors, now guarded by two doughy security guards. They probably couldn't defend us from clawing kittens, but at least they'd deter unsolicited social-media pictures.

"What did you guys witness in there?" Dad asked. Anyone else would probably just see the town sheriff collecting information for his case, but I knew him better. He wanted to know how screwed up we were from what we'd seen.

Dustin took a step forward like he was reporting for duty. "At approximately seven oh five, Mr. Kline was found hanging from the lobby ceiling in front of the trophy case. Jacob and I were two of the first to see him. The halls were empty at the time."

My father nodded with appreciation at such a thorough report. Dustin, my dad's protégé. He'd always wanted to be a police officer, just like my father. Unsurprisingly, he followed my dad around like a puppy, always picking his brain about the law.

"We came in early today to meet with Principal McKenna about Pride Week. Since it's during playoff season, the basketball team wanted to wear rainbow patches on their jerseys to show their support." He offered Jessica a small smile. "When students started filing in, I pulled the fire alarm. I thought it would clear the halls out." He shrugged. "I guess people don't really care if they burn to death. Pretty much everybody just stared until the teachers started yelling."

Jessica and I had been among them. We'd heard about the other two school hangings, but to see one in person? Nothing could have prepared us for that. The shock had tugged me under a fog. I'd hardly registered the fire alarm or its meaning.

Dad put his hand on Dustin's shoulder. "Nicely done." He turned to the rest of us. "You should go home. This is now a crime scene. School will be canceled for the next couple of days."

Jessica pulled her keys from her purse. "I can drive Pepper and Liv home and stay over until you get back," she offered. Jessica's parents worked late hours, and her girlfriend, Tiffany, went to a private school several hours away. Chauffeuring us around benefited her too. She hated being alone.

"I think that's a good idea. Dustin, why don't you join them?"

Dustin saluted.

"I'll call your parents and let them know the four of you will be at the house doing your schoolwork until I get home. We can order pizza for lunch later." Dad snapped his fingers at Pepper, who was staring sullenly at the ground. "You. Shower. I can smell the smoke on you from here."

She grimaced but acquiesced. Fighting him wasn't necessary. We all knew she'd go home, lock herself in her room, blast her music, and not come out until dinner. Eating was the only group activity you could count on her to show up for.

Dustin grabbed my bag from me. "I've got it," he said as he flung the backpack over his shoulder.

We trekked toward Jessica's car. Not two steps in, a shiny black 1972 Ford Bronco, dragging a trailer hauling a black motorcycle, pulled into the parking lot. I'd know that car anywhere. It was my dream car, the one I had been saving for since my sophomore year. I was practically drooling as it pulled in, ten spaces down from Jessica's silver Volkswagen.

While I gawked at the exterior, three people emerged from the car.

I scrunched up my nose the way I did whenever I sensed Pepper lying or trying to distract me. Something about them was just . . . off.

The driver, an older man around my dad's age, wore a brown trench coat, black suit, and black scarf, possibly government. At least he looked like the government officials on television. He walked around the car and tossed something at the gorgeous teenage girl behind him. About Pepper's age, she had wavy blond hair past her shoulders and wore jeans, a cream turtleneck, and a fitted navy peacoat. Barbie-doll pretty. She caught the foreign object and pointed it at the school. It looked like a plain black box, the size of one of my favorite novels, but as the girl held it up, orange and red lights flickered on its side. She tossed it back to the older gentleman, who placed it in his pocket.

Oh my God, was that a detonation device for a bomb? My pulse raced. I opened my mouth to call for help, but only a wheeze came out.

But when nothing went boom, my fright transformed into bafflement as the third person crossed in front of the other two.

He appeared to be around my age, tall and wide like Dustin, but slightly leaner. My heart gave a mighty thump in my chest as my eyes traveled from his black boots, up faded blue jeans that molded to his muscular thighs, to his black leather jacket and stretched-out white T-shirt pressing against his defined chest. He looked nothing like his sharply dressed, professional-looking companions. He had darker hair than the girl, similar to the older man, with a touch of douchebag swagger, but he had plenty going for him.

I bit my lower lip, studying his face. I pressed my fingers to my mouth as if I remembered his on mine.

But that was impossible.

As if he could feel my stare, he turned and looked directly at me.

Warmth seeped up my neck and overtook my cheeks. His narrowed eyes trailed over me, heating me like a brand. I jerked as if he'd lunged at me, and to my surprise, he started to laugh. He leaned against the car and crossed his arms over his chest. His critical gaze gave way to a stupid grin. Though the other two spoke to him, he never took his eyes off me. I didn't realize I'd stopped following my friends and stood alone in the parking lot, mesmerized by this stranger, until the horn of Jessica's car sounded, startling me.

She lowered her window. "What are you doing? Get in."

Jessica, Dustin, and Pepper waited with the door to the backseat flung open. When I looked back, the three newcomers were gone, and in their wake, an uneasiness settled in my core.

Something had gone incredibly wrong at Falkville Falls High, and my gut told me they were here because of it.

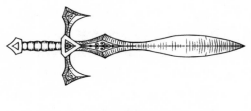

2

LIAM

Another school, another hanging.

We'd been following this case for almost a year now. Five schools in Wisconsin, each with at least one dead nurse. The electromagnetic force (EMF) reader confirmed supernatural activity, but our little black box couldn't tell us the details.

Falkville Falls High School differed, though. Out of three victims, only the second was a nurse. The Hunterland message board picked up the chatter last week sending our investigation here. Damned if we could figure out why this school was an anomaly.

We stepped into the lobby, where the police were lowering the body from the ceiling. Several school employees stood off in the corner, sobbing and holding one another. Grieving the deceased or fearing for their own lives, I had no idea and didn't really care. Mr. Kline, thirty-nine years old, lived alone and had worked as the athletic advisor at this school for the last sixteen years. No priors or known enemies. Lived a simple life, just like the other victims. The only significant connection with the other casualties was occupation. The sheriff barked detailed orders at his subordinates, and we watched as they scrambled to obey.

He stood about six feet tall, was in shape, and worst of all: He appeared confident. Too confident. We dealt with a lot of overweight idiot cops who lost their breath during press conferences. Most of those guys were the paper-pushing, donut-eating types who'd never worked a serious case in their careers. Dad and I loved them. They stayed out of our way and let us do our job.

But this guy? This guy screamed pain in the ass.

As if on cue, the sheriff homed in on us.

Jac, my younger sister, mouthed the words *You folks can't be in here*, just as the sheriff shouted them in our direction. He had a deep, intimidating voice.

But we weren't easily intimidated.

I chuckled under my breath and crossed my arms, making my heavy leather jacket creak. We'd heard that sentence a thousand times, and we'd ignored it a thousand and one times.

Dad opened his credentials and held them up for the sheriff. "Agent Jack Hunter," he announced, using the surname our ancestors took on generations ago. As expected, the sheriff's eyes widened at the sight of Dad's badge. "And I can be anywhere I damn well please, Sheriff."

It was a statement my dad made so often even *I* almost believed him.

"FBI?" The sheriff raised an eyebrow. He crossed his arms, mirroring my stance. "And why would the FBI be interested in a small town like Falkville Falls?"

Other officers gathered around him.

"They send us big boys to handle things the locals can't." Dad flipped his wallet closed and shoved it into his blazer's inside pocket. "Sheriff . . . ?"

"It's Sheriff Matthew Davis." His pursed lips said he was anything but pleased by our presence. Our arrival into new towns had brought on a variety of reactions over the years. Some were ecstatic to get federal assistance, but small towns like this one—the ones that likely needed us the most—normally weren't. I'd bet everyone in this place knew each other, and their basketball games were like backyard barbecues. There was probably a Billy Bob's convenience store in the center of town.

Sheriff Davis glanced at Jac and me. "And who are they?"

"My kids," Dad answered, offering no further explanation. He slipped his notebook and pen from his brown overcoat and started his usual line of questioning. "What connection do the three teachers have to one another? Were they friends? Lovers? Enemies? Anything odd about their deaths?"

Sheriff Davis grimaced. "Other than the obvious, no." He glared at my father before his eyes found mine; they then changed to worry as he looked over at Jac. "I'm not answering any official questions with your children around. They are too young for this conversation."

Dad kept his cool, but I couldn't help it. I burst out laughing.

I was the brawn, Jac was the brains, but even she was no saint. At fourteen, she had already gotten her hands dirty a time or two: beheaded a bunch of vamps, slaughtered several shifters, burned more ghost bones than I had, and even slew a few rare banshees and ghouls. She'd been waiting for her chance at a zombie.

My dance card, however? Completely full. I'd eliminated every kind of creature known to man and this guy thought I was too young for this conversation. *Hilarious.*

"And that's funny to you?" the sheriff said.

"Very," I answered, pretending to wipe a tear from my eye.

Dad glared at me. "You don't need to worry about my kids," he told Sheriff Davis with his gaze still hard on me.

I shrugged. We'd be gone in a couple of months, anyway. What did I care what this homegrown official thought? I had a job to do: find the monster who was killing teachers.

I'd be nineteen in six months, and Dad and I agreed after that I could no longer pull off the student routine. Internally, I couldn't wait for that day to come. Acting like a high schooler was starting to wear on my nerves. I knew I could play a very convincing agent after all these years of watching Dad do it.

"If they were my kids, I'd want to keep them away from this trage- dy." The sheriff glowered—a papa-bear sort, it seemed.

Dad took three steps forward. The sheriff stiffened. I had to hand it to him; most would've crumbled. Two of his officers moved to flank him, but Sheriff Davis held up his hand for them to stand down. At six foot four and as wide as a Mack truck, Dad usually won stand-offs. This tiny department's balls would've been more impressive if it wasn't such an inconvenience. We didn't have a lot of time before the next teacher fell victim, and we needed to act fast. The gap between murders had decreased, and time was of the essence.

"It'd be in your best interest to work with me. We're here to help." Dad slipped out a phony business card made by an online print store and handed it over to the sheriff.

When he took it, his sleeve rose, and I noticed a fraying string bracelet on Sheriff Davis's wrist. It looked like he'd been wearing it for decades. Probably an arts-and-crafts gift from his kid.

The sheriff flipped my dad's fake business card over a couple times as if even he doubted its authenticity and then slipped it into his chest pocket.

"We will be staying at the Rose Motel, down the street. If you can think of anything, let me know," Dad said. He placed his arm around Jac. "Let's go. I've got to feed you weeds. Let's see what culinary delights this town has to offer before we bunk down in that little room."

Before we made it halfway to the exit, the Sheriff called to us. "You're *all* staying at a motel, for the whole investigation?" I looked back to see his eyes crinkled in concern, bouncing between Jac and me.

Dad's pace slowed, but he kept walking. He'd played his cards per- fectly, never intending to take us to any local diner. Meals typically in- cluded ramen noodles, canned soup, and fast-food runs. However, if we were lucky enough to get a room with a kitchen, Jac cooked. Our own vegetarian version of Betty Crocker. But most of these dumps barely had fully intact mattresses and working plumbing, let alone enough space to prepare food.

Nah, Dad wasn't worried about our food intake. This was a ploy for sympathy. Dad could find a weakness in the toughest audience, and Sheriff Davis just gave his away.

I could hear the hesitation in the officer's voice as he said, "Do you and your family want to join mine for pizza? I'm a great chef. I dial the number to the local Italian restaurant like no other."

At first, Dad ignored him. But then the sheriff added, "We can talk about the incidents in *my town* while the kids eat."

His town. Of course. We were on his turf now. Small-town sheriffs were so territorial.

"My daughters are around your children's ages. I'm sure they would get along." The strain in his voice told me he was anything but confident about that.

I watched my father's lips peel back into a grin. He always liked using us as bait.

We already knew Sheriff Davis had two daughters. The eldest, Olivia Davis, who they called Liv or Livy, just turned eighteen last week, and she was squeaky clean. Not an outcast, but not winning any popularity contests either. She probably looked both ways before crossing the street. His youngest, Patricia "Pepper" Davis, age fourteen, wreaked havoc, destined for juvey before her senior year. Mom, also Patricia, died during childbirth. High-school sweethearts, Patricia and Matt went to school here at Falkville Falls High and were married after graduation.

There wasn't a town we stepped into without doing our homework.

Dad dropped his smirk before turning around. "We'd love that. Wouldn't we?" He squeezed Jac into his side.

Sheriff Davis pulled out his phone and dialed. I couldn't hear most of the conversation but by what I could make out, whichever daughter he had on the other end wasn't over the moon about strangers coming over for lunch.

"I have a couple things to follow up with here. Why don't you meet me at our house?" He scribbled his address on the back of his own official business card and handed it to Dad. Not that we needed it.

We piled into the Bronco, and Dad started the engine. "Watch yourself, Liam," he warned as he pulled out of the school parking lot and onto the main road. The Bronco growled as if in agreement. Figured, since it was technically Mom's car and she had always sided with Dad when on a hunt.

I kicked up my heels on the dash. "That guy's going to be a problem."

Dad focused on the road as we drove up and down several hills, following winding roads filled with potholes. We passed signs for developments like "Basking Ridge" and "Clinton Community," before we located "Falkville Falls Family Homes."

Jac leaned over the center console. "Dad, I agree with Liam. I think Sheriff Davis is going to be an issue. He's stubborn and old school. I noticed none of his deputies had updated gear or tech in their cars. They are archaic and stuck in their ways."

Dad, an inventor by trade, was unimpressed with official tactical gear, so he couldn't care less that Sheriff "pain in the ass" Davis didn't have modernized equipment. His interests lay in his DIY inventions currently crammed in the trunk. In his defense, some of his gadgets were pretty freaking cool. Jac used to say we had our own "Q" from the old James Bond movies. I argued he acted more like MacGyver, using whatever trash he had in arm's reach to invent a solution.

"We've dealt with worse. Why is this guy bothering you both so much?" Dad asked, making a right onto Sheriff Davis's street.

"His daughters attend that school, which makes him emotionally invested. He won't let this go," I said. "He's either going to be dead weight or get in our way, or worse, get himself killed."

The worst type of complication in our line of work happened when people got involved when they really should just stay the hell out of the way. Didn't matter if it was other hunters, nosy law enforcement, or stubborn officials. We were the best, but to be the best, we needed to be left alone to do the job. Sometimes that meant coloring outside the lines of the law, and a good cop was the last person keen on breaking it.

"You handle the daughters; I'll handle the sheriff. Got it?" Dad pulled into their driveway as Jac and I agreed.

The house reminded me of any suburban community stuck in the late eighties, early nineties. It had a brick chimney on the side, a white wraparound front porch complete with a porch swing, and a red front door with a small etched-glass window.

From the car, I spotted Olivia on the second floor, pulling back the curtain. She gawked when she saw me. She'd clearly had no idea her houseguests included the guy who'd laughed at her in the school parking lot. This was going to be fun, maybe too fun.

"Oh, I'll take care of Olivia. I'll take such good care of her, she'll cry the day we leave." I swiveled around to face my sister. "You think you can handle the juvenile delinquent, or should I have my go at both of them?"

Dad smacked me across the chest. "Do not be 'Liam the Romance King' around these two! Get information and get out. No relationships whatsoever."

I rubbed my bruised chest.

Jac laughed. "Yea right, like Liam can keep it in his pants! They'll be making out by sunset. That girl will be doodling his name in her notebook before week's end." Jac winked. "Isn't that right, Romeo?"

Dad shifted in his seat. "Knock it off, the both of you. Seven people are dead, and we're eleven months in without any real leads. It's no laughing matter."

I groaned. He was right. The duty of monster extermination was an enormous honor and no joke.

"Sorry, Dad."

When I looked back up at the second-floor window, the hairs on my arms stood at attention.

A familiar, faint flicker of light danced behind Olivia's outline.

I grabbed the shotgun resting at my feet and darted out of the car.

3

OLIVIA

I watched the mysterious boy shoot out of the Bronco, charging toward the house. Instead of the doorbell, a loud crash and Pepper's screams announced his arrival.

"What the hell?" Jessica jumped up from my bed, disturbing our spread of chemistry worksheets.

Heavy footsteps climbed the stairs, and before I could reach the door, Mystery Guy darted across the threshold, aiming a shotgun at my face. My brain stuttered, gluing me to the floor while it processed the two black mouths of the double barrel. My breath hitched.

"Duck," he commanded, forceful enough to unstick my brain. "Now!"

I dropped to the floor, pulling Jessica down with me. An explosion of sound, like a car backfiring, followed a cascade of shattering glass. My eardrums vibrated as the pieces clicked together in my scrambled head. He'd shot the mirror of my dresser. Splintered wood scattered over the rug confirming my thoughts.

"Oh my God. Oh my God!" I shrieked, over Jessica's hysterical screams. "What the hell is wrong with you?" I pushed myself up with a trembling arm, keeping the other wrapped around Jessica. Tears spilled down her cheeks, and I realized I was crying too, the droplets tickling my jaw. Thankfully, we weren't pierced by any of the debris, but my room hadn't been so lucky. Healing crystals and stones from the dresser had flown all around. Remnants of my mirror reflected dozens of prisms onto the ceiling.

The shotgun settled by the psycho's leg, giving me the courage to glare into those piercing blue eyes and scream, "Are you insane?"

Ignoring my questions, he offered me his hand. I refused, pushing myself up on wobbly knees. I aided an equally unsteady Jessica to her feet, then heaved out a shaky breath as I took a step forward. To do what, I had no idea.

His cobalt irises appraised me, lips forming a smirk. My heart fumbled a beat, and dread curled into a knot in my gut.

"How come the ladies never say thank you?" he said to no one in particular.

"What. Was. That?" Jessica jabbed a finger at the obliterated mirror and nearly lost her balance.

"A gun. It goes boom and things break," Mystery Guy answered, rolling his eyes. "Typically, it kills something bad, but in rare instances like this, it just busts stuff up." He leaned the shotgun against the wall.

The bathroom door burst open, and Dustin, who I'd almost forgotten about, launched himself at Mystery Guy in a perfect linebacker tackle. The whole floor shook, and my side table tumbled, spilling homemade healing ointments and balms. Some of the lids broke open and rolled toward the heap of tangled masculine limbs. The shotgun toppled next, and I flinched as it thudded harmlessly to the rug. I thought Dustin had him pinned until I saw my friend soar backward into my bookcase. Paperbacks fell on his head as my mouth dropped open in complete disbelief. Dustin had fifteen or twenty pounds on this guy, easy, yet Mystery Guy threw him like a rag doll.

"Enough!" an older gentleman yelled from the doorway. The trench-coat guy from the parking lot. He stood shoulder to shoulder with the pretty girl. Pepper peered at them, a Cheshire-cat smile spreading across her face. Of course she would think this was funny, but at least she was safe.

"Liam!" Trench Coat yelled as he picked up the shotgun from the floor. Mystery Guy nodded and stepped away from Dustin. The older man turned to me. "I'm Agent Hunter. The boy who shot up your room is my son, Liam." He pointed at the blonde. "And this is my more responsible child, Jacqueline."

Jacqueline waved. "Everyone calls me Jac," she said with enthusiasm, like we were meeting at freshman orientation.

"Agent, like FBI agent?" Dustin said, now standing and brushing drywall off his pants.

Agent Hunter nodded, then turned my way. "The sheriff invited us for lunch." He shot Liam a sidelong look of disappointment. "But I am sure there will be a change of plans very soon."

Liam stepped out of his father's shadow, giving Dustin an earnest smile. He extended his hand and said, "You okay, buddy? No hard feelings. I mean you did go after me first, right?"

Dustin smacked away his offered handshake.

"Dustin, he's trying to apologize," I said. Pepper, Jessica, and Agent Hunter all looked at me like I had lost my damn mind, but Jac smirked.

"Doodling by week's end, I tell ya," Jac said, and Liam laughed in response.

"Downstairs. Now!" Agent Hunter barked, finding no humor in Jac's perplexing comment.

Whether he meant all of us or not, we filed downstairs and took up occupancy in the living room. Agent Hunter waited for us to be seated before excusing himself to wait for my father in the front hall. Jac and Liam settled on the love seat. Liam sat with an arm laid casually across the back of it, his right leg crossed over his left knee, as if he owned the place. Jac, however, crossed her ankles and folded her hands in her lap, very ladylike. How were they even related, much less brother and sister?

Then again, Pepper and I weren't exactly alike either.

Jessica, Dustin, and I took up the sofa while Pepper perched on the ottoman across from Liam, staring like a lovesick puppy. Great. My impressionable sister had a crush on the gun-toting, leather-jacketed hooligan who'd destroyed my room and the front door like he was in a shooter game.

"So how long have you been firing guns?" Pepper batted her eyes like she had something caught between her lashes.

"Pepper!" I cautioned. She scowled in my direction.

"Since I was four. Why? You interested in guns?" Liam answered with a devious grin aimed at my baby sister like he had her in the cross-hairs.

Pepper tucked a strand of blue hair behind her ear. "I'd love to go shooting with you. Is it hard? Do you think I'd be a quick learner?" She gave her best suggestive smile, and my stomach turned. "I bet I'd be great if *you* taught me."

Liam uncrossed his legs and leaned forward, resting his forearms on his thighs. "Sure. I'd love to teach you." In a softer voice, he added, "The trick is focus. Anyone can pick up a gun and shoot, but to be great, you have to be aware of your target, your surroundings, and the type of ammunition needed to kill the monster you're after."

Liam winked at Pepper, and I swear she swooned sideways with an audible sigh.

"Okay, enough!" I chimed in. Monster? Could he be any more dramatic? Dad called them bad guys like the rest of the sane world. Did he think calling them monsters made him sound cooler?

Acting like I was invisible, Pepper smiled at Liam. "You think we could go this weekend?" She leaned forward and crossed her arms to create cleavage in her V-neck shirt.

"No," Dustin, Jessica, and I answered in unison.

Liam laughed, resting back against the love-seat cushion. "You'll have to get through the wardens first." He thrust his chin in our direction.

Pepper stuck her tongue out at me, crinkling her nose so her piercing danced. Regrettably, that was one of her nicer responses to my efforts to keep her alive.

"You as good as your dad?" Dustin asked, mockery slinking between words.

"No one is as good as my father, but I did manage to attend the FBI teen academy my freshman year, so I have some knowledge," he said as if telling us he'd taken AP math for a semester.

"Whoa!" Dustin's eyes bugged from their sockets. Great, this guy's fan club already multiplied by two. "That is so freaking cool!" He turned to justify himself to me and Jessica by saying, "That program is super hard to get into."

Dad's car pulled into the driveway, and his door slammed harder than usual. My mouth went dry. Before I could move to warn him, confirm we were all okay, his voice echoed in the hallway. "What the hell happened to my door?"

Around the living-room doorjamb, I could see the top of our front door laid out on the ground. Liam had broken it down to get to my room and kill . . . and kill what? My reflection? My choice of décor? The doorknob had rolled under the little hall table that held family photos. How was this teenager so strong? To break down a door and toss Dustin around took some serious strength. He looked fit, but this was almost inhuman.

Agent Hunter peeked into the room. "Stay here. I'll explain what happened." He mumbled something that Liam found amusing and then disappeared to confront my father.

None of us spoke, too concerned with the yelling in the other room. Dad never once ran in to make sure we were in one piece. Instead, I heard him hollering at the FBI agent about kids with guns and laws and parenting. He went on and on and on, but whatever Agent Hunter said in subdued undertones was enough to make my dad feel validated and confident that we were safe.

Why did this feel like they had done this before?

I finally broke the silence with a question for Liam. "Wanna tell me why you shot my mirror?" I crossed my arms over my chest.

"Thought I saw something in your room." Liam shrugged. "It must have left when it heard me coming or smelled the rock-salt bullets."

"Liam, don't," Jac hissed.

"Like she'll believe me anyway." Liam patted his sister's leg. "Why does it matter what I say?"

"It matters because she will think we're crazy, and it'll be harder on us."

My last nerve was frayed. Harder on them? He'd just fired a damn weapon in my room. I pulled one of the couch pillows next to Dustin and clutched it in my lap to anchor myself.

"I'd believe you if you told me the truth," I said, a sliver of uncertainty nagging at my mind. I wasn't sure I'd believe anything this guy said, logical or not.

"You can't handle the truth," Liam said in his best Jack Nicholson voice.

Dustin laughed. "Dude, I love that movie." He eased deeper into the couch. The second he heard Liam went to FBI camp or whatever he'd called it, Dustin's anger had vacated the premises. That boy had major respect for law officials. He was probably already hoping for a bromance that could open doors, completely forgetting he had just been flung across a room like trash.

"Right? *A Few Good Men* is such a classic." Liam laughed along with Dustin.

I had never seen the movie, but I knew that Jack Nicholson line from memes. Hell, that film was almost as old as my dad, but Dustin loved that era of cinema. Figures these two would have the same stupid interests.

I wriggled my fingers at Liam to reclaim his focus. "Um, hello. I asked you a question. The least you could do is explain to me why I'll be sleeping in the guestroom tonight?" I twisted the pillow as if I was squeezing Liam's neck.

Liam stood and paced the length of the fireplace, hands linked behind his back.

What the hell was he doing? He cleared his throat, continuing his Nicholson impersonation.

Oh, so we're still playing games?

"We live in a world that has walls, and those walls have to be guarded by men with guns, men like my father, my sister, and myself." As if getting on a soap box, he jumped onto the raised brick hearth. "Who's gonna do it? You?" He pointed at Pepper. "You, Olivia Davis?" He swiveled his finger to me. To avoid being poked, I moved back on the couch. "I have a greater responsibility than you can possibly fathom. You weep for the teachers who have died. You have that luxury. You have the luxury of not knowing what I know."

Pepper slid off the ottoman to watch his monologue like an adoring fan, hands folded at her chest.

Liam stepped onto her unoccupied seat for extra height and continued: "And my existence, while grotesque and incomprehensible to you, saves lives! You don't want the truth, because deep down in places you don't talk about at parties, you want me to be here in the flesh, defending you from the monsters out there." Liam pointed to the front hallway and then up toward the ceiling. "You need me to break your doors down and shoot at your mirrors. I have neither the time nor the inclination to explain myself to a girl who rises each morning beneath the blanket of the very freedom that I provide, and then questions the manner in which I provide it! I would rather you just said thank you and went on your way." He jumped down and crossed his arms over his chest. "Otherwise, I suggest you pick up a weapon and stand at a post. Either way, I don't give a damn what you think!"

Jac and Dustin stood, clapping wildly alongside my googly-eyed sister.

"Nicely done, my man! Colonel Jessup would be proud!" cheered Dustin.

Liam bowed in my direction, then Dustin's, then to the window, extending his genuflection all around the room.

Jessica leaned against my shoulder and whispered, "Am I the only one not buying the crap this guy is selling? I think he might be insane."

"I'm with you. He's absolutely crazy." I shook my head. "Something's off about the whole family."

Liam turned to me the same way a dog pricked its ear at a rustle in the woods. He strode over and knelt at my feet like a supplicating sinner, a forearm rested on one thigh. Something sharp and shrewd danced across his face. "You have no idea how off we are. So be a good little girl and listen to us."

My chest rose and fell before words found my lips. "And why should I do that?" I gripped the pillow until my nails dug into the foam. This guy exuded confidence.

Too much for my liking.

Jac swooped in, looking over her shoulder as if she sensed they were about to be escorted out. "Because we are the only hope your school has at stopping the killings. And there *will* be more."

I flinched. How could anyone predict that?

So close I could feel his radiating body heat, Liam lifted my fingers like a man proposing.

His were calloused as if he had worked construction his whole life, but they were also warm and gentle, surprising me. He pulled a marker from his pocket and scribbled on my palm. He stroked my skin before closing my hand into a ball. I sucked in a breath. As his thumb rubbed over my knuckles, déjà vu washed over me. For a moment, I thought he was going to say something.

Instead, he focused on Dustin.

"Sorry again, man," he said as he rose.

"We're good," Dustin said, extending his hand to shake.

And with that, the two Hunter children walked toward the hole where a front door used to be. Their father stood there glaring before ushering them out.

I opened my hand to find a phone number in red ink, along with the words, "For emergencies." Emergencies? This guy was delusional. Like I'd call him for anything. I'd be washing this hand immediately.

My dad walked into the room rubbing the bridge of his nose and closed his eyes. Without opening them, he said, "Dustin, Jessica, I think it's time you went home. I need to speak with my daughters." He exhaled hard. "Alone."

The two scurried upstairs to retrieve their things before heading out to Jessica's car.

From the window, I watched them disappear down the street before I joined my father. "Dad, what's going on?"

Pepper slouched deeper into the couch. Her cheerful disposition had left with the Hunters, apparently.

"Pepper, why don't you go upstairs and start your homework?" I offered, realizing that dad and I should maybe have this conversation privately.

She pushed off the couch. "Not like I give a rat's ass about whatever you guys are uptight about anyway," she said, stomping her way up the stairs.

I waited until Pepper was out of earshot and then placed my hand on Dad's arm. "What happened?"

He sighed. "I don't know who or what is killing the teachers at your school, but I am pretty sure I'll need that family's help to figure it out." He gazed down the hall as if watching the Hunters leave all over again.

Why was he drinking their crazy Flavor Aid? How could he want to work with such lunatics? "What did Agent Hunter say that has you so unraveled?"

Dad placed his hand over mine and gave it a squeeze. "We aren't the only school that's been targeted. There's a long list of dead people throughout the state with the same pattern, and they aren't accidents or suicides. Something . . ." He paused, and the uncertainty on his face unnerved me. "Teachers are dying, in my town, under my watch." He drew a deep breath and with his exhale said, "And I need all the help I can get to stop it."

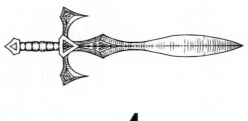

4

LIAM

Back at the crappy motel, a mopey Jac handed out the fast-food burgers and fries we'd picked up on our way back from the Davises' house. To call her annoyed with our greasy cuisine was an understatement. The bright yellow and orange wrappers clashed garishly with the drab gray interior design. Two beds, a sagging cot, and an old couch upholstered with thick plastic sheeting over dingy beige fabric decorated the room, yet somehow, it managed to feel bare and sterile despite the obvious grime. It was a place far more suited to struggling single parents and traveling salespeople than a family of three. Not that we were a normal family by any means. Nevertheless, Jac had intended to bake a casserole, or something equally overloaded with vegetables, in the tiny kitchenette. Finding only a single saucepan and a banged-up baking sheet, her plans were thwarted. Dad promised her we'd do a little shopping tomorrow for the extra cookware she needed to make what she considered an adequate meal. It's not like we could fit all our weapons *and* an assortment of home goods in the trunk. The former took precedence.

That promise was the only sentence Dad uttered the entire ride home. Otherwise, he'd stayed eerily quiet. He wasn't too excited I'd shot up Olivia's bedroom, but he also knew my intrusion, impulsive or not, most likely saved her life. What we couldn't figure out was why a monster would even go after Olivia. All the other victims had been educators and nurses in schools—not a single student, and never in a residence.

"Do you think there are more related deaths off school premises, and we just missed them?" I sat on the squeaking plastic of the couch. Kicking up my heels on the stained wooden coffee table, I clicked on the TV.

"Possibly. That's an angle we haven't pursued," Dad said between chews. He was so hungry he didn't even take his coat or scarf off. "Jac, why don't you search suicides in Wisconsin, then do your fancy computer thing and map them out for us?" Mustard rested in the corners of his mouth. "Maybe there's a pattern we haven't seen yet, and your nifty technology can bring it to light."

Jac rolled her eyes at our father. "It's crazy to me how someone so brilliant can be so completely incompetent." She pulled out her laptop and put it in a patch of slatted sunlight on the two-person kitchenette table. "What are we thinking here?"

The blue screen illuminated Jac's face. She looked so much like Mom, it rammed a stake through my heart.

"Maybe a witch who has a thing for teachers?" she mused. "Or specifically school nurses?" Her pink painted nails tapped a rapid beat on her keyboard. "Maybe a vamp or werewolf with a vendetta?" She wrinkled her nose. Even Jac didn't believe that.

Vamps killed for food, and these hanging victims still had every ounce of their blood. Werewolves killed humans to eat their hearts so they could shift back into their human forms after a full moon, and we hadn't had a full moon in weeks.

Both types of revenants had no motive.

"What about a vengeful spirit?" I said, flipping through channels until I found the perfect movie to watch with my meal—*Indiana Jones and the Temple of Doom*. Such a classic. Without turning from the screen,

I continued: "The figure behind Olivia flashed bright just like a ghost before taking form."

"A spirit is stuck in one location. It can't jump a party bus from school to school," Jac countered. She threw her napkin at me. "Are you even paying attention, or are you too invested in that dumb movie?"

I muted the TV and shifted on the hard couch, crinkling the plastic. "First of all, this is a classic. It's not my fault you have terrible cinematic taste. Secondly, I like entertainment with my meal."

Jac's gaze went to my untouched food, then back to me. "You're an ass."

"All right," Dad said, finally wiping his mouth. "He is an ass, and you do have poor taste in movies. Can we move on?" He stood, kicking off his polished black shoes, which fell short of the closet. "As I was about to say, I agree with Jac. I think a witch's spell sounds like the more feasible option. A talisman exploding could explain the light you saw. There may be remnants of it still in the Davis home."

Solid theory. Witches liked working their magic from afar by leaving magnetic energy talismans in places they wanted to manipulate. It could look like a locket, a small jewelry box, or a charm, but it was always cut glass with a hexagon shape or etching.

"We should get back in there and do a search." Dad finally removed his scarf and jacket before sitting back on the bed. "A spirit would have to be attached to an object that was either somehow coincidentally at all these places or carried on someone's person to each location, including the Davises' home. Both ideas seem farfetched." Dad paused, tapping his chin. "Unless Matt's been to these schools on official business of some sort. I'll ask him."

I swiveled back around. "A witch's talisman does sound feasible. That burst of light expanded, like an explosion." I pulled an impish grin. "Guess I'm going to have to get closer to Olivia so I can investigate her bedroom for any ritual anchors, charms, or hex sigils." Getting some action with a hot girl on a hunt didn't seem so bad. And Olivia *was* hot, not that she knew it. She was one of those overprotective older-sister types who acted like a mother hen rather than a frisky high schooler. What a waste.

"Liam Noah Hunter, if you so much as touch that girl, I'll cut off your weapon of choice," Dad thundered. "This is an in-and-out job. Let's find the witch, or whatever evil we're after here, and move on."

I clamped my teeth on the inside of my lower lip to stop a broader grin. All I wanted was to go in and out. But by the look on my father's face, I doubted he'd find that joke amusing.

"Fine. So, what do we know from Sheriff 'pain in the ass' Davis?" I asked, throwing my hands behind my head, internally sulking about Olivia. That girl had *virgin* written all over her pouty face, and I loved a good challenge. "How did he take the monster speech?"

"Not well at first, but eventually he came around." Dad started to unbutton his shirt. "Matt said they originally thought the first killing was a suicide. No sign of foul play was discovered until death two. After today, he was positive they were related but had no reason they should be." Dad laid his button-down on the bed and kicked his feet up. "Mr. Camber was a health teacher, married, two kids, quiet guy. Lived a simple life. Mrs. Dreyfuss was the school nurse, which adds up with the other five victims. There's some sort of pattern there, but I'm not sure why this school is different."

Jac tapped her nose with a fry. "Hmm, what if the health teacher is considered a medical professional like a nurse. A witch with a serious grudge against the medical profession? Maybe a nurse ruined a spell or couldn't save a powerful witch's loved one?" She tossed the fry into her mouth.

"Could be, but what about the guy dangling from the ceiling today? What did he teach?" I leaned back in my chair, annoyed as the tenth commercial interrupted one of the few pleasures in my life. Why did all the local channels bombard you with fifteen minutes of ads when only dumbasses like us living in hotel rooms even watched them anymore?

"Mr. Kline was the athletic advisor, young, dating a nurse. Maybe that's the link." Jac grimaced at her food. "Dad, can we please go shopping tomorrow and buy some pots and pans? I want—no, I *need* to cook a healthy meal. I can't live like this." She wrapped up the vegan patty and tossed it in the waste basket.

I lifted the top bun of my burger. No ketchup. How? Why? My condiment curse continued. They always forgot it. "You start the mortality board, and have it done by dinner, and I'll go get you whatever your little heart desires right now," I said, landing on the perfect excuse to get ketchup and avoid unpacking four evidence boxes. Dad and I had carried them in from the car earlier, along with our bags of weapons. Each time we moved to a new hotel, one of us kids had to retape the evidence to the wall.

So annoying. And Jac was better at it anyway.

"Deal." Jac jumped out of her chair, ready to attack the containers.

That was too easy. What did I miss?

Dad chuckled. "She asked me earlier today if I would occupy you while she put up the board because all you do is get in her way and complain."

I threw up my hands. "Nice, Jacqueline. Real nice."

She hit me with a know-it-all smile. "What? It's true, isn't it?" She dropped a fat file on the counter with a *thwap*.

"Write me a list." I grabbed the keys to the Bronco. Jac pulled a piece of paper from her pocket and handed it to me. "How long ago did you make that?" I asked, reading the tidy itemization.

She shrugged her shoulders. "It's the same one I give you guys every time we find a place with a working kitchen." She pulled out a stack of papers for me to see. "I have like twenty copies. Neither of you pays attention." I threw Dad a look, wondering if he had any clue that we always picked up the same supplies. His one lifted brow said he had no idea either. "Anyway, it's nice to leave a collection of cookware to the local church or food pantry. I like that part of our job."

I mussed her hair and kissed the top of her head. "I like that part too."

Jac loved helping others. Living on the road meant never having anything of your own, and although we were rich—probably too rich— we never got to enjoy it. Only Dad knew where the Hunterland money came from. Jac and I joked that we had a wealthy grandfather, or that we were secretly working for the government, or that Dad robbed banks behind our backs, but Dad never confirmed or denied any of our theories.

Instead, he'd say, "When Liam turns twenty-one, it goes into his name, and should anything happen to Liam, then it goes into Jacqueline's name. That day, and that day only, you will find out where the money comes from."

As I touched the door handle, Jac called, "Hey, when was the last time you had your serum shot?"

I frowned. "Can't it wait?" I rarely "forgot"; I just hated needles. But I kept taking it because it made Jac and Dad feel better.

Dad looked at the food I'd barely touched and told Jac, "He can wait a few hours, once he's got some sustenance in his stomach." He narrowed his eyes at me. "But don't put it off forever. We are on a hunt, and you'll need your strength."

I dipped my chin and headed out the door.

The serum was our secret weapon. Developed by our forefathers back in the 1800s and more recently perfected by Doc, our fearless medical and historical liaison at Hunterland, the magic drug heightened our senses, gave us super strength, and quickened our reflexes. It made us effective against monsters and meatheads like that Dustin dude.

In truth, tossing him into that bookshelf was an accident. I rarely used my extended strength on humans. We tried not to, but occasionally, shit happened. I'd started using the serum when I turned fourteen, and even then only on big hunts. Hunterland protected the recipe and monitored the dosages, allowing only the Hunter bloodline and some special exemptions the usage. Jac started last year, not long after we'd almost lost her in a hunt. Now we were one lean, mean, monster-fighting machine of a family.

The Bronco roared as I twisted the key. I circled out of the motel lot and took two turns to the main drag—this place was homely, that's for sure. The streets were dead this time of day, the crooked sidewalks blistered with weeds, the pavements old enough to turn brown. The architecture along Main Street was straight from the 1950s—like the little Oregon town in *Stand By Me*—only it was worn down and dusty. White paint peeled from the facades of the local no-name bank and tiny corner pharmacy. There was even a shuttered-up, two-screen, old-timey theater. An awesome spot for movie marathons if they'd restored it, but they just left it to rot. A serious shame. A little farther along, the street was cleaned up—some kind of Main Street revival area. Boutiques selling ridiculously expensive soaps or local artisanal, handmade whatever-the-hells lined the freshly poured sidewalks. Of course, this was the area I had to go shopping for Jac.

I swallowed my pride and pulled into the three-car side parking lot of the Falkville Kitchen and Pantry Store. Small and quaint, like every other joint in this town.

As I pulled the store's front door open, chimes sounded. I'd be hard-pressed to guess whether I'd wandered onto the set of a horror movie or a made-for-TV romance.

I walked down each aisle, getting Jac everything on her list. By the last row, I cursed her name under my breath. There were only three mouths to feed, not an army of hunters.

"Liam?" Someone shouted from down the aisle. Dustin jogged toward me. A hunter-green apron dangled from his neck. "Dude, what are *you* doing here?" His gaze found my cart, and I watched his mouth silently count to four. "That's a lot of ketchup bottles."

I shrugged. "Yea, well, fast-food restaurants tend to forget my condiments, and I cannot live without ketchup." I waved my hand over the pots and pans. "The rest? My sister. Let's leave it at that." Dustin caught my gaze wandering to his abandoned cart filled to the brim with cereal.

He laughed. "My mom owns the place. I'm restocking." He adjusted his lopsided apron. "Hey, I can get you a reduced price. My mom's real keen on military and police discounts, especially since it looks like your family is redoing your kitchenware . . ." He trailed off, giving me a side-long look. I wanted to shout, *Yes, Dustin, I know this is too much for a family living in a motel.* But I also didn't feel like being hounded by questions, and Dustin seemed the inquisitive type. Most wannabe cops are. What most daydreaming detectives don't realize is that actually working in the field looks nothing like the movies. Swap the glamour and glory for a minimal, backpacking lifestyle and the eureka moments for long hours huddled over piles of homework in a hard chair.

I waved off his discount offer. They definitely needed the money more than we did.

"So, what do you think about all these murders? Crazy, right?" Dustin said, trailing me as I pushed my cart toward the register.

"Yeah. Dad's hoping we catch the guy here, and the case is closed sooner than later. Followed the bad guy through all five schools, starting at Montgomery High." I pulled each product out and laid them on the conveyer belt.

"Montgomery?" Dustin questioned.

"Yeah, it's about thirty, maybe forty miles from here." I grabbed the last item.

"Oh, I know where it is." His brows furrowed. "But there was a hanging in Falkville Falls almost two years ago." He cocked his head to one side. "That's the first teacher to ever hang themselves at our school. I'm thinking it started here."

I dropped the pot in my hand, and it clanged off the cement floor. Dustin powered on like he hadn't noticed.

"It's gotta be the same guy, right? I mean, same MO anyway. Ms. Daryl was a retired nurse from Falkville Falls Hospital. She was really quiet and weird but nice. Hung just like the other three. She was working part-time at our school assisting Mrs. Dreyfuss."

The wheels in my head started spinning. "Dustin, you are a genius." I handed the cashier my credit card as another employee bagged my items. "Come by the Rose Motel this week. Room 212."

Dustin straightened his spine, and I thought he was going to salute me.

I patted him on the shoulder. "Thank you."

I nearly upended the cart racing the groceries across the lot, then drove like the wheels of the Bronco were on fire. Finally, we had a starting point for this string of murders. The first real lead since ... well, our only lead.

I threw open the motel-room door.

Jac jumped back from the mortality board and gawked at me as I rushed over to scan her map of the murders. If I added them together, drawing a line from the first murder location to the last, it made a complete circle, a radius.

Dad sat at the table tinkering with his newest invention, a light box. It was supposed to mimic natural sunlight, weakening vamps in their nests, making it easier to take them down. So far, the box, which resembled a Rubik's cube, only worked for thirty seconds. Dad wanted it to work for a full three minutes.

I walked up to the red tacks Jac had laid out on the table. She and Dad watched as I pinned Falkville Falls High school with a fifth pin. I dragged the red yarn to Montgomery High, closing the circle with the strand.

"The murders started here two years ago." I turned around. "Our monster came home!"

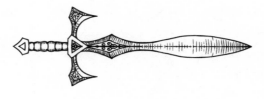

5

LIAM

Exciting as my revelation was, we couldn't do much about it yet. So, when Doc called the next day about a possible vamp nest about thirty miles northeast of Falkville Falls, we jumped on the chance at a little side investigation.

After all, the only good monster was a dead monster, and only we could take them down.

"Working yet?" I motioned to the device in Dad's lap, taking one hand off the wheel. Dad hated when I drove, but he was set on getting the light box to work. While he toyed with it, I played chauffeur.

"Almost there but not yet." Dad gave it one last inspection and then tossed the box into the backseat. He grabbed the weapons bag from the floorboards, pulling it into the passenger seat with him. He started hiding stakes under his jacket, then slid three into the custom ankle sheath concealed by his pant leg.

We pulled up to the rest stop closest to the campground. According to the material Doc sent over, four campers had died last night, their bodies drained of blood. Yet somehow, the local police had written it off as an animal attack. I often wondered if they really believed their own crap, or if they just wanted a simple way to close a mysterious case and move on.

"Planning on staking a coffee addict?" I eyed Dad's armaments and pointed at the "Hot Coffee" sign in the rest-stop window before shutting off the car.

Dad threw me a mischievous grin. "It's good to always be prepared."

Besides two humble pickup trucks, the only other vehicle in the gravel lot was an abandoned bus with broken windows, sitting lopsided on two flat tires by the dumpster. As dusk fell, the lights hanging over the entrance switched on, flickering like a candle's flame. This place screamed vamp feeding ground. No prying eyes. No town ties. No one to look for the missing. Sure, a vamp couldn't just walk in and attack, but the tree-lined perimeter, inadequate lighting, and dead roadway made for easy pickings. Dad had the right idea.

We were about to enter through the attached coffee shop's door when a woman's scream echoed around the corner. I took off in a full-on sprint.

"Liam, wait," Dad yelled.

My leather jacket moved with my screaming muscles. The serum shot I'd finally given myself this morning coursed through my bloodstream, and I flew, my legs pushing to their ultimate limits. The bite of cold air against my skin woke my senses as I charged into the clearing behind the building. The cry came again, and I pinpointed the direction.

My boots churned up frozen mud as I raced into the thick trees. Shadows darted in front of me—here one second, gone the next. I twisted my head to follow, and a hand grabbed me in a bone-crushing grip. Claws pierced my jacket, stinging my skin, and launched me clear across the wood line. I faceplanted into the freezing hard ground, reminding me of my one miserable attempt at ice skating. The impact jammed my spine, like I'd taken a hammer between the shoulder blades, and clacked my teeth together. I rolled to distribute the blow and stood.

Ten feet away, Dad raised a stake, eyes dilated and shining from the adrenaline high. I started toward him, but he yelled, "Stop!" With his head, he motioned to the ground between us.

Skidding to a halt, I stood over a figure in the grass.

We were too late. She was dead.

"No." I took a knee, reaching out for the girl. I couldn't make out her age or even what she was wearing because of all the blood oozing from her. She'd been mutilated . . . neck, stomach, wrists, and thighs . . . shredded.

Once those bastards tasted blood, there was no stopping them. The bloodthirst took over like a violent addiction, a sickness that had no treatment or cure.

"We need to find out who she is." I turned her onto her side, hoping to locate some sort of identification. Her purse laid open, its contents covered in dirt and viscera. I slipped her license from her wallet and held my breath as I read. *Jennifer Sutherland. Age twenty. Organ donor.* I wasn't sure she'd be able to make good on that selfless promise.

The air behind me rippled, making a soft *pop* against my right eardrum. I cocked my head that way and saw Dad aim his stake.

"Liam, roll," Dad said as he lunged forward.

I leaped over the girl into a somersault as Dad flung his wooden dagger like a carnival knife thrower. I stood and turned, now shoulder to shoulder with my father. Heat radiated off him. I wasn't the only one pissed off.

The stake caught one of the two oncoming vamps in the shoulder. His blood-covered arm snapped back, but without hitting the heart, all we managed to do was annoy him. He squinted crimson eyes at the sliver of the falling sun on the horizon and growled like a puma. The second vamp sank into a crouch and crinkled his milky-white face, lips peeling back in a hiss that revealed needle-like fangs dripping saliva.

The lead vamp yanked the stake from his shoulder and mumbled, "Dead." Foaming red spittle flew from his mouth onto the ground as his pointed incisors extended past his lips. The other chittered back in an animalistic language, grunting and squealing. He extended his arms like a Hollywood mummy, and his claws grew from his blackened nailbeds.

Anger prickled down my arms, and I curled fists by my sides, flexing until veins pushed against my skin. They'd killed an innocent girl, leaving a body no parent should have to bury.

"Shall we teach them a thing or two?" Dad asked, voice thick with the same rage simmering inside me. He handed me a stake from his crossbody bag.

"With pleasure, old man." My fingers curled around the weapon's hilt.

The vamp to the right went for Dad. He moved fast, but Dad jumped clear of his grasp. The other vamp charged me, and anticipation coiled my muscles and sharpened my vision. I waited till the last possible moment, then leaped into a spinning kick, burying my heel in the vamp's gut. I heard the spike Dad installed in the heel of my shoe spring free on impact, and the vamp reeled backward, clutching the hole I'd gored in his side.

He howled but shot right back up. I rarely played with my prey, but knowing we'd been seconds away from saving that poor desecrated girl ate at me. I'd make him suffer as she'd suffered.

The vamp slashed at me with his talons, but I dipped under his arm and whirled, slamming my left fist into his face. My knuckles burned, but I welcomed the pain. He swayed like a drunkard, dazed.

"Stop screwing around," Dad ordered between heavy breaths. "Let's end this." Dad jammed his stake right into the heart of the vamp he had pinned.

"With pleasure," I said, grinning.

The vamp roared straight into my face, displaying all his fangs and spewing the stench of rot. A scare tactic wasted on me. Idiot!

I threw a low kick, sweeping the vamp's legs out from under him. His fall made a dent in the grass that I deepened by leaping onto his stomach, knees first. I slammed the stake through the vamp's chest, right into his revenant heart. His right arm lifted for a feeble, last-ditch swipe at my side, but I shifted out of his reach. Sealing his damnation, I twisted the weapon back and forth until I felt the hard ground on the other side. Dark arterial blood seeped from the vamp's lips as his chest rose for the last time, and then the entire body collapsed into formless dust. After a few seconds, there was nothing left.

A warm hand squeezed my shoulder. I looked up and saw my father's sympathetic gaze. "We can't save them all, son." He gave me a second squeeze as my eyes returned to Jennifer's disemboweled body. "But we never stop trying."

The remoteness of the area played in our favor. We moved Jennifer's body farther into the woods and made an anonymous call to the local precinct, alerting them to another animal attack.

We might not be able to save them all, but Dad was right, we'd never give up. That was our hunter's oath.

Back at the Bronco, we changed out of our soiled clothes and tossed them into a bag we would most likely burn back at the motel. Vamp guts never came out in the wash.

Dad took the driver's seat while I climbed into the passenger side. It was too late to go after the nest tonight. Best to take care of the vamp hideout during daylight. And after killing our only two leads, we had no idea where to start looking. But we'd come back and hunt them all. Where there were two vamps, there were most certainly more.

The only noise aside from the snarl of the Bronco's engine came from the radio—"light tunes," as Dad called them. Consumed with images of Jennifer's mangled body, I brooded with my forehead pressed to the cool window. If we'd only come a couple minutes earlier, if we'd had better lighting, if the light box were working. All the ifs and whys consumed me.

Dad turned down the radio as we passed a sign for Falkville Falls and asked, "What do you think of the Davis family?"

I turned my head, squinting at my father. Sheriff Davis was annoying. Olivia was hot but off-limits. Pepper was witty as hell and reckless. But I doubted those were the answers he was looking for. "What do you mean?"

"Let's say your vengeful-spirit theory is right. You think Sheriff Davis is the one carrying the object, or do you think it's one of the daughters?" Dad liked to give Jac's and my theories a shot. He'd prod us to do investigations on our own and come back to him with supporting evidence. I always wondered if we were really helping or if it was just his own brand of homeschooling. Not that it mattered. The end result was the same: kill the monsters.

"The sheriff has a bracelet that looks old and handmade. Possibly a gift from someone who's dead? I'm sure he's lost a lot of people with the job he has. Maybe he wears it as a reminder of someone he couldn't save." I crossed my shin over my thigh, letting the tattoo of a broken clock peek out from the hem of my right pant leg. The hour and minute hands were set to the moment we lost Mom. The time my world stopped.

I studied the starless sky and the poorly lit street. "Or Jac's right and it's a witch. We found EMF readings at the school, but Jac said she didn't get anything when she used it in Olivia's room."

We pulled into the extended stay parking lot.

"What do you think?"

Dad stayed silent, but his head tilted and his eyes narrowed. I followed his line of sight.

"Dad," I breathed, seeing shadows cross the flimsy white curtains of our motel room.

Dad threw the Bronco into park, and we both shot out of the car, guns in hand.

Jac wasn't alone.

6

OLIVIA

After a week of being closed as a crime scene, the school finally re-opened. Everything had fallen back into place, except for one thing—or should I say, one person—and he was currently leaning against Dustin's locker after homeroom as Jessica and I approached.

What was Liam-freaking-Hunter doing casually chatting with *my* friend during *our* usual meet-up time in a school he didn't even attend? My bedroom was still under repair from my last encounter with the maniac. Needless to say, I prayed I'd never see him again, but now he was invading my safe space.

Every night, I stared up at the guestroom ceiling, cursing the blue-eyed, dark-haired delinquent. I didn't care that he was kind of hot in a break-you-out-of-jail-and-throw-you-on-the-back-of-my-motorcycle sort of way. What bothered me the most wasn't his snarky personality. It was our fathers' weird reactions. Sure, my dad wasn't too pleased that he'd spent the whole weekend with one of his police buddies fixing the holes in my room, but he didn't threaten jail time or demand restitution for the destruction. He'd just brushed it all off, and continued on like he needed the Hunter family to solve his murder investigation. I, on the other hand, thoroughly believed the Hunters, more specifically Liam, needed therapy, yoga, and a lengthy time-out like I used to give Pepper when she was younger.

Jessica crossed her arms over her chest and said, "What the hell are you doing here?"

Liam slowly turned his head. "School. Same as you."

Jessica's face burned, the red splotches along her high cheekbones matching her fiery red hair.

"They let you in?" I asked. "Security's gotten lax."

"Liam's enrolled here now," said Dustin. He patted Liam's shoulder. "Don't worry, ladies. He's not here to blow up the school or anything."

Liam opened his leather jacket, revealing his heather gray T-shirt, as if to confirm he wasn't armed.

"See?" Dustin smiled too broadly for my taste. "He made a list of eighties movies he thought I might like, and we were just deciding which one to watch first."

My hands flew to my hips. "Why are you even speaking to him? Why would you take his side?"

Dustin tilted his head. "Sides? There aren't any sides, Liv."

Liam flashed his pearly whites in a condescending smile. "Listen, sweetheart, you are wound a little too tight for me." He twirled a finger. "So, if you're worried about ulterior motives, don't flatter yourself. The only way I'm going back into your bedroom is if I need to search your house for a link to the monster who's killing teachers." His lips slanted upward, part playful, part alluring.

My hands curled into fists. Everything about this guy made me want to scream.

What he said, about a correlation between my room and the teacher murders, was complete nonsense. More infuriating was the fact that no one other than Jessica seemed to contest his delusional theory.

Flustered and furious, I scrunched up my face and tried to think of a decent comeback, but the pause stretched, and he continued.

"Did you put your thong on backwards?" Liam tilted his head. "What's that face you're making?"

"You're an asshole!" Jessica snarled over my sputter of embarrassment.

Liam laughed. "I'm way worse than that!"

"All right, Liam. They'll only hate you more if you keep this up," Dustin said.

Liam shrugged.

Dustin patted his back. "It'll be more work on my end if you don't play nice."

Liam laughed, mocking eyes swiveling my way. "I'd love the chance to play . . ."

Oh, that was my breaking point. I raised my hand to smack him, but he caught my wrist in midair. I heard Dustin and Jessica suck in a breath.

"Don't," Liam warned.

My stomach clenched while my brain tried to catch up to his inborn reflexes.

He released his hold and turned to Dustin like nothing happened. "I'm telling you, *From Dusk Till Dawn*. Great movie. Stellar, A-plus cast. It's about vamps. Couldn't be farther from the truth but still entertaining as hell." He squeezed Dustin's shoulder. "See you at lunch, buddy."

Lunch, Jessica mouthed to me, incredulous.

Not missing a beat, Dustin nodded good-bye in return. Liam walked down the hallway without another word.

"Okay, so he's a little rough around the edges," Dustin said, palms up in surrender. "I'll talk to him." He grabbed his bag and headed toward his first class. Jessica and I exchanged confused expressions, then followed after him like ducklings. Before we could press him, he spoke. "Can you believe his dad is an FBI agent? Dude, this guy's skillset is pretty amazing. He has all his quals for shooting at an agent level because of his father. And the equipment he has . . ." Dustin let out a low whistle—"is state of the art. Some of it I haven't even seen on the market." He shook his head as he slowed his pace to match ours. "I mean, his whole family was FBI, and he's planning on following in his dad's footsteps. I could learn a lot from him."

My mouth hung open like he'd slapped me. The traitor, drooling over that stuffed peacock. "Um, Dustin." I snapped my fingers under his nose, hoping to bring him back to reality. "You realize that jerk has a serious ego problem and is completely insane, right? He thinks he's a vigilante but the only thing he's taken out is my dresser, which he claims is connected to the murders. Doesn't that seem ludicrous to you? A murderous dresser?"

Like a boy struck by Cupid's arrow, Dustin said, "Yeah, I could see how it appears to you. He doesn't communicate with girls well. Not sure why. I saw a few drooling over him just this morning. You'd think he'd like the attention." He lifted one shoulder and dropped it. "But I swear if you got to know him like I do, you'd like him."

Okay, now Dustin was worrying me. *Know him?* He spent less than thirty minutes with the guy.

"Give him a chance." He threw his arm around me and squeezed.

Jessica's face twisted, and she released a sound like hawking up a loogie. "You've met him once before today, and he tossed you across the room." Jessica clutched her books to her chest like they could anchor her in reality.

Dustin flashed an apologetic smile. "Yeah, about that . . . He totally apologized again when we, well, we kind of hung out. In fact, he and his dad almost shot me when I showed up at their motel room, but they apologized for that too. Guess they saw my shadow from the window and thought I was a bad guy." He chuckled, dropping his arm from my shoulder. "I've been there almost every day since we met. Honestly, they're really cool."

"What?!" Jessica and I squawked in tandem.

But before Dustin could explain himself, the bell rang.

"See you ladies at lunch. And try to be nicer to Liam. He's a great guy once you get to know him." Dustin waved as he headed in the opposite direction.

"Did you hear that or am I dreaming?" Jessica asked me as we walked into science class. "*That's* why we didn't see Dustin once while school's been out. He dumped us for the Hunter family."

"Between my lovesick sister *and* Dustin's bromance, I'm really starting to hate this guy."

I couldn't help but relive my sister's nightly gushing sessions. That girl hadn't set foot in my room in years, but after the Hunter family's visit, she'd been climbing into the guest room bed with me to talk about Liam. Part of me loved that she was turning to me to talk about a boy, but couldn't she crush on someone more worthy of her time? Someone who would be a positive influence? I was already contending with Billy Lyons, Falkville Falls's honorary delinquent. He'd gotten Pepper wrapped up in vandalism and, if I had to guess, was also the reason she'd been labeled a thief.

With a deep calming breath, I hurried to my seat before Mr. Romano addressed the class.

I retrieved my textbook and notebook from my backpack, and by the time I looked up, Liam had appeared at the front of the classroom, and Mr. Romano's hand was resting on his shoulder.

"We have a new student today: Liam Hunter. Give him your best Falkville Falls welcome and introduce yourselves after class." He gave Liam a dutiful grin. "Nice to have you. Impressive school records."

Jessica turned to me and mouthed, *What the hell?*

Liam smiled in response and headed to the back of the room, taking the seat right behind me. I swiveled in my chair. "Really? There are three open seats and this one is the one you want?" My brow rose.

Liam's lips curled in a Grinchy grin. "I always sit close to the exit." He tossed his head toward the door. "In case I need to help in an emergency or, you know, tackle any gun-toting maniacs."

"Like you?"

He leaned in so close, his breath grazed my cheeks. "Exactly." He tapped me on the nose. "But it's cute how you think everything I do has something to do with you."

I swatted his hand. "Well, it's not cute how much crap you get away with because of your high-powered daddy. Does he tell you you're special? Because you act like every other entitled douchebag to me."

His cocky grin dropped into a dark frown for a moment so brief I could have imagined it. "Well, you look like every other uptight, self-righteous, vanilla Goody Two-shoes." Though a smile played at his mouth, he scanned me with fierce eyes. "Too much effort for a mediocre personality and church-girl kisses." He leaned over the desk, our lips a sheet of paper's distance apart, like he wanted those boring church-girl kisses after all.

Hot in the face, I backed up and said, louder than intended, "You are such an arrogant jerk!"

"Olivia," Mr. Romano barked. "Is that any way to welcome a new student?" He shook his head. "I'm disappointed in you."

"Are you serious, Mr. Romano?" I responded without thinking. "You don't even know this guy. He's a complete—"

Mr. Romano stalked toward my desk, silencing my rant. "You just earned yourself detention. Friday, after school. Congratulations."

My jaw dropped, but I said nothing. I'd never gotten detention before. This guy elicited the worst in me, and I was letting it happen.

For the next sixty minutes, my anger broiled on high heat. After repositioning myself in the chair half a dozen times, I grabbed a calming stone from my purse and squeezed the life out of it. To my dismay, nothing relieved the resentment that was coiled around my lungs like barbed wire. This jerk waltzed himself into my life and started taking over like he was God's greatest gift.

The second the bell rang, I shot out of my seat, not even waiting for Jessica. I did happen to catch a glimpse of Liam approaching Mr.

Romano's desk, probably awarding me a week's worth of detention. I hurried down the hall toward my locker and barreled right into Jac. "Watch where you're going!" I growled and continued along my path. Sure, I might have overreacted, but she shared *his* DNA and that alone made her Team Liam.

Jac laughed and followed me. She even walked pretty, hips sashaying like a dancer in a music video.

"In my experience, there are two reasons a girl gets this angry. One is a monthly, biological curse, nothing we can really do about that one." She shrugged. "And the other, which is way worse, is my brother."

When I stopped at my locker, Jac leaned her shoulder against the neighboring door. "So, did he pull your hair, make out with your best friend, steal your homework?"

I scrunched up my nose. "He steals people's homework?"

Jac smiled. "As far as I know, just mine. Although, Liam is an idiot savant. He speaks three languages and has a four point oh, but that little weasel loves having me do his homework." She unzipped her bag. "In his defense, it's because he works nights with my dad sometimes." Jac showed me a stack of papers in a manila envelope. "So, I make sure he has plenty of prewritten work for his classes."

"But you're not even in the same grade. You're telling me you do senior math?"

"Technically, I'm at a college level in all subjects, so yes. Senior work is easy." She tucked the papers back into her bag and zipped it up. "We call it progressive homeschooling."

"Who *are* you people?" My blood boiled, riled by the Hunters' seeming perfection—a pretty, glossy coating hiding their reckless insanity. Their father was one bizarre role model.

"We're the Hunters," Jac said, batting her thick lashes. "But in all seriousness, don't let my brother get to you." Jac moved a step closer and whispered, "If you want him to drop the act, tell him something personal. Vulnerability normally throws him off guard."

"How do you expect me to do that?" I slammed my locker shut. Vulnerable? I didn't have any secrets or hidden fears. What could I tell him? And why was I even considering it? Who cared what he thought?

"Tell him about your mom?" Jac offered. Before I could scoff my outrage for her bringing up the subject, she continued: "I'm not saying it to be a jerk. I'm saying it because it's something the two of you have in common. We lost our mom." She threw her bag over her shoulder, pink lips tipping upward. "It's just a suggestion." And with that, she walked away.

My mom? I never talked about her. I took a page out of my father's book on that one. What would I even say? She died in childbirth. I didn't know the particulars, and I didn't want to.

I slammed my locker and reset the lock. My hand slipped into my pocket to find my soothing stone when I heard Jessica call me, her shoes slapping the tiles. Her red ponytail bounced against her back as she ran over.

"It's Pepper," she said, somewhat out of breath, when she reached me.

"Is she okay?" My heart pounded.

She shook her head. "She's in Principal McKenna's office." Jessica held her chest, nostrils sucking in air. "Your sister assaulted a teacher."

7

OLIVIΛ

Pepper physically assaulted a teacher. I waited for the surprise to drop, like the first descent of a roller coaster, but sadly, it never came. Instead, my stomach caved as I released a heavy sigh, wilting me like a plucked flower.

Between me getting detention and Pepper getting suspended—or worse, expelled—Dad would lose it.

"Thanks," I told Jessica. I darted toward Principal McKenna's office. I turned two corners and was about to hit the third when a hand snatched my arm.

"Where are you going so fast?" Liam asked as I swung around him and nearly tumbled. He steadied me with his firm hold and peered down his nose at me, eyes suspicious.

I tugged my arm out of his grasp as the bell for the next class shrilled. "Why do you care?"

"Why does it matter why I care?" He looked around at the empty halls. "Spill it, speed racer. Where are you off to?"

"My asshole sister probably got herself expelled from school," I said, briskly walking toward the office. I found myself playing with the soothing stone inside my jeans pocket, hoping it would rid me of stress's constrictor hold on my guts.

Liam matched my pace. "What did she do?"

"Assaulted a teacher." I had no idea why I even entertained his questioning. It was probably easier than fighting him, though.

When I got to the principal's office, I turned the knob and walked into the waiting area. Four upholstered wooden chairs were lined up against the wall. I chose the one that allowed me a better view of our principal reading Pepper the riot act. Her office door stood ajar, and I saw Pepper slouched in a chair, her chin dipped to her chest. I couldn't hear all the words, but I got the general gist. Pepper kicked Mr. Bailey, her Western Civilizations teacher.

Instead of taking the seat next to me, Liam burst through McKenna's door.

I jumped up and scurried after him, hissing, "What the—?"

"Pepper, what did the teacher do to you?" Liam asked, glaring. Pepper's arms were crossed against her chest. Blue hair curtained her face, but I saw a sliver of flaming red cheeks. "What did this Mr. Bailey do to make you assault him?" Liam asked again, emphasizing each word.

"Young man, you cannot be in here," Principal McKenna said, now standing behind her desk. Her tented fingers pressed on the oak hard enough to whiten the tips below her red polish.

Liam ignored her and walked to Pepper's chair, crouching with an arm thrown over the back.

"She's not going to tell you anything. She hasn't said a word this whole time," Principal McKenna said. "There's no excuse for her behavior."

Liam aimed a glare at the principal before returning his focus to Pepper, softening his face. "I don't need to know you well to know you didn't assault a teacher who didn't deserve it." His voice shook with such conviction that it almost made me feel guilty. But I knew Pepper better than he did. She thrived at sardonic commentary and was perfectly capable of lashing out at an authority figure. "What happened?" Liam asked with a gentleness I couldn't have imagined he possessed. He tucked back the blue hair veiling her eyes.

Pepper turned her head revealing her puffy, red eyes and the mascara streaking her cheeks. I wanted to run to her and take her in my arms. Instead, I stood paralyzed.

She averted her gaze as she murmured, "He grabbed my ass." Tears spilled over her lashes, and Liam wiped them across the dark smudges, erasing both before confronting Principal McKenna. His hand rested on Pepper's shoulder, giving it a gentle squeeze.

"You were screaming at Miss Davis two seconds ago, for what? Defending herself against a teacher who sexually assaulted her, and *she's* treated like the criminal?"

Principal McKenna's jaw dropped.

"Do you normally start yelling first and ask questions later? Or do you not care about your students' side of the story?" Liam didn't stop. "You should be ashamed. I assume you'll at least have the sense to fire Mr. Bailey. While I *will* make sure he is investigated." His stormy blue eyes watched Pepper wipe away her own tears. "Because if this happened to her, you know damn well it's happened to other students, and for all we know, those other instances could have been worse."

Principal McKenna closed her mouth, then reopened it, trying to find words. I could sympathize.

I struggled finding my own voice.

Heavy breathing behind me alerted us to someone else in the room. I turned, and my eyes widened. Jac. How the hell did she get here? How much had she heard?

"Dad's on his way," Jac answered from the doorway. Her chest rose and fell as if she had run here. Liam nodded to her.

Weird. I'd add this to my ever-growing list of Hunter eccentricities.

Liam placed his palms on Principal McKenna's desk. "You've got three dead teachers and now a sex offender on your hands. I'd be very careful if I were you, Principal McKenna. People lose their jobs over far less." He retreated and patted Pepper on the back. "Let's go."

Principal McKenna's gaze followed us out the door, seemingly still too stunned to speak. The Hunters flanked Pepper for the whole walk to the parking lot. I followed in complete silence.

"Come on, Pepper," Jac said, pointing to their Bronco. "I'll take you home."

Liam tossed the keys to Jac, who caught them in one hand. "Be careful," he said. "Apparently, there's more than one monster in this town, and I doubt the local law-enforcement officers would be as chill with you driving underage as me and Dad are." Liam winked at his sister.

She gave him a "yeah, yeah" look, flicking him away like a bothersome bee.

Liam helped Pepper into the car. Before he closed the door, he whispered something that made her smile. It was the first genuine grin I had seen on her face in years. Every muscle in my body knotted. Jealousy squeezed my heart until I thought it might pop.

Liam closed the door, and we watched in stillness as they drove away. I had said nothing, just stood there. I wasn't even sure what to say. Liam started to walk back into school. I hurried after him.

"How did you know?" I strode alongside him, which proved to be a workout.

At the front door, Liam whirled on me, eyes darkening into sapphires. He looked pissed . . . at me, like I had done something wrong. "The better question is, how *didn't* you know?" His lips thinned into a straight line.

"Are you actually mad at me?" I asked, completely taken aback. Pepper was *my* sister, *my* responsibility. Not his! Where did he get off?

He laughed—a sinister sound weighted in the back of his throat. But when he spoke, his tone stayed frightfully even. "The fact you are even surprised that your sister was the victim is sad. I wouldn't for one second question Jac if she struck someone." He crossed his arms and squinted at me like I was a bug on his windshield. "Do you ever wonder why your sister is so mad at you and your dad? Why she hangs out with kids who defile walls and steal things? Have you ever sat down and asked her?"

I squared my shoulders and jutted my chin. "Are you serious right now?" I mimicked his posture and crossed my arms over my heart. "You don't know the first thing about my sister and me. You don't know the first thing about my family. How dare you judge us! Or me for that matter!"

Liam raised a brow. "I don't have to know about you specifically to know about family." His features softened along with his tone. "She's hurting, Olivia, and she doesn't know how to talk about it."

Whether he had a point or not, who did he think he was? He had no right to take charge of my sister or accuse me of not caring, of not making an effort. We weren't perfect, but it wasn't like Pepper made it easy. She fought me every step of the way no matter how hard I tried.

"Oh, and you are completely in touch with your feelings?" I mocked him.

The muscle in his jaw popped. "No. I suck at emotions, at being open, but"—he held up his finger—"when it comes to Jac, I'd bleed my heart out to any stranger if it meant helping her. In fact, I'm sure she already gave you the vulnerability speech." He waved his hands around the parking lot. "Go ahead, open up to me." He laughed. "She says that to people because she thinks I'll react the same way I do to her, but I don't love anyone like I love my family. So, hit me with your best shot, but it's gonna bounce right off." He yanked open the door but didn't go inside, tossing a few final daggers over his shoulder. "Maybe you don't allow Pepper to come to you because you're afraid of what she might ask."

And with that, he disappeared into the school.

Dread twisted in my belly. Maybe he was right. I could still hear the last serious question she ever asked me . . . those haunting, pleading eyes and the huge silence that hung between us, pushing us apart. But I didn't know the answer when she'd asked me if she'd killed our mother.

By the time I made it home from school, Pepper was already locked in her room. She didn't even come down for dinner, which curdled my own appetite. I hoped I could make things up to her in the morning. Not that I had any idea how. Back in my own room at last, I went to bed.

At some point in the night, a creak in the floorboards pulled me out of my slumber. With my face in my pillow, drool dripping from the corner of my mouth, I froze, all my senses on high alert. It's not like I believed Liam had really seen something in my room, but the seed of doubt he'd lain had started to bloom. An ice pick of fear rammed through my skull.

In truth, I'd never felt completely alone at night within these four walls or even in my dreams. Déjà vu plagued me often; snippets from my sleep would be plucked straight out of my head and become a reality. Stupid things, like a question Dad asked or a shoe Pepper left on the stairs. It was the freakiest thing.

Our floorboards always made weird noises, especially in Pepper's room. I had mentioned it once at dinner. Dad's reasoning was "It's an old house with old bones," but Pepper—well, she downright told me it was all in my head and that she didn't hear a thing. But I knew that wasn't the truth.

Right around two years ago, Pepper started talking in her sleep, and ever since then, our home's strange creaks and cracks woke me at all hours of the night. It wasn't like I feared the boogeyman, but at first, the phantom sounds creeped me out. Then, when nothing became of them, my fear lost its credibility, and I found myself laughing at my delusions.

Turning my head a fraction of an inch, I saw a shadow stretch across my floor. It started to move, and my heart cantered. Sweat prickled the back of my neck. Having no choice but to face my fears, I flipped around, confronting the window next to my bed and whatever horror had managed to get through the row of protective black tourmaline stones. Nothing. Just the oak tree in the front yard swaying. I checked the floorboards and watched the shadow move in time with the branches. My breathing slowed. Relief set in. The moon had cast the tree's shadow in sharper relief than usual.

Several minutes passed before my pulse returned to normal. I rolled back over and closed my eyes. The sound of my own breathing began to lull me back into a slumber until I heard Pepper sleep talking across the hall.

"Don't do that again. I don't want them to hurt you." There was a brief pause. "And I don't want you to hurt them. They're my friends."

I glued my eyes to our adjoining wall, waiting to hear more over the thud of my heart and at the same time praying she'd keep quiet. My mind soared with a million possibilities but landed on the only thought that ever stuck.

We weren't alone.

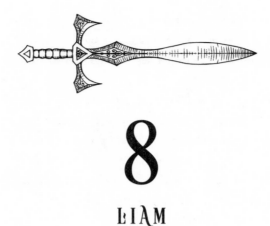

8

LIAM

Jac rubbed her temples as we sat in the precinct's waiting room. My butt lost feeling in the blue plastic bucket seat.

Sheriff Davis wanted Pepper to give an official statement about her teacher's assault, and Pepper asked Jac and me to be there for it. We'd agreed to all go together the following day. But before we left, Dad and I had taken a detour to Principal McKenna's office, and he chewed her out a hell of a lot worse than I had.

When she'd tried to bring up my "inappropriate" behavior, Dad stopped her. "I'd be less worried about my son's actions and more concerned with yours." He'd pivoted and walked out. In the Hunter family, we had each other's backs. Always.

Jac pointed at our matching black watches, calling me to the present. "Dad thought there was another school attack yesterday when the app registered your pulse at hunting levels."

Jac had developed an app that monitored our heart rates and tracked our location. The idea came to her about six months ago, when we had gotten separated during a windigo hunt, and it almost cost Jac her life. Windigos are nasty-ass creatures, abnormally tall and gangly, with barely-there lips and jagged teeth. They'll eat any human who ventures into their territory, and Jac had almost become a midnight flesh snack. Thankfully, we caught the monster, cut its icy heart out, and then melted the beating flesh in a roaring fire. But that had lit a fire under Dad too. He'd decided from then on that we needed a way to quickly locate one another in times of distress.

When our pulse got higher than a certain range, the app alerted all three of us with a push notification. You'd press the app icon on your watch, and the location of the family member would be pinned.

Jac's and Dad's watches had alerted them to my angry outburst, amplified when I'd seen the tears in Pepper's eyes. I'd heard my cadence rise to screams and plummet to growls at roller-coaster speeds. Apparently, my pulse had taken a ride of its own. Too bad Mr. Bailey wasn't a supernatural monster, because then that fucker would be dead already.

"Probably for the best that you came when you did. It took all my self-control not to stalk the halls searching for this Mr. Bailey," I said, pressing the icon to see my current heart rate steady at eighty-six. "Principal McKenna is a blind old bat in more ways than one."

"You were doing fine on your own. You handled it just like Dad would have," Jac said with a proud smile.

I returned it with one of my own.

"So, I did more research on this town." Jac lowered her voice. "The volunteer nurse who died a couple years ago has a sealed file."

My ears perked up. "And did we break said sealed file open?" Jac could hack the Department of Defense if we needed her to.

To my surprise, Jac shook her head. "No. The file was erased. Like someone went into the hard drive and completely wiped her record. Maybe the hospital?" She leaned closer. "That's not the only weird thing. Sheriff Davis submitted a request to have her removed from Falkville Falls High School soon after they had hired her."

My brows furrowed. "How did you find that out?"

"I hacked Principal McKenna's email." She smiled, handing me her cell where she'd pulled up the email.

For official reasons I cannot divulge, it would be in the best interest of Falkville Falls High School if Ms. Daryl was removed from the assistant nurse position. Although I understand this is a part-time job, it is not one Ms. Daryl is suited for. I caution that her assumption of this role is not in the best interest of Ms. Daryl and/or the school.

Sheriff Davis

"That's it? There's no response or anything?"

Jac shook her head. "She was killed the next day. Hung exactly where they found the athletic advisor, with another gym rope."

I sucked a breath through my teeth. It couldn't be a coincidence.

"Did we get her case files? Anything unusual from this one compared to the others?"

"Yeah, just one variation from the others." Jac paused, eyeing the room. "She had bruising in the shape of hands around her neck. Someone choked her, and yet no one labeled this a possible murder? It was deemed a suicide. What suicidal person tries manual strangulation on themselves first?" She rolled her eyes and answered her own question. "No one."

I squinted. "Who was the officer in charge of the case?"

A shadow fell over us, and Jac gulped. "Hey, Sheriff Davis, how's it going? Having an excellent day, I hope?"

Well, my sister's blathering answered that question. Intel was her strong suit. Deception was mine.

As if it were a real inquiry, the sheriff answered, "Hasn't been my best." He had his arm around Pepper, who wasn't fighting the affection. "Thank you for what you kids did yesterday for my daughter." He gave her a little squeeze. "I truly am grateful."

I stood up. "We always have our friends' backs." I winked at Pepper.

She slipped from her father's embrace and threw her arms around me. In a tone so low I could barely hear her, she whispered, "Thank you."

I returned the hug. "You're very welcome."

"Sheriff." A deputy approached with heavy strides. "We've got a problem. You know the situation the station up north told us about?"

Sheriff Davis nodded.

"Apparently, they think the"—the deputy flashed a glance at us—"perpetrator might be coming our way."

Sheriff Davis's brow creased. "Kids, can you wait here? I need to talk to Officer Apple."

Jac threw me a sidelong glance.

"Sure, Sheriff," I said, holding up my cell. "I was going to call my dad to see where he is anyway."

The sheriff and officer moved into the sheriff's office. I waited until their backs were turned before I slipped past another deputy, headed for the station's main lobby to listen with my serum-enhanced hearing.

"Matt, the pictures are gruesome. Another two campers were mutilated. Skin torn right from their bones and"—I heard the officer suck in a breath—"there were teeth marks on their necks. What type of creature would do such a thing? Real animals don't attack like that. It's like the psycho drank their blood before murdering them."

That's all I had to hear. The vamps were closer than I thought.

I'd started back toward Jac when Olivia barreled in. She ran for Pepper, but a glaring Pepper backed away from the oncoming embrace. She hadn't forgiven Olivia yet for standing there like a raccoon caught in a garbage can while Principal McKenna yelled at her.

I took Olivia's wrist and pulled her back. "Who's hungry? How about Olivia and I go grab some pizza?"

"Good plan, son," Sheriff Davis said, stepping out of his office. "This time, why don't you leave your guns at home?"

"Perfect. Wasn't feeling like target practice tonight anyway." I smirked.

Sheriff Davis chuckled. "Will your dad be joining us?"

"I'm sure. I'll leave him a message and let him know to meet us on his bike. Olivia and I will pick up the pie. Cheese sound good?" I didn't wait for anyone's response. "Jac, go with the sheriff and Pepper." I mussed her hair before leading Olivia toward the exit.

"She hates me. She wouldn't even acknowledge me last night at home," Olivia whimpered as we walked through the snow-dusted parking lot. The overcast sky reflected a dull sheen off the white powder. "Not that I blame her. I just stood there, even after she told us what happened." She huffed. "How could I have stayed silent?"

I moved my hand down her wrist to lace my fingers through hers. The small gesture sent an unexpected warmth up my arm and to my heart. The need to protect Olivia and Pepper—from anything the world threw at them, not just monsters—had become palpable. "Nah, she's a kid. She'll forgive you. Just give her time."

Olivia looked from our interlocked hands to my face. Whatever thoughts hid behind her eyes, she didn't share. Instead, she gave me a gentle squeeze and bit her lower lip.

As we approached the car, she said, "Nineteen seventy-two Bronco. You know this model is built on a ninety-two-inch wheelbase." She swept her free hand over the hood, leaving finger trails in the thin layer of snow. "The Bronco used box-section body-on-frame construction. All cars were sold with four-wheel drive; a shift-on-the-fly Dana Twenty transfer case, and locking hubs. The rear axle was a Ford nine-inch axle, with Hotchkiss drive and leaf springs; the front axle was a Dana Thirty, replaced by a Dana Forty-four in nineteen seventy-one."

I released her hand and clapped. "Okay, that was impressive and kind of hot. How do you know so much about cars?"

She pressed both hands onto the hood. "I don't know much about all cars. But this one . . ." She sighed. Her eyes may as well have become cartoon hearts as she ogled the automobile. "I know everything about this one." I thought she was going to hug it, she was so enamored. "Maybe we got off on the wrong foot," she said, turning to face me. Her hazel eyes softened when they found mine.

I remembered how I snickered at her my first day in town.

"I did laugh at you in the parking lot, then rearranged your room with a bullet. If you think about it, it'd be weird if we started out on any other foot."

She perched her hands on her hips. "Why? Why do you have to ruin a good moment?"

I leaned against the car. The cold snow soaked through my jeans, but I didn't care. My lips twitched as I watched Olivia unravel in front of me. "We were having a good moment. Do tell?"

She threw her hands in the air, waving them around. "I thought we were moving past you being an ass. I thought we were—"

I laughed so hard I practically keeled over, and her mouth snapped shut. "We were what? You think because I held your hand while walking in a parking lot together and you sweet-talked me about my car that I'm what? Done being myself?" Olivia was cool, but chemistry or not, I had to stopper any curiosity or connection. Hunting monsters took precedence over everything but family, and we'd be leaving soon, so why risk getting attached? After a minute of waiting, the passenger door opened, and Olivia climbed in.

"Fine, Hunter. If you don't want to be civil, we can continue this song and dance, but if you think I'm the only messed-up person here, you're fooling yourself."

She crossed her arms, closing herself off physically.

I allowed a devilish smile to spread across my face. "Oh, Olivia, I'm as messed up as they come. The only difference is I can acknowledge who and what I am, while you're afraid of what you are."

She ground her teeth so loudly, I feared she might break them. "And what's that?"

"Willfully ignorant."

Needless to say, we didn't talk much after that.

The rest of the night at the Davis house was tame. Dad and Matt drank whiskey and smoked cigars on the back deck after dinner while we kids relaxed in the family room. We streamed a classic movie, *Teen Wolf* with Michael J. Fox. Apparently, the Davis girls had never seen it. What a limited childhood they had!

During the movie, I caught Olivia watching me. She'd toggle between biting her lower lip and grinding her teeth, an internal battle playing out across her mouth. A mouth I wouldn't mind playing with myself.

Unfortunately, according to my father, she and her pretty lips were off-limits. It was better that way, really. If I thought about it, I was doing her a favor, fighting off that I-want-you look she'd been flashing me from the moment I saw her in the parking lot. I remembered her eye catching mine. I'd known who she was within seconds, thanks to Jac's preemptive research. But her inquisitive look across the asphalt sent all the right feelings through me. Realizing my job at Falkville Falls High would go a lot smoother with her as a captivated audience, I'd started to laugh.

But now, having gotten to know her more, I was laughing less.

As the credits rolled, Pepper snickered. "Man, how freaking cool would it be to be a werewolf?"

Jac shot me a sideways glance.

"Too bad they aren't real," Olivia said, shitting on her sister's good time.

"Shifters are totally real," I said, facing Pepper.

I wasn't sure why I blurted it out. Maybe because I hated how Olivia dismissed Pepper's excitement, or maybe because keeping my whole life a secret weighed on me, but I couldn't help myself.

"But werewolves aren't that cool in real life. They don't just magically shift back when the sun comes up. They have to eat a human heart to become human again. If they don't, the wolf hunger kills them before the next full moon." Pepper's mouth hung open, while Jac's lips pressed into a tight line. But I didn't stop there. "Easy to kill them, though. Silver bullet to the heart does the trick in seconds."

"Is that what you blasted Livy's room with?" Pepper asked, hovering on the edge of her seat.

"Nah, I used rock-salt rounds." I crossed my ankle over my thigh, ignoring Jac's searing glower. I liked a captive audience, and Pepper was all ears. "Those puppies can dissipate ghosts or other undead fiends." Pepper looked like a ghoul herself, suddenly pasty and wide-eyed. *Probably a superstitious type*, I thought. In my world, we called that perceptive. "Unfortunately, it's not a permanent solution," I concluded. "They can appear again moments later, depending on the strength of the spirit."

Jac popped to her feet. "Hey Liv, any chance I can see your room?" she asked, entirely too peppy. "We travel so often with my family, I've never had my own. I like meeting new people and seeing how they set it up."

Smart. Leave it to Jac to get back on track with our objective. We needed to search for any remnants of a witch's talisman to corroborate the burst of light I saw.

Olivia didn't acknowledge Jac, too busy glaring at me.

Jac added, "And it'll be a great chance for a little distance between you and my brother."

Apparently, that was all the motivation Olivia needed. "Sure. I just moved back in last night. It took my dad and his friend all weekend to put it back together." Olivia pushed to her feet.

"Great. Can't wait to see it," Jac said, rolling her eyes and pulling Olivia out of the room toward the stairway and away from me.

Pepper leaned back on the couch, throwing her hands behind her head. Color had returned to her cheeks. "You know she likes you," she said, smiling like a fool. "I've never seen her so twisted over a guy before."

I kicked up my heels onto the ottoman, matching Pepper's recline. "Oh yeah? How do you know?"

"She bites her lower lip when she gets all tingly in the pants, and she's practically bleeding from all the gnawing she's been doing." Pepper laughed. "So, you like her back or what?" She crossed her arms like she was about to give me "the talk."

"I thought *you* were interested in me," I joked, tapping her feet with my boots. "Gonna give up on me that easily and hand me over to your big sister?"

"You're too old for me." She sat upright and tucked a loose strand of hair behind her ear. "Plus, I could use a friend like you." She studied the floor. "I don't have many."

I shifted forward, resting my forearms on my thighs.

"Pepper." I drew out her name and waited until she looked into my eyes, allowing herself a moment of exposure. "I am your friend. And if you ever need me—whether we still live here or not—you call me. You got that?"

She dipped her chin. "Thanks." With her pointer finger, she tapped her lips. "I think you should kiss my sister and see what happens."

I rubbed my jaw, imagining Olivia's reaction if I tried. "I think I like having all my teeth, thank you very much."

Pepper and I laughed together, but then she grew serious. "Maybe one day you can teach me how to kill werewolves, and then I can hunt with you."

My eyes widened. She'd placed weight behind the word *hunt*, as if she knew what it meant to me. Before I could ask her any more questions, Dad and Sherriff Davis burst into the room, faces awash with fear.

I jumped out of my seat. "What? What happened?"

Dad cleared his throat. "Mr. Bailey was found this evening in the detainment cell at the precinct"—he paused, shoving his hands in his pockets—"hung to death."

9

OLIVIA

Dad, Agent Hunter, and Liam all left within minutes of the announcement, leaving Jac to stand guard at the house. Why my dad thought a fourteen-year-old would be suitable protection was beyond my wildest comprehension. Pepper made it through three minutes of arguing about wanting to go with them before my dad threatened a grounding sentence and she stormed upstairs, each step so heavy I worried her foot would plunge through the wood.

Before Liam left, he pulled out a revolver and handed it to Jac without my father seeing, ignoring the "no gun" request. Jac stuck it into the back waistband of her jeans. Liam mussed her hair and walked out.

"I saw that," I said, pointing to the bulge in her sweater.

"Great, then you know the danger is real and that having me here is a good thing." She smiled. "There are things you don't know and can't even begin to understand, Liv. Just let us handle this."

"Handle what?" I waved my hands around the family room. "It's not like you go around solving serial killings."

Jac placed one hand on her hip. "Actually, that's exactly what we do." She huffed. "Let's go back upstairs. Since we are being candid now," she looked up at the closed bathroom door as if making sure Pepper couldn't hear while showering, "I needed to get into your room to do a search, not to see your pretty decorations." Her grin didn't match her eyes. "I've been looking for something that would explain why my brother assaulted your room." She started toward the stairs. "Mind if I have another look?"

"Be my guest," I said, waving her forward. "Like I have a choice," I mumbled. I walked with her to my room, mentally noting that insanity ran in the Hunter family gene pool.

I observed as Jac checked behind books, pillows, stuffed animals, my crystal collection, and thoroughly examined each nook and cranny of my nightstand. I leaned against the door frame and scrutinized her every move.

Finally, after ten minutes of watching her flit around my room, inspecting it like Sherlock Holmes, I spoke. "This is ridiculous." I huffed. "What are you even looking for?"

She lay flat on her belly to search under my bed, her voice muffled. "You won't believe me, so I'm better off saving my breath."

I laugh-coughed. Taking the bait, I said, "Try me. The worst I can say is that I think you're just as crazy as your brother." I moved across the room, keeping my eyes fixed on her. "But maybe if I know more, I can help."

Why not? I had nothing better to do while Dad, Agent Hunter, and Liam were at the jail assessing the fatality. I still couldn't believe my father let Liam accompany him to a closed crime scene. What help would an eighteen-year-old boy offer?

Jac wiggled her body out from under my bed and pushed herself up to her knees. Her gaze drifted to my desk, focusing on all my essential oils and homemade balms. She straightened her posture, but not fast enough to hide the wave of apprehension that rolled over her demeanor.

I fidgeted, unable to control the unease that had taken over my body with her long pause.

"Oh, just spit it out."

"I'm not really good at 'the talk,'" she said using air quotes.

"The talk?" I raised a brow.

She smacked the dust off her hands before using my bed post to stand up. "Yeah, the one about who we are, what we do." She bit her cheek. "You really should clean under there. It's gross."

"Yeah, thanks. I'll get right on that." I tossed her the no-rinse hand cleaner that I had on my desk. She caught it one handed and squirted it onto her palms. "So, about the talk?" I said, bringing her back to the conversation.

She flapped her hands in the air to dry them off. "Well, your dad kind of freaked when he heard it, so I'm not sure if I really should . . ."

"For the love of God, out with it." I rubbed my eyes with the heels of my hands.

Jac sat cross-legged on my bed. "Okay. But let's note you're my first, so if this goes badly, remember, I'm working the kinks out on you."

"Whatever that means," I mumbled.

"My dad, Liam, and I are hunters." Before I could assure her I was well aware of their last name, she clarified. "Yes, our last name is Hunter, but we are monster hunters. We are part of an organization known as Hunterland, an online community with members all over the world."

"Monster hunters? Like the kind you were just looking for under my bed?" I said, half joking. I pointed at the flipped dust ruffle that was stuck in between my box spring and mattress.

Jac laughed. "No, silly. I was looking for any ritual anchors, charms, or hex sigils that a pissed-off witch might have left." She adjusted her legs. "You mess with any witches lately?" She half smiled.

I crossed my arms, gripping my biceps so hard, I was sure there'd be a mark. She was right, I didn't believe her, not one word, but her confidence impressed me enough to let her continue.

"Anyway, we hunt vampires, ghouls, ghosts, shifters, banshees, zombies, wraiths—pretty much anything damned. Fiends, soulless, revenants, that sort of thing. Witches can be good but there are also evil ones. They love to mess with the undead, so technically they fall into the same category. I always argue with Liam that they are the most dangerous, but he's really stuck on banshees being the worst. Figures, because they are women. He always thinks women are annoyingly more complicated. I just think it's because . . ."

I waved at her, cutting her off midsentence. "I'm sorry. Your family hunts things that aren't real?"

"Undead. Revenants. Definitely real. I'll show you." She pulled up her right sleeve and pointed to an inch-long scar on her forearm. "This is from a werewolf claw. A very hungry lycanthrope, who believed I was her next meal ticket until my brother shot her with a silver bullet." She rolled up her left pant leg. "This one is from a vamp fang, but he only broke the skin, never fed, so don't worry, I'm not turned or anything. Dad stuck a stake right through the vampy's heart." She moved her hair away from her neck, exposing her collarbone and pinkish raised skin in an oblong shape. "This one hurt the most. A wraith got me. He was a complete asshole." She rubbed the spot. "I actually killed him with the silver dagger I got for my twelfth birthday. It's really pretty. I even had it engraved with—"

I exploded from my seat. "You're nuts!" I started to pace. "Your whole family is nuts." I gestured to her calm posture. "Your everything is . . ."

"Nuts?" Jac finished my sentence, her eyes watching me wear out the carpet as I marched back and forth. "Seriously, I'm new at this but I think I did a great job. You're calmer than most people would be." She smiled proudly, showcasing all her perfect pearly whites. "You haven't run out of the room screaming or called me a liar. Although I'm not too keen on being called nuts, I'll take that over the names my father and brother have been called during the talk."

"You think this is a good reaction? You think this went well?" I questioned, shocked.

"Totally. I mean it would be odd if you just accepted my crazy story right away." She stood but kept her distance. "Your dad freaked out too, but my dad had some pretty convincing evidence on a kanima case your father could never solve that helped win him over."

"What? What is a kanima?" I flicked my hand. "Never mind. I don't even want to know." I shook my head. "My dad believes this crap? There's no way."

Jac crossed her arms and pressed her lips together. "Listen, good cops are logical and follow patterns. And when it comes to monsters, there isn't always a pattern—or at least not one that makes sense to law enforcement—so cops like your dad are always looking in the wrong places, and most of the time they jump to the wrong conclusions." She lowered her arms. "Like when a werewolf or a kanima attacks and eats hearts, most cops say it's a wild-animal attack." Jac shook her head and rolled her eyes at the same time. "Like an animal bite from a bear or coyote could do what a werewolf could. Anyway, most of the time the police go on how they were trained, their protocols. They aren't really out-of-the-box thinkers because they don't know that monsters are what is encircling their box. So yes, while your dad freaked at first, *my* dad," she said, pointing to her chest, "used police logic to show the how and why your dad's officers missed what is so obvious to us." She nodded. "You're welcome!"

My mouth opened to protest, but before one syllable sounded, a bright white light flashed. I attempted to speak but the words got stuck in my throat.

Jac threaded her arm behind her back, pulled out the gun, and pointed at a figure I could barely make out. The bright light blinded me. I closed my eyes and only reopened them when I heard Jac scream. "Get Pepper and get out of here. Now."

The starburst glow sizzled to life and began to take shape in the form of a woman. Her pale skin with a pearlescent sheen glistened in the glow from the light fixture. My eyes narrowed in on her face, but her straggly long hair covered most of it. Despite her fair complexion and barely solid clothing, shadowy darkness dripped from her translucent form, reminding me of the shadow I briefly saw in my room the previous night.

My heart thumped, my pulse raced. I pointed my trembling hand at the figure. "What is that?" My voice shook as tentacles of fear wrapped around my neck, choking the words out of me.

Gunfire sounded, and I jerked.

"Run!" Jac yelled, shooting more bullets into the being. The image dispersed into the air like a bag of flour being shot. Then another bright light from the opposite corner exploded, and the form started to take shape again. Jac twisted and fired again and again into each flicker of light. A scream threatened its way up my throat, but I hadn't found my voice yet, so I simply swallowed.

Pepper's shouts echoed from the hallway. "Stop shooting!"

I charged through my bedroom door. A purple terry-cloth-robed Pepper in matching fluffy slippers stood with a slack jaw and a pale face.

"Let's go!" I yanked her by the hand, leading her down the stairs and out the front door. Jac followed right behind us, shooting every couple of moments at a new eruption of light.

"Seriously, stop," Pepper repeated.

"Jac knows what she's doing!" I had no idea if that was true. She looked comfortable with a gun, but God, she was only fourteen years old. Who were these people?

"Get in the Bronco. Now!" Jac yelled as she threw me the keys. "You drive. I shoot!"

I caught the keys with one hand as I pushed Pepper toward the back door with my other. I jumped into the driver's seat, started the ignition, and drove like my heels were attached to a cement block, pressing the pedal to the floor of my favorite car. Nothing like a crisis to ruin the first time I drove my dream vehicle. We were two streets away from the house when Pepper cried out, throwing herself forward.

"My necklace! It's in my bedroom. We have to go back."

Jac twisted to face Pepper, her gun still in her hand. She cupped Pepper's face. "We will get it tomorrow, okay? But for now, we need to drive to the motel." Pepper sniffled, causing Jac to lower her voice. "My brother has got a sweet spot for you. I know he'll make it a priority. I promise. He's never let me down."

I looked in the rearview mirror and saw Pepper nod her agreement. Liam Hunter might not be the most courteous guy in the world when it came to me, but with my sister he acted like Prince Charming. And since the Hunters had come into our lives, Billy dumbass Lyons had barely even come up in conversation, much less been to the house. I had to be grateful to Liam for that, regardless of how he treated me. His compassion toward her softened my insides, sweeping aside the logical part of my brain that knew he was trouble.

Jac's phone sounded, breaking my internal thoughts. She picked it up on the first ring.

"Yeah. We are okay. It's not a witch. It's a freaking ghost!"

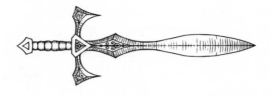

10

LIAM

We returned to the motel shortly after I hung up with Jac. Sheriff Davis asked for our room number, and as soon as we pulled into a parking spot, he shot out of his truck. We watched as he ran up the decrepit iron stairs to the second floor and threw open the motel-room door. We followed hot on his tail. Inside, he grabbed both daughters in one huge embrace.

Jac handed me back my revolver. "You're an ass. Rock-salt bullets, really?"

I smiled. For a witch, I would have given Jac a gun loaded with 9 mm rounds. But I gave her rock-salt bullets instead, which were used for fighting spirits. They would still incapacitate a witch, just might not kill them.

"Lucky guess," I said, mussing her hair. She swatted my arm away.

Last month, Dad told me to give Jac more reign. If she was wrong, she'd figure it out like we did when we first began hunting. Even though I was only four years older than Jac, I started in on the family business at a much younger age. Mom and Dad wanted to provide Jac with a normal childhood for as long as they could. So, we kept her away from hunting until she turned nine, the year my mother died by the canine teeth of a monster.

Dad placed his hand on my shoulder. "Nicely done, Liam."

Jac pushed me. "Why didn't you just tell me you thought it was a ghost?"

I pulled out a chair at the table and grabbed the closest potato-chip bag. "Because I wasn't positive. I just had a gut feeling."

Jac grabbed the bag. "Next time your stomach has rumblings, just man up and tell me." She opened the bag, took one whiff, and handed it back. Jac's taste buds were more like a rabbit than an average teenager. Carrot sticks and grapes for days—I didn't know how she managed. "I'm not a baby. I can handle being wrong."

The Davis family finally released one another but remained close together.

"Are you okay?" Sheriff Davis asked Pepper.

"Yeah, I wasn't scared," she said tying the robe string tighter around her waist.

Olivia draped her arm over Pepper's shoulder. "It all happened so fast." Her fingers wrapped around Pepper's damp hair, and she started methodically braiding it neatly down her back. "Bursts of light came out of nowhere. Then Jac would shoot it and the brightness would reappear across the room, never fully taking shape. Only once, I think I saw a woman." Olivia shivered. "But I couldn't be sure."

"We will go to city hall tomorrow and see if there were any deaths in that house before you bought it," Dad said, directing his statement to Matt. "It's an easy fix once we find out who the spirit is."

"I can have my boys run that info tonight." Sheriff Davis pulled out his phone. "If they find something, what do we do?"

"Burn the bones," Jac answered. "We find out where the remains are and scorch them, sending the spirit to its final resting place. Easy peasy."

Olivia finished the braid and wrapped her arms around Pepper, who wiggled herself out of the embrace.

"And then that's it, the killings will stop? At all the schools?"

"If it's the same vengeful spirit in your school, then yes, but there's always a possibility that there's more than one case here." I didn't mention that if this *was* the same spirit, one of the Davis family had to be carrying something on them that tied them to the ghost. But if we were dealing with multiple cases in Falkville Falls, the overlapping evidence would be hard to sort out. I'd love to find just one simple, straightforward hunt.

Sheriff Davis stopped mid-tap on his phone and let out a low whistle. His eyes trailed over the mortality board plastered on the wall above the tiny desk. "What in the world is this?"

Dad casually walked over to where the gaping sheriff stood pointing. "It's all the murders and evidence we've collected from the schools," he explained, bypassing the map and blocking it with most of his body. He directed the conversation to the pictures we had hung of the deceased, starting with the Montgomery High School nurse.

Jac tilted her head in my direction, motioning to the picture of Nurse Daryl we still hadn't tacked up. I meandered behind my father, swiping the image clipped to her file. I slipped it under my leather jacket, tucking it into my jeans. I glanced up to find Olivia shooting me a dark look.

"I need something to drink," she said, glaring and gesturing with her chin at my backside.

Caught red-handed.

"Finding out ghosts are real kind of leaves a girl parched." Olivia waved at her throat. "I'm sure there's a soda machine somewhere." She ground her teeth but managed the next words with painful execution. "Liam, would you mind escorting me? I'm a little nervous given my recent supernatural encounter."

I wasn't confident anyone else picked up on her deception, but her sour face reminded me of the time I convinced Jac to suck on a lemon for five dollars.

My father turned toward me. "There's one on the first floor. Get a couple sodas for the rest of us," he said. "I think the Davis family should stay here tonight, and tomorrow we will figure out the next steps."

"What?" My voice overlapped with Olivia's as we said the word in unison.

"I agree," Sheriff Davis said with authority. He didn't even look away from the comprehensive board.

As much as I wasn't keen on the idea, it made sense. If one of them was toting the spirit around with them, we'd find out tonight.

Pepper darted to the closest bed—mine. When I caught her eye, she winked. I couldn't help but laugh. She was fearless, I'd give her that. Already settled into her new environment and not phased one bit by a ghost appearing in her home.

The reactions varied from case to case, person to person. But Pepper acted like she belonged in our world. I shook the feeling and moved toward Olivia.

"I'll take the floor," I said, so Dad could keep his bed and Jac her cot. "Sheriff Davis can sleep on the pullout couch." That left Olivia the option of sleeping with her sister in my bed or with me on the ground. "I'll keep you warm if you want to sleep next to me." I waggled my brow at her.

"Absolutely not," Sheriff Davis said as his eyes broke momentarily from the board to narrow in my direction.

"Liam," my dad warned.

I held my palms up in surrender. "I was kidding. Calm down. Trying to lighten the mood, that's all." I motioned to Olivia. "Come on. Let's go get some hydration for everyone. I have a feeling it's going to be a long night."

The streetlights cast a muted glow over the old motel as we walked down the winding iron staircase to the first floor. It wasn't until we were in front of the illuminated vending machine that I noticed Olivia's pinched brows and scrunched-up nose.

"What are you hiding behind your back?" she asked, crossing her arms.

I grabbed my wallet and inserted my credit card. "How many you thinking? Like two sodas per person?"

Olivia smacked my arm. "I'm serious. What are you hiding from my dad?"

I tapped on the number pad for eight caffeinated colas. That should be enough.

She folded her arms again. "Okay, so monsters are real. You guys are the experts. Law officials, according to your sister, don't know anything about how to fight these creatures or whatever ghost was in my room." Her tirade stopped as she took in a deep breath. On her exhale, reality came crashing down. Moisture pooled in her eyes, and her body trembled. "Just tell me what you know, what you are hiding, tell me anything." Her words broke in her throat. "Maybe I can help. It was my room. The thing tried to attack or maybe kill—oh my God, I could have been hung, couldn't I?" She started to cry, no longer able to hold back the overwhelming number of emotions that must have been bubbling up inside.

I abandoned my credit card in the machine and turned to wrap her in my arms.

"It's okay." I ran my hands up and down her back. I threaded my fingers in her hair, hoping to soothe her. I continued the motion until her quivering body settled and then, if I'm being honest, a moment or two longer after that.

Placing my hands on her shoulders, I pushed her away a couple inches and lowered my head, resting my forehead against hers.

"I know it's scary, and I know it's really overwhelming, but you and your sister are doing great."

She sniffled.

"And I'm sure you have a million questions. So why don't you let me take you back upstairs so you can try and get some rest, and then tomorrow, I'll answer everything I can."

Her eyes went from red and swollen to shrewd and pointed. She backed up a step, creating space between us. Her sudden absence left my forehead colder than I'd expected. She threw her hands to her hips. "Are you trying to downplay this? Tell me that everything is going to be okay?"

My compassion vanished, replaced with irritation and confusion. "No. But I *am* trying to bring you peace. You need a good night's rest in order to process everything."

She pursed her lips. "Consider me processed. Now explain what you're not telling us."

Practically baring my teeth, I growled, "You are the most frustrating woman I have ever met." I looked up, recalling the banshee I had met last year that really pissed me off. Yeah, Olivia topped that.

She pushed me out of the way and stomped back toward the stairs.

Abandoning my credit card and drinks, I chased after her. I grabbed her by the hand, swinging her around to face me.

"I'm sorry, was the ghost in your house not enough trauma for one night?" She struggled to break free, but I held her fast, tugging her in closer. "Did you need more bad news? Like how the murders in your school have something to do with Nurse Daryl's death two years ago? How someone tried to cover it up? Does that help your anxiety? Will you sleep better tonight knowing the image I hid from your father is because a vengeful spirit might have some correlation to your dad or the school or the hospital itself?" I raised my voice at the end of my sentence for dramatic effect. Confusion clouded her eyes while the skin around her lips pinched. I tilted my head.

"Did you say Nurse Daryl?" She backed away from me, stopping when her backside hit the railing.

In a calm voice—since I had no idea why she just retreated from our closeness—I said, "Yes, we realized the murders started here, making a complete radius, and now they've come back home. Nurse Daryl was the first murder. That's the picture that's under my jacket."

Olivia gave me the once-over.

"I remember Nurse Daryl." She paused, gathering her thoughts. "My dad had a strong reaction when he heard she had been hired by our school. Not a *bad* reaction per se." She shook her head.

I reached for her, and this time she let me touch her wrist. "How so?" I wrapped my fingers around her and pulled her back into my personal space. Was it necessary? No. Did it make me feel better to be close to her again? Yes.

"Nothing really. Nurse Daryl sought me out at school, called me out of Ms. Dunne's creative writing class. It was strange. She was awkward, playing with her bracelet and fidgeting, but she didn't really say much."

I wondered if it was the same bracelet Sheriff Davis wore. Maybe we were looking at this wrong. Maybe Nurse Daryl was the vengeful spirit killed by a human and that's how it started at Falkville Falls.

Olivia looked to the side, as if remembering. "She introduced herself and then that was it. I told my dad about it."

Almost involuntarily, I tucked a stray hair clinging to Olivia's face behind her ear, her skin feeling chilly to the touch from the crisp winter air. "How did your dad react?"

Olivia shrugged. "Unnerved, maybe. I remember he wrote the school board a letter asking for her removal from the position." She shook her head. "I never asked why, but then she died, and he didn't say much else." She quickly added, "He wasn't relieved or anything that she was dead. He just didn't bring it up again. There was no need to."

"Did he know her?"

"Not that I know of." I could see the seed of doubt in her eyes. "I just assumed he had reacted that way because he thought it was inappropriate teacher behavior."

I thought about it for a second. Although it might be a cause for concern, a request for her removal instead of calling the principal for a sit-down seemed a bit drastic, even for Sheriff Davis.

"It could be. Or it could be something more," I offered.

Olivia started to pick at her nail polish. "I shouldn't even have brought it up. I'm sure it's nothing. It's not like my dad had anything to do with her murder, or any of the recent murders. He is the one trying to stop them. What would her death have to do with a ghost, anyway?"

I wrapped my arm around her shoulders and pulled her to my side. "I have no idea. But that's what we're going to find out." We retrieved the sodas and my credit card and headed back to the room.

I don't think I slept longer than an hour. Pepper's bulldog snores and Olivia's groans weren't exactly lullabies. All that noise made me toss and turn all night. Not to mention that my makeshift bed, comprised of old motel carpet and a thin sheet, did nothing to lull me to sleep. But my struggle didn't hold a candle to Sheriff Davis's when he woke and found out we would be going back to his house to get the girls' things. He paced in front of the window, making me wonder if there would be permanent footprints in his wake.

"In and out, right?" Sheriff Davis asked for the tenth time as the sun rose that morning.

Dad reassured him. "Yes, they will get their things and come right out. I'll go and salt the whole house while they are at school, and no spirit will get in there after I'm through. You can all be back in your house before nightfall."

I drove Olivia and Pepper to the Davis house to get ready for school while Sheriff Davis and my dad went to the station to continue their investigation into the murder of Mr. Bailey during his incarceration.

Jac and I kept watch in the hallway while a well-rested Pepper and an overly tired Olivia went inside their respective rooms to get dressed.

"Find out anything from your make-out session with Olivia?" Jac asked.

She rested her head against the wall and closed her eyes. I guess Pepper kept her up too.

I stared at Olivia's bedroom door, not wanting her in there alone. What if the spirit came back? But when I'd suggested I stay with her, Olivia fought me and said she needed privacy to get dressed. So, I cleared the room, lining the perimeter of both sisters' bedrooms with salt. If the spirit did appear, it couldn't harm them if they stayed inside the salt line.

"There was no spit swapping last night," I replied, assuring Jac of my good intentions.

Jac lifted her head and shot me a cynical look, making it obvious she didn't believe me.

"Seriously, we just talked." My leg bounced up and down. I really should be in there with her. As a precaution, I told myself.

"Glowering at her door like a creeper is not going to make her get dressed any faster." Jac put her hand on my thigh. "You are giving me secondhand anxiety with all your staring and twitching. Their rooms are lined with salt, and if for some reason this spirit is sneaky and breaks the line, we are seconds away." When I didn't acknowledge her logic, she continued: "If you see a bright light, we break the door down." Jac motioned to the rifle in my hand. "Okay?"

I nodded.

"I think Sheriff Davis knew Nurse Daryl," I said, changing the subject.

Jac's brow rose. "Did Olivia say that?"

"Not exactly, but she did mention Joanne Daryl wore a bracelet when they met, and Sheriff Davis wears one around his wrist that seems out of place." Not that a man can't wear jewelry. It just didn't appear to be a usual police officer's accessory.

"Did Olivia say what it looked like?" Jac asked.

I pursed my lips. "No, but remember when you said to trust my gut?"

"Yes."

"Matt Davis knew Joanne Daryl. I'd bet my life on it."

Both girls stepped out of their rooms. Pepper bounded down the stairs as Olivia, Jac, and I followed. We started toward the car and Olivia fell behind to lock the front door. I turned to look for her, and that's when I saw them: various school patches on Olivia's book bag, staring back at me. The patches didn't just represent Falkville Falls High School, but also Montgomery High School, Summerset High School, Franklin High School, and Levittown High School. All five schools who fell victim to the vengeful spirit clung to her bag, making a very good case for Olivia Davis as the reason the spirit appeared, killing at each school.

Holy crap! It had been Olivia all along.

My heart sank into my stomach. How many more would she put in danger before we could stop her?

11

OLIVIA

We pulled up to the school in the Bronco just as Jessica parked her car in the spot directly in front of us. I rubbed my temples and slouched in my seat, not daring to glance upward. My door opened before I could plan a stealthy escape.

Liam wrapped his arm around my waist and helped me out of the car. A chill ran through my bones, matching the cool winter temperature.

"You going to be okay today?" he asked, gently bringing the hood of my jacket over my head. I silently thanked him, hoping the cover hid my face from Jessica.

Little snowflakes swirled through the air, one landing on his nose. Without thought, I reached up and wiped it away. Liam gave me a small smile, but something dark hid behind his sunken, sleep-weary eyes. Before I could question his look or answer him, a familiar voice startled me.

"Seriously? Did I fall through a black hole and end up on some bizarro version of Earth?" Jessica stared over Liam's shoulder and squinted. "I know that shit happens. I've seen it on TV." Her eyes followed

Liam's hands resting on my hips, and heat rushed to my cheeks. I wiggled out of his grasp as he turned around and leaned against the car, his arms crossed.

Pepper and Jac rounded the car, and I swore Jessica gave them a double take with wide eyes. "Are you now living together? One big happy family?" She waved her hands at the four of us. "Why the hell are you and your sister getting a ride from this one?" She pointed her thumb accusingly at Liam.

"We slept in their motel room," Pepper chimed in. Hers and Liam's lips tipped up, making them a matching pair. I wanted to smack the shit-eating grins off their faces.

"They sure did," he added, winking at Pepper as she crossed in front of him. She reached out and grabbed her bag from my hands. If I hadn't brought it with me, she'd totally have forgotten it. "It was quite the slumber party," Liam said, but his eyes lost the mischievous glint as he watched Pepper, studying her book bag like it was about to sprout wings.

Looping my arm through Jessica's, I yelled over my shoulder. "Thanks for the ride. I expect the same service on the way home or no five-star rating." I dragged a confused Jessica toward the school entrance. A blast of heat hit us as we crossed the threshold.

"You slept in his family's motel room?" Jessica removed her gloves and held the cool palm of her hand to my forehead. "Do you have a fever? You feel warm." She gawked at me. "You two were acting like a couple back there. Tell me I haven't lost you to the dark side. First Dustin, now you?"

"I'll explain." I pulled her into a corner by the side stairwell, checking all around to see if anyone was in earshot. When the coast was clear, I continued: "Mr. Bailey was killed last night at the precinct."

Jessica sucked in a breath, her eyes wide like saucers. "What?"

"Agent Hunter and my dad are working on the case together so . . ." I paused, trying to think of a reasonable justification as to why we would have had to sleep at their motel room. Before I could answer, Jessica cut me off.

"Pepper, right? She never listens to you, and she's awfully fond of Liam. Bet he could get her to sit and stay." Jessica rolled her eyes. "Your dad must have thought it made more sense with a killer out there to have you both babysitting her. Probably a smart idea, to be honest, but you must have been miserable."

Huh? That's actually a really good reason. Inaccurate maybe, but her explanation sounded more believable than the truth. I nodded feverishly in agreement as she continued her rant.

"I mean, with all the nights Pepper sneaks out and goes to other schools with her idiot friends defiling their walls, it's probably nice to have her stay in one place and not have to worry." She pulled strands of hair off my shoulder. "I'm surprised you aren't going gray from that child."

"Wait, what?" I asked knocking my locks out of her grasp. "What do you mean she goes to other schools?"

Jessica tilted her head and pursed her lips, her eyes searching my face. "You didn't know? She's been to at least four schools in the last year. Their 'art' pieces are huge. Haven't you seen them?" When I shook my head, she grabbed her phone from her pocket. "That twig with the dreads and the low-hanging pants, like ridiculously low, the one Pepper is always with . . ."

I groaned. "Billy."

Billy Lyons railroaded me every chance he got. He'd enter our home like he owned the place, then make a mess, steal our food, and leave without even a thank-you for our hospitality. My dad called him Hurricane Bill.

"Exactly. He posts them on his social media page. He uses a fake name, but I was following the account when it was still Billy Lyons, now he's 'Art King of the Beats.'" She swiped to his page and tilted the screen for me to see. Graffiti wall after graffiti wall plastered his social account, like a rainbow threw up on itself. Talk about overstimulation. Several pictures were posted of Pepper and him. One specifically irked me, where he had his arms around her like they were a couple. Using her two pointer fingers, Jessica zoomed in on Pepper's tag in one of the more recent photographs.

Son of a . . . "I'm going to kill her," I said, fire burning in the pit of my stomach. "Actually, I'm going to kill Billy Lyons too." I shook my head. "I'll see you after homeroom." I took to the halls to find Pepper. But instead, Mr. Romano found me.

"Miss Davis, could I have a word?" Mr. Romano waved me over to where he was standing outside his classroom.

I walked slowly, my anger cooling to nervous agitation.

He placed his briefcase on the floor and pulled out a stack of papers. "As Liam might have mentioned, I revoked your detention. He told me what he said to you and why you responded the way you did." He swallowed. "Liam expressed his remorse. Nevertheless, I did task him with tutor duty to make up for his conduct."

My mouth hung open. I had no idea what Liam said, but holy crap, just the fact he took responsibility shocked me. I decided to play along and would ask Liam for the details later.

Mr. Romano held my exam up for me to see the large red "D" at the top of the paper. My heart sank into my stomach, quenching the remains of my temper. How would I ever get accepted into the biology department of Lawrence University, my dream school, if I failed science class?

"I know how hard it must be as the eldest woman of the household. Your father has confided in me how much he relies on you, but you really mustn't let your grades slip. I have a favor to ask you, and of course feel free to say no. Mr. Hunter needs a student to tutor and you need the help. How would you feel about allowing him to aid in your studies?" My eyes widened as Mr. Romano held up his finger before I could object. "Just one session and if it doesn't work, we will make other arrangements."

I nibbled on my nail as I gave Mr. Romano's request some thought. "One session?" I questioned.

"Yes, just one and we can reevaluate." He sighed. "I feel for him and his sister." His lashes lowered. "They've never had a place to call home. I think he's rather fond of you and although he may have a poor way of showing that, you'd be a good influence on him."

For the first time since meeting Liam, I realized we had more than just our deceased mothers in common. We both didn't have a childhood, ripped away for different reasons but still having to grow up faster than our peers. And for that, I understood him a little more.

"Okay, one session," I conceded.

"Wonderful. I will schedule you for a private session in the science room today during your study-hall period. No one else will be in there to distract you." Mr. Romano looked down at his watch. "We'd better get to class. The bell's about to ring." He picked up his briefcase, then added, "I hope you can help Liam adjust to school. Maybe this can be the place they end up calling home."

With a final nod, he stepped into his classroom just as the bell echoed through the halls.

I walked into the empty science laboratory and saw Liam sitting in the back by the exit door. He must have changed after gym. A long-sleeve waffle shirt clung to the lithe muscles under his leather jacket above his staple-distressed denim jeans. Wet black hair curled around his ears. Just looking at him sent butterflies to my stomach. With his lips sealed shut, he reminded me of a sexy cologne model, attractive and allusive. Not that I'd ever admit that out loud.

His eyes scanned a stack of papers as his mouth moved ever so slightly with whatever he read. As I got closer, I realized the articles weren't school related.

Newspaper clippings fell out of a cracked leather-bound notebook open in front of him.

"What are you looking at?" I peered over his shoulder. Scribbled notes covered every open space, twisted in so many directions, I had to wonder how Liam kept them straight.

Without looking up, he said, "Have you ever heard of a class of serial killers called Angels of Death?"

"No, is that some other kind of monster?" I pulled out the chair next to him and sat down. Our knees touched, causing me to suck in a breath. Liam didn't pull away, so neither did I. The closeness of our bodies made my heart rate kick up a notch.

He lifted his chin, so our eyes were aligned. "No, not a monster. But it is a theory." Liam pushed one of the newspaper articles toward me. "Read it."

ANGEL OF DEATH: AFTER A SERIAL KILLER TARGETED A MATERNITY UNIT AT A HOSPITAL, FAMILIES ASK WHY

Nursing assistant Rena Mayers killed patients with insulin injections at a hospital in Clarksburg, WI.

In March 2018, Sally Shaw began to experience weakness and trouble breathing while recovering from the birth of her twin boys at the Johnson Medical Center.

Hydration helped Shaw, 31, improve quickly. Doctors told her husband, Norm, that Sally and their boys would be discharged soon.

"She was feeling better," says Norm, who was anxious to get his wife and sons home. "Then all of a sudden, she fell in the hallway on the way to visit our sons in the NICU, where they were being held."

After the fall, everything in her body started deteriorating, including her mind. No one knew why she got dizzy, no one knew why her blood sugar dropped, no one knew why her memory had gone to nothing. Not one doctor could diagnose her.

"It's like she was trapped in her body," Norm, 36, tells *PEOPLE* in this week's issue. "She couldn't talk, couldn't get up."

Nineteen days after being admitted, she died, leaving a devastated husband to care for two newborn sons alone.

Three months later, a knock on Norm's door brought a cataclysmic shock. FBI agents told him they didn't think Sally had died from natural causes—and they wanted his approval to exhume her body. Norm's jaw dropped, he says. "It just confirmed the fact that we knew something was not right."

It was a year before he learned the truth: Sally Shaw had been murdered—and was neither the first nor the last new mother to fall prey to a serial killer stalking the maternity ward.

In an extensive investigation that spanned two years and included more than 250 interviews and hundreds of pieces of evidence, authorities uncovered a chilling murder spree undertaken by a calculating killer armed with syringes: nursing assistant Rena Mayers, 28. On July 14, 2020, Mayers pleaded guilty to seven counts of second-degree murder and one count of assault with intent to murder an eighth victim by injecting each with lethal, unprescribed doses of insulin.

In October the following year, the U.S. government settled a civil suit naming Mayers and blaming oversight failures at the hospital for the similar death of a ninth patient. Additional suits are pending.

"We will never truly know how many mothers Rena Mayers killed," says attorney Anthony Delano, who represents several of the victims' families.

"You think the vengeful spirit is killing nurses because of the serial killings?" I asked after finishing the editorial.

He grabbed the newspaper article and stuffed it back into the binder. "Not exactly. I think the vengeful spirit that was in your room came back to right a wrong, or at least that's what the spirit thinks it's doing."

"Okay, so the spirit is a what? Another nurse, a cop, an attorney?" I thought back to the attorney for the victim's families in the article. I could imagine this being a difficult case to unravel. Any kindhearted lawyer would feel responsible for righting this extreme wrong.

Liam shook his head. "Maybe. Could be any of those but I'm leaning toward it being a nurse. I think it could be Nurse Daryl. Maybe she knew of a serial killer at her hospital. Maybe that's why she was let go so many years back," he explained. "I've looked in all Hunterland lore and I can't find anything. Then I remembered my mom had a notebook filled with official police cases. I've been going through them and found this," he held up the book. "These are notes of unsolved cases." He tapped his pen on the desk and continued: "She sometimes left leads in the corners, and she wrote 'Falkville Falls' in this one." He pointed to the upper right-hand corner with my town's name written in cursive. "Mom had a weakness for a good mystery, supernatural or not."

"Okay, so if the ghost I saw in my room is Nurse Daryl, you think she might have been killing school nurses to avenge a nurse serial killer who killed her in this school?" I asked, scratching my head. That was a lot of information based off pretty much nothing.

As if reading my mind, he said, "I know it's a farfetched theory, but I've investigated more with less and it's the only nurse-related article I could find online, in the Hunterland Library, and in this book that would make sense of this all." He shrugged. "It's worth a try. Wanna ditch school and go to the hospital with me to check it out?" Liam waggled his brow. "Maybe someone knows something there about other nurses who were employed around the same time as Joanne Daryl."

I puckered my lips. Ditching school and getting a real detention would not go over well with my father, but the thought of sleeping in my own house, in my own room with a prowling ghost unsettled me even more.

"Come on, live a little. I could use the company too," Liam said collecting his things and stuffing them into his bag.

I shifted in my chair. "Sure, why not? I'm already failing science class. How much more trouble could I get into?"

Liam smiled a devious attagirl smile. "I'll make a deal with you. I'll help you pass science, like I promised Mr. Romano, if you help me with the hospital. Sound good?"

"Okay." I narrowed my eyes. "So, what did you tell Mr. Romano that got me out of detention?"

A faint blush dotted Liam's cheeks. "I told him I acted like an asshole. That I have a sister and I wouldn't want some jerk treating her the way I treated you. You didn't deserve that."

My eyes widened. "Liam Hunter, is that an apology?" I placed my hands over my chest, feigning surprise.

"That depends. Did it work?" Liam winked sending my heart into overdrive.

I recovered with a fake eye roll. "All right, let's go to the hospital."

We stood at the same time, and our bodies collided. But instead of pulling away, Liam wrapped his arms around me, steadying us. He pulled me in tighter, and although my brain protested, my body ignored the warnings and leaned into his embrace.

He stopped moving. His arms still trapped me, but his muscles tensed. His tone turned gruff. "You know, your sister has this wild idea you're kind of into me." He brushed my hair off my neck and leaned his face in closer to my ear. His breath tickled my lobe as he spoke in a whisper. "She'd be crazy, right?"

My pulse quickened in response to Liam's touch. I prayed he couldn't feel the intense thumping of my heart. "She's young and has wild ideas. She still secretly believes in Santa, so I'm sure she's . . ."

Liam cut off my sentence by pressing his fingers into my neck.

"I don't know. Your pulse feels frantic." His hands traveled down my arms and settled at my wrists. He pulled my right one up to his mouth and kissed it. "It's a good thing we're going to the hospital. Your heart rate is abnormally fast."

"I . . . I don't think . . ." I stammered. A familiar sound rang in the distance and Liam grunted. He stepped back, creating much needed space between us and pulled his phone out of his pocket. The screen illuminated his face as the corners of his lips turned downward. He tapped the screen and held the phone to his ear.

"Doc?"

He paused, listening.

"You found the vamp nest? Where? How many?"

He stared into my eyes, his blue irises so dark they practically blended into his pupils.

"No, nothing important. Yeah, I'm on my way."

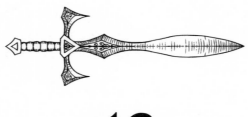

12

LIAM

Thick green vines clung to the sides of the old dairy plant, climbing across the façade and in and out of the broken windowpanes. The parking lot asphalt splintered, also being reclaimed by the surrounding woodland, whole swaths of it overgrown with milkweed and other tall grasses.

"Is that it?" Jac whispered, pointing to the abandoned building.

"I believe so." Doc's directions weren't the most specific, but how many neglected warehouses could there be in this area?

We'd parked the Bronco half a mile away and hiked here. Despite all my complaining, I was glad Mom's car wouldn't have to brave the broken pavement that spread out around the dilapidated facility. Or worse yet, the soaked grass from last night's rain that caused the usually frozen dirt to sink under our feet. Mud already covered the tops of my boots.

"Dad is *so* buying me new shoes tomorrow," Jac practically growled, sharing my irritation.

Dad and Sheriff Davis were back at the house going through all the previous residents since the 1980s, when the first homeowners bought it. I told Dad to look for nurses as well as question Sheriff Davis about a relationship with Joanne Daryl. They were knee-deep in research, so he sent Jac and me to handle the vamp nest Doc found about sixty miles north of Falkville Falls. I'd hoped it was the same nest the two vamps we killed were from. My eagerness to avenge Jennifer's death stirred my adrenaline.

"I say we make him buy us new jeans too." I pulled on my mud-soaked pant hem, which weighed me down as I trudged through the marshy woodland.

Jac shushed me with a finger to her lips. She pointed to the opening in the back of the building. The rapidly receding sunlight casted long, distorted shadows across the eerily quiet lot. I scanned the busted old windows of the factory building for sentries, but they were vacant. We crossed the few yards of cracked pavement, stopping at the big steel double doors to listen. I'd say it was as quiet as a grave, but in my experience, cemeteries could get pretty loud under the right circumstances. Either way, we heard nothing—no movement, no voices. Even the wind had stopped whistling, as if holding its breath along with us.

Jac gave me a nod, and the double doors creaked ever so slightly as she gently inched them open. No locks to pick this time, but that wasn't much of a surprise. Vamps were cocky bastards. Little did this nest know, we were at the top of the food chain, not them.

Inside, the cavernous space smelled musty. Stray orange rays of a setting sun reflected off the towering stainless-steel milk tanks that studded the floor in front of us. We inched through them, using each as cover, crossing the expanse. My adrenaline spiked in anticipation as we crept closer, hunched behind the old scaffolding and abandoned crates.

"There," Jac whispered. "In the old cow pens." She pointed ahead. The vamps had hung swaths of cloth around the old pens to block out the sunlight, turning them into a macabre version of a kid's blanket fort. In the next fifteen minutes, the sun would be gone, and the vamps would come out to play.

"Do you have the light box?" I asked Jac, pointing to the satchel she had draped over her shoulder. Dad finally got the damn thing to work and wanted us to try it out on the nest. He'd instructed us to throw it in the middle of the den, where it would send a burst of artificial sunlight through the room. The UV rays would weaken the vamps in their nests. While their skin incinerated, we would take them down with wooden spikes to the heart or behead them with our machetes.

The small cube had a new record of two and a half minutes, so we needed to be fast. Plus, I wanted to get back to Olivia. Even in this life-or-death situation, all I could think about was her, the smell of sage and vanilla that engulfed her. If I closed my eyes, I could envision her confused and irritated expression when I'd left.

We crossed the open expanse between us and the pens, but before we could deploy the light box, my body prickled. My personal alarm system reacted to the vacant space. The vamps' sleeping chambers were empty. Where were they?

Hissing sounded from the rafters above me, and before I could call out a warning to Jac, I felt a bony knee ram itself into my lower back. Pain radiated up my side. Instinct took over and I whirled on the opponent behind me. A smiling vamp, fangs extended, had blood smeared across his lips. He howled in my direction. I slipped my weapon out of my pack and raised it to strike, but the vamp moved faster and knocked it clear out of my hands. Bastard.

I cocked my closed fist and punched him square in the jaw. Pain flared across my knuckles as he smiled like I hadn't even made contact. Sure, I wasn't as strong as he was, but how could I be so . . . And then I remembered. I'd given my dose of serum to Jac. Doc's shipment hadn't arrived yet and we'd stored only one extra shot. Dad and I wouldn't let Jac go unprotected, so we gave it to her. She didn't know it was the last one.

Thus, my current situation: pure human frailty, head to toe.

Jac called from less than twenty feet away: "Are you okay?"

But before I could answer, the vamp grumbled, "Dead." Spit and blood trickled down his chin as if he'd just fed. Either they had human captives or blood bags—I couldn't be sure of which. The bad news was, that meant he was at his strongest.

The even worse news: He was raging with bloodlust. Feeding never quenched their hunger, only aggravated it.

Lucky me.

He grabbed me by my shirt and tossed me like a frisbee across the room. I hit the ground several feet away from Jac with a loud groan. My teeth clanked together, sending stinging torrents throughout my jaw. She rushed to my side.

"Are you okay? How were you thrown so . . . Oh." Realization dawned on her disappointed face. "You and Dad gave me the last dose," she whispered in her angriest quiet voice. The pinch of her nails pricked my skin. "Why would you do that?" She followed up with a smack to my arm.

I half smiled. "I could do without the sibling abuse." I sucked in a breath. "I'll be okay." Shaking off the pain, I climbed to my knees. "Deploy the light." She hesitated. "Go! I'm fine. I'll lead them to the middle and signal you when the time is right."

I staggered out into the open floor of the warehouse and rolled up my sleeve. Taking the knife I had in my pocket, I sliced my forearm and balled my hand into a fist, letting my blood drip onto the cement floor. "It's feeding time," I shouted, using the ichor's scent to distract the vamps to follow my pulse instead of Jac's.

Eyes popped out from every corner like stars in the night sky. There must have been twenty vamps in this nest, all exposing themselves at my scent. They started toward me, slinking out of the shadows and into the quickly fading twilight. The sky above the apertures darkened, and the stars began to pepper the navy-blue atmosphere. Saliva shimmered as it dripped from the vamps' mouths, their needle-like fangs protruding over their bloodstained lips. I waited until they were close, until I could see their bloodshot eyes, the dark, fully dilated pupils so large their irises were nearly overcome with the inky blackness.

Only when they had me surrounded did I shout, "Now!"

Jac threw the light box toward me, and it skidded to a stop at my feet. A thousand rays of light shot forth from its core, mimicking the direct glare of a clear, sunny day. I shielded my eyes with my arm as I dodged out of the fray. The screams and cries of the vamps blared as their skin sizzled and crisped. Most of them dropped to their knees around me. The smell of dead, burning flesh filled the air, but a couple stronger vamps, the ones farthest from the light box, continued forward.

I kicked out, sending the heel of my mud-covered boot into the face of a larger vamp, catching him in the chin. He swayed, and before he hit the ground, I drove the stake I grabbed from my bag into his heart. Like the off-road dust from the back of the Bronco, the vamp's remains fluttered into remnants of ash. That's for you, Jennifer Sutherland.

My cockiness faltered when my leather jacket tightened from behind. The angle was so awkward, I couldn't see who—or what—had grabbed me. Jac breathed heavily on the other side of the room, taking head after head off the decaying vamps with her machete. There was no way she would get to me in time. The vamp turned me around, clamping his blackened hand on my windpipe. His crisp skin scratched like sandpaper against my neck. Only the thinnest amount of air flowed through to my lungs. One more squeeze and I'd pass out. But instead of finishing me off, he picked me up like a surfboard over his head and threw me clear across the room. I landed on my stomach, slamming into the cement floor for the second time this evening. Pain lanced my ribs as the air rushed out of my lungs. God dammit, where were these super-charged vamps coming from?

I flipped over to get a good look at how many we had left only to be met face-to-face with a female vamp. Her eyes were red and swollen. Streaks of fresh blood covered her face. Her gray, emaciated skin clung to her bones, but it was intact. She must have avoided the light box. She stood with her hands behind her back as if she were hiding something. I heard Jac in the distance getting closer to me. If I could reach down to my ankle sheath, I could grab my spare stake and take the vamp out. Before I could move, she shifted forward, shouting, "Stop!"

Instinctively, I obeyed.

A crazed vamp couldn't make much sense. Words like *dead* or *kill* or *eat* were as profound as vamps could be. But moments like these, when they seemed to be coherent, made me question everything I'd ever learned from Hunterland lore about their kind.

The woman pushed what she was hiding behind her back in front of her.

Pepper!

"Jac," I shouted making sure she wasn't nearby. "Get out now!" I needed my sister out of here so she wouldn't become another hostage. Something about these vamps wasn't right, and until I could figure out what that was, I wouldn't be taking any chances.

"Pepper, it'll be okay," I said, taking in a deep breath. "Just focus on me. Okay?"

Pepper nodded frantically. I took inventory of her body, and other than the blood on her shoulders from where the vamp held her, she seemed completely unscathed. No marks on her neck or wrists, the typical areas a vamp fed from.

"What is going on?" Jac said as she came closer, covered in splattered blood and rotting flesh. "Oh my God. No," Jac whispered when her eyes landed on the captive Pepper.

I held my hands up, ignoring the pain in my side.

"Give me the girl," I said, pushing off the ground so I could stand, all the while praying this vamp could understand me. Jac rushed to my side and wrapped her arm under my shoulder, helping me upright.

The pain was manageable, but the idea of Pepper being hurt was not.

"Stop killing," the vamp said as her body trembled with effort, possibly . . . fear? "Stop killing us." Moisture flew from her lips, dotting the ground in red.

Pepper looked up at her captor, her eyes wide.

"Pepper, look at me," I warned, watching the tears stream down Pepper's face. Although she seemed unharmed, this could end up causing her some serious emotional damage, and the less branded into her memory the better.

I stepped closer to Pepper, keeping a watchful eye on the vamp's body language. With that much blood on her, she should be full of bloodlust. But instead, she looked frail. Her clothes dripped off her as if they were meant for a larger person, and her bones pressed against her lax skin.

"I don't know how you can understand me and why you are holding her prisoner, but I can promise you this won't end well for you." I took another step forward.

"Stop!" the vamp shouted again, but this time the words were sent over my head. I threw a look past my shoulder and saw two vamps standing behind us. Suddenly, I could feel their breath on my neck. The female vamp gestured with her head, and the vamps took off in the other direction.

The noise and heat from their bodies vacated the room as fast as they had come into it. Jac and I exchanged confused looks. A different kind of fear blasted my system, but I pushed it down deep and focused on saving Pepper.

"Pepper, start walking to me." I waved her forward. She looked up at the vampire holding her shoulders as if asking her permission. The vamp nodded, and Pepper started for me.

Within five steps, she was in my arms. My chin rested on her head as my gaze narrowed on the female vamp. My hold tightened around Pepper.

"Go," the vamp ordered.

Jac placed her hand on my shoulder, and the three of us retreated backward out of the abandoned dairy building. Jac covered our path with her machete held high, while I took up the rear, making sure the female vamp didn't charge at us. Her swollen, bloodshot eyes remained on Pepper until we reached the door.

Then, something unimaginable happened. The vamp's head twisted, and her eyes closed briefly. She held a shard of wood—a makeshift stake—in her hands over her chest. With one last look at us, she drove it deep into her heart. Her body exploded into ash that quickly faded, leaving the barest traces of dust behind.

She'd destroyed herself, and I had no idea why.

13

OLIVIA

Knowing Liam and Jac were going after a vamp nest while my father and Agent Hunter were researching obituaries made me feel completely helpless. It's not like I wanted Liam to bring me on a hunt with him, but I wanted to be useful. I hated not being able to do anything at a time like this. Slamming my locker shut, I rested my forehead on the cool metal.

"Hey, you okay?" Dustin asked. His black-and-red sneakers came into view during my bleary-eyed stare at the floor.

"Yeah," I mumbled with a sigh. I picked my backpack up from the ground and swung it over my shoulder. I stared at my phone as Dustin and I walked to the front of the building. Pepper had texted—which was never good.

Apparently, she'd gotten in trouble—again—and Dad and Agent Hunter had to pick her up early from school.

Not surprised at all.

"You want a ride home?" Jessica came up behind me and threw her arm over my shoulder. "I saw your boyfriend leave earlier without you."

I rolled my eyes. "Liam Hunter is not my boyfriend."

As I looked away, my gaze fell on the last person I wanted to see. Billy Lyons. He was leaning against the water fountain, surrounded by that crew of delinquent lackeys he always had in tow. They were throwing their heads back, laughing. His eyes caught mine, and a conniving smile spread across his face. Then he blew me a kiss.

Anger rolled violently like thunder from my core to my throat. Without thinking, I marched over to him, Jessica on my heels. He turned his whole body toward me as I got close—perhaps too close—invading his personal space.

"What trouble did you get Pepper into now?" I pointed at his chest.

He looked down at my finger, then back up into my eyes, raising an eyebrow. "Why are you always accusing me? You seriously need to get laid." He crossed his arms over his chest. "What has you all twisted today, Big Sis?" he scoffed, wielding the nickname like an insult.

My fists clenched at my sides. "Pepper. What did you make her do?" I asked, ignoring his glare. No doubt, whatever sent her home early directly correlated with Billy Lyon's corruption.

"I don't make Pepper do anything," he replied, looking to his group. "She's a willing participant of our crew." They all nodded in confirmation, smiling like conspiratorial fools.

"Yeah, well," I said awkwardly. I didn't have an end goal for this conversation. My resentment stemmed from his bad influence on her and that her troubles had started when Billy first came around. "Stay away from my sister!"

He quirked his lip and looked me up and down. "She can't get enough of me. What can I say, Big Sis, I'm just her type." He turned his back to me, chuckling with his friends.

Ignoring the possibility of detention, I lunged forward, my last nerve frayed. Dustin put a hand on my shoulder, physically pulling me back from doing something I would regret.

"C'mon," he said, steering me away. I tried to ignore their laughter as we made our way back to the school's main entrance.

"That kid is a punk but not worth detention or worse." Dustin threw his arm over my shoulder and squeezed. "So, back to Liam? I thought you couldn't stand him." He released his embrace and pushed open the door, motioning for Jessica and me to walk through.

I avoided making eye contact as I stepped into the crisp winter afternoon air. "It's complicated."

"It always is," Jessica said. "When Tiffany and I first met, she swore she wasn't into girls. Now *that* was complicated. Three nights of making out and she still swore it. Thankfully, I'm beautiful, and she caved to my charms, but it was a rough go for a while."

Tiffany wasn't Jessica's first girlfriend, but Jessica was Tiffany's first, and she fought her feelings for the longest time. I think that's why Jessica was so into her from the start. Was that what was going on with Liam and me? Were we fighting our feelings and that made us want each other more? Or maybe I was reading too much into everything. He did say Pepper thought *I* had a thing for him. He never said he felt the same.

A headache formed behind my eyes, and I rubbed my temples.

"You want to study together or something at your place?" Jessica asked. "Tiffany's got after-school stuff going on, and I've been painfully bored at home. Mom and Dad are away on business trips this week. Again."

And that's when it hit me.

I could be useful while Liam and Dad were busy. Jessica and Dustin, especially Dustin, could help me locate information at the hospital that Liam wanted us to investigate. This way, I'd be contributing to the case and hopefully ridding my bedroom of any lingering ghosts. "Actually, if you two are up for it, there's something I wanted to look into at the hospital." I studied their engaged eyes. "A former employee, actually. Interested in helping?"

Dustin rubbed his hands together. "Retrieving intel?" His lips tilted up toward his ears. "Oh, now this is up my alley! I'm in!"

Jessica shrugged. "Sure, why not?"

We loaded ourselves into Jessica's Volkswagen and headed over toward Eisenhower Medical Center. Clouds rolled overhead, and I could almost sense the rain threatening to fall from the graying veil. As Jessica drove, I explained the article Liam found, and to no one's surprise, Dustin knew all about it.

"Oh, that story is huge! Angel of Death serial killers happen everywhere. Is that what they think this is?" In the side mirror, I saw Dustin scratch his head. "So, a nurse is killing other nurses at schools? Does your dad know about this theory?" He paused and removed his winter coat. "Or maybe it's a serial killer attacking those he or she thinks had something to do with the Angel of Death killings . . ."

I certainly couldn't tell them it was an avenging ghost. "We wanted to check it out before going to my dad with info. Honestly, we don't even know if it's related. Liam just had a hunch."

"What's the plan when we get in there?" Jessica pulled the car into a visitor's spot at the front of the hospital.

Across the parking lot, a mother and child walked toward the entrance, a bouquet of flowers in the mother's arms and a balloon floating from the boy's hand. A vision of a sick relative, possibly a father, took shape in my mind.

The patient in my imagination looked about my dad's age. I shook my head, pulling myself out of my weird thoughts and back to the task at hand.

"Liam thought it would be best to start in the maternity ward and ask if there has ever been a nurse with a poor record, meaning a lot of fatalities while she was employed here."

I unbuckled my seat belt as Jessica put her hand on my knee. "Okay, maybe you have lost your mind," she said.

I looked up into her concerned green eyes.

"That's confidential," she continued. "The hospital will never give us that info. Maybe we should leave this to your dad, Livy." She chewed on her finger. "I think we are in over our heads here."

I thrust myself back into my seat. She was right. How the hell did Liam think we could get that information? Steal the records? Charm a nurse? Knowing that conniving pain in the ass, probably the latter. Something curled inside my belly at the thought. Jealousy? Sucking in a breath, I willed myself to get it together. I refused to fall for Liam Hunter.

Dustin leaned forward, resting his bare forearms on the center console. "I have an idea. Remember Kevin Archer?"

Jessica and I wrinkled our noses. "You mean our old babysitter, Kevin Cool?" I asked. That's what we used to call him when we were little. As our babysitter, he'd let us do whatever we wanted when he was in charge, and we thought he was so cool. Our parents thought he was an angel since he had manners and kept the house clean, but it was really us kids. We were allowed free reign if we made the downstairs sparkle before bed and that literally meant we could do anything our little young hearts desired.

Dustin's lips tipped upward. "Yep. He works here now. Not sure he's in the maternity ward, but he owes us." He paused, looking down at his forearm. A six-inch keloid scar stared back at him. "He owes us big time!"

When we were little and messing around, Jessica and I chased Dustin up an unsteady stack of plastic chairs he'd piled up to avoid capture. The pile collapsed, bringing Dustin down with them and through the glass-topped kitchen table. A long, sharp piece caught his forearm and tore it open. A distracted Kevin Cool, playing tonsil hockey with his girlfriend at the time on the living-room couch, hadn't been paying attention. We covered for him, saying he was using the restroom, and helped the girl sneak out of the house. Couldn't even remember her name. Kevin told us he'd owe us a favor, and we'd never collected.

We were nine at the time. We wanted to wait for something big.

Jessica beamed as she recalled the story. "Oh, hell yeah. Took one for the team, Dustin."

We hurried into the hospital lounge. The room was two-thirds full of people waiting for loved ones or waiting to be seen. People coughed and shivered, and one little girl sobbed quietly against a young man's shoulder in the far corner. My heart hurt for her, seeing her in so much pain, and I wondered who her tears were for. I paused, taking everything in, and then I sensed it. A tingle ran up my spine like an answer to my question, and I knew for certain she cried for a close family member. I thought of all the healing crystals I could give them, like I did with Pepper when she hurt as a child.

"Liv? Hello, Earth to Olivia?" Jessica waved her hand in front of my eyes, and I refocused. I shook my head, collecting myself.

"Sorry, I just . . ." Just what? Got distracted by a crying child? Wake up, Olivia. "I just don't even know where to start." I took in the myriad of signs and hallways. "There are so many departments—how do we find Kevin?"

"I know a way," Dustin replied, a cunning look dancing on his face. Before I could argue, he pulled the attention of a pretty nurse who didn't look exceptionally busy. Within a minute, she told us exactly where Kevin worked and what floor, and we headed straight to the cardiac ward. Apparently, Kevin Cool was still cool enough to get the attention of the ladies on staff.

Kevin sat behind the desk in light-green scrubs that reflected his big hazel eyes, and I was happy to find he was still just as handsome as I remembered. Way too old for me, but a girl never forgets her first crush. His eyes lit up like a Christmas tree when he saw us.

"Well, this must be my lucky day. The Three Musketeers. What are you guys doing here?"

Dustin rolled up his coat sleeve and leaned his scarred forearm on the counter, smiling. "We came to collect."

Kevin's eyes dipped to Dustin's scar, and he frowned.

He rounded the desk and led us into the currently unoccupied staff lounge. The smell of antiseptic assaulted my nostrils as we stepped inside. Kevin didn't say a word until he pulled a chair out from one of the bare circular tables and motioned for the three of us to do the same.

"Okay, what's this about? You can't seriously be collecting on a promise I made to you kids eight years ago."

"We can and we are," Dustin said, crossing his leg over his thigh.

Kevin shook his head and chuckled. "Fine. I guess I owe you. How illegal are we talking?" Kevin's bushy brows were knit together. "Your big eyes scream trouble."

We told Kevin the whole story about the Angel of Death article and blamed our visit on school research. Kevin sat there and listened. He barely moved a muscle, he was so laser focused. When we were done, he leaned back in his chair, the two front legs lifting off the floor. "So, you want me to snoop around and see if there was a nurse here who had a history of patients dying?" His brows rose. "Doesn't really sound like a school project."

"Then think of it as a civic duty," Dustin said, ignoring Kevin's motive questioning. "And you'll have to go back some years. It could be someone from a decade or so ago that's no longer here."

"Maybe look up nurses that worked around the same timeframe as a nurse named Joanne Daryl," I offered. If she was the vengeful spirit trying to find retribution, she would have known the killer, which made me wonder how she was flitting around our house. Maybe Dad did know her.

"Hmm." Kevin tapped his bottom lip, shifting forward in his seat. The metal legs tapped the floor. Jessica and I leaned in. I don't think the two of us were even breathing. "It'll take me a few days, but there are some residents here who owe me favors, so it shouldn't be a problem." He scooted his chair back, the metal screeching against the linoleum. Then he stood and took his phone out of his pocket. "I'll see what I can do about finding out if there was—or is—any suspicious activity." He handed me his oversized phone. "Not like you nose boogers had cell phones when you were little. Save your numbers in here, and I'll text you all when I have something."

I punched my digits into his contact list and passed the phone to Jessica. She did the same and gave it to Dustin. Before he handed it back to Kevin, he added, "This is time sensitive, so act fast!" Dustin looked at Jessica, then me. "Ya know, for our school project."

Kevin swiped his phone out of Dustin's hands. "Sure. Whatever you say." He shook his head. "I liked it better when you kids were begging to stay up an extra hour, not blackmailing me into a felony." Kevin winked, catching me off guard. "But if we can catch a killer, hey, even I can't argue with that." Kevin slid his phone back into his scrubs. He started to walk away, then pivoted on his heels. "Consider us even. Debt paid."

Dustin, Jessica, and I walked out of the small room and were about to head back the way we came when my eyes landed on the sign across the hallway.

MATERNITY WARD

I knew we couldn't get in without proving we had a family member there. But something about it called to me. I headed in another direction, a confused Jessica and Dustin on my heels as I took a few turns and ended up in the right department. There was a second waiting room, this one full of pacing men and nervous-looking women. The door to the ward was plastered with warnings about allowing only approved guests. I was glad they took infant care so seriously, but it certainly was going to make finding anything out harder. I looked over at the blue plastic chairs and a memory flashed.

I had just come out to sit with Grandma while waiting to meet my new sister. My legs dangled, never meeting the ground. Mid-swing of my

feet, I froze. My father's agonizing screams filled the air. My gaze shot
to the room he and Mother were in. He fell to his knees. His hands
covered his face. Grandma jumped up from her blue chair and ran to
him, closing the hospital door behind her. I was all alone. Scared. I
clutched the rainbow stone my grandmother had given me for my
birthday. Later, I found out it was a chakra stone, one of the most
powerful worry stones, able to guide the mind into an instantly more
relaxed state. My vision blurred before a final image passed. A nurse
exited my mother's room. Her lips twitched. She turned and stared at
me for a long time. Then her head tilted as her lips tipped downward.
The door behind her opened causing her to jump and within seconds
she ran in the opposite direction. Her familiar face blended into the
background of my subconscious as the present moment reappeared.

A real-live nurse approached us. "Are you kids here to visit someone?"

I couldn't speak.

In the background, I heard Jessica answer. "Sorry. We were just on
our way out." Her fingers wrapped around my elbow as she led me toward the elevators. "You okay?" she whispered. "You like blacked out
or something."

"Sorry." I shook my head. "I had a weird flashback to when my
mom died here."

Dustin wrapped his arm around me. "Aw, Livy." He pulled me into
his body. "Let's go. We did our part. I don't want you to have to relive
any more of those memories."

Silently agreeing with Dustin's assessment, the three of us headed
out of the hospital and back to Jessica's car with our chins held high and
shoulders back. Liam would be damn proud of how we handled that,
and maybe, just maybe, this would pay off.

"Where to now?" Jessica asked as she buckled her seat belt. Excitement filled her tone. Great. I'd created an investigative monster.

"I better get home to see what kind of trouble Pepper is in." I rolled my eyes. Who knew what she had done this time?

Jessica stared at me in bewilderment. "What do you mean?"

I buckled my own belt and turned on my heated seat to rid the winter chill from my bones. "She texted me that Dad picked her up from school because she got in trouble earlier today."

Jessica tilted her head and furrowed her brows. "Well unless she's calling Liam 'Daddy' now, I doubt that's the truth." She shook her head. "I saw her leave earlier, it looked like she was trying to catch up with Liam and Jac in the school parking lot. I just assumed they took her home."

The Wisconsin weather had nothing on the ice that settled in my stomach when reality hit me.

Pepper had gone on a vamp hunt.

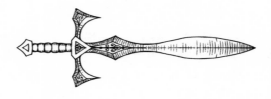

14

LIAM

Nothing about what had just happened in the abandoned plant made any sense. As Jac, Pepper, and I sprinted through the thick fog back to the Bronco, I revisited everything. Not only had a vamp conversed with me in a somewhat intelligent way but she had also protected us from two other vamps and then taken her own life. None of it added up.

Every part of my body hurt, but I didn't slow down until the Bronco appeared in my sight. Jac swung the car door open and pushed Pepper and our weapons into the backseat while I started the engine. Within moments, the tires were screeching against the wet, dark road back to Falkville Falls.

Relief washed over me the farther we drove. But the cold fear in the pit of my stomach began warming into a boiling rage.

My eyes found Pepper in the rearview window. "How could you be so stupid? Why on earth would you follow us? How did you even get here?" I spit out question after question as Pepper clung to the back of my seat. Every time she tried to speak, I cut her off with another rage-filled inquiry.

Jac placed her hand on my forearm. "Let her talk, Liam."

"I'm sorry," she whispered behind me. "I just wanted to go on a hunt with you. When I saw you leaving school with Jac, I knew you were going somewhere important, so I climbed into the backseat while you were arranging things in the trunk. I thought I could help."

I turned my head for a moment in complete shock.

"I told you I heard something," Jac said, hitting my arm. She had mentioned a noise when we pulled out of school, but I dismissed her. I guess I forgot she had supersonic hearing and because of my lack of serum, I didn't.

"Sorry," I gritted out.

Jac must have sensed I was on my last straw because she waved me off. She turned in her seat and faced Pepper. "I know it must seem like what we do is fun and exciting," Jac said. "But it's also very dangerous. Liam and I have had years of training, and we still make mistakes." Jac shot me a sidelong glare, her gaze burning into my cheek.

"But I really can help!" Pepper stammered.

"You almost got killed. How could that be helpful?" I attempted several calming breaths, but they weren't working. I couldn't imagine what Sheriff Davis or Olivia would do to us if anything happened to Pepper.

My anger consumed me so much that I completely ignored the cold, prickly feeling creeping up the back of my neck.

"But I'm fine."

I growled, narrowing my eyes at her in the mirror.

She tugged at her bloodstained clothes. "Not a scratch on me. This isn't my blood. And that woman wasn't going to hurt me."

"You mean that *vampire*," I corrected her. If she thought of vamps as people, she'd be in for a surprise if she ever faced off with one again. "She's not human. She's a revenant. And she's got nothing to lose by killing you and everything to gain by making you a meal."

Pepper threw her back against the leather seat and crossed her arms over her chest.

Great. Teenage pouting. She pulled a stupid stunt like this and somehow blamed me.

I wanted to shake her.

My focus returned to the road. Pattering rain flushed out the feathery clouds of fog floating above the dark highway, making it easier for me to see where we were going. You'd think someone could invest in more than the occasional streetlight on a curvy back road like this.

"As a vamp, she doesn't know right from wrong anymore," Jac said, turning back around and securing her seat belt as the pitter-patter of water on the windshield grew in volume. "All vamps care about is feeding. You could have been killed, or worse."

"What's worse?" Pepper asked her voice not as confident as her previous tone.

"Being turned into a bloodsucker, that's what's worse!" Venom soaked my words as I gripped the steering wheel, envisioning wringing her neck. Sure, she wasn't accustomed to our lifestyle, but she was smarter than this.

I heard the sound of the impact before I registered the dark silhouette of a body skidding across the hood of the car. Pepper and Jac screamed as I slammed on my brakes. The tires skidded on the slick road, the car fishtailing as the steering wheel spun wildly in my hands. I desperately grabbed hold of it and jerked it in the opposite direction, trying to steady us, but we still pitched over the shoulder and into the grassy incline along the road.

Each hill sent the Bronco to fly and crash, again and again. White pain burst behind my eyes as my head slammed into the roof above me. I clamped my jaw shut for fear that the agony would escape from my lips. Finally, we came to a stop. I revved the engine and put the car into reverse, but the wheels only spun. The tires spit out mud in front of us.

"How did they track us?" Jac shouted in disbelief. The silhouette thumped against the windshield, sending a spiderweb of splintering cracks across the glass.

Pepper yelled, "Is that one of them from the warehouse?" I heard her reach for the door.

I turned in my seat. "Stay in the freaking car. Do not move, and do exactly what I say." The dark shadow disappeared over the edge of the hood. "Grab my stakes," I yelled to Pepper, indicating the bag of weapons next to her. Pepper froze, so Jac unbuckled her own seat belt and climbed into the backseat.

The dark figure of a male reappeared in front of the car, allowing the one working headlight to illuminate his face. I squinted at him. He was dressed in a black suit with a dark button-down and tie. Too fancy for a monster. He smiled, and the hairs on my arms stood erect. Needle-like fangs dropped down from his mouth and hung past his lips. I couldn't see any blood on him, which meant he hadn't fed. On the one hand, he wouldn't be bloodthirsty. On the other, he was probably looking for his first meal of the evening.

He closed the distance between us, placing his palms on the hood of the car and staring right at me. His eyes flickered black, not bloodshot like the vamps we had just slaughtered. I had never seen a monster like him before. "Jac?" I questioned, having no current defense that would kill this guy.

He pressed his hands onto the car and jumped up on top of the hood, causing it to indent. Mom would have killed this monster just for the destruction of her baby. In a crouched position, he stared at me, teasing me with the unknown. It wouldn't have been so odd if he was drooling or blathering in monosyllables, but he just continued to glower like some sadistic New York attorney, not a bloodthirsty animal.

"I'm trying to find them. Did we use them all at the nest?" Jac asked as I heard her clanging metal on metal. Bullets and guns wouldn't work. I needed a stake or a machete.

"That would be considerably bad luck, especially since we left the light box back at the warehouse," I said. The vamp slunk closer to the windshield. His hands curled into fists.

He smiled sadistically, right before he pounded the already weakened glass.

"Found one," Jac said. I heard her moving behind me. "Better make this one count! It's the last one we've got."

No pressure. "Thanks." I extended my arm overhead to grab the weapon, refusing to turn away from my opponent's lethal stare. Just as my hand connected with the stake, the creature's fist came through the windshield in an explosion of crystal safety glass. His bloodied fingers fumbled over my shoulder, clamping around my arm and the weapon. If I could pull him through, I could attack him in the car, but I needed the girls safe first.

"Get out of the car!" I shouted.

"But you said to stay in the car!" Pepper squealed.

I resisted the urge to glare at her, keeping my eyes on the vamp. "And now I'm telling you. Get. Out!"

The vamp held on, digging his sharp claws into my flesh. They punctured my leather jacket and needled through the skin of my wrist. Wet, warm blood escaped from my wounds and was absorbed into the fabric of my clothing. I sucked in a breath as pain radiated down my spine, causing my eyes to water.

"I'm going to have fun killing you," I said, smiling as I tried to take my focus off the agony.

"Are you sure it won't be the other way around?" he asked through his razor-sharp teeth, raising a manicured brow.

Startled by his conversation skills, I loosened my hold. Rookie mistake. The vamp tumbled into the car, pushing my seat back and practically straddling me. He pressed the hand with the stake above my head.

"How would you feel if I killed your family? Would that make you an angry hunter?" He twisted his head to the side window. "What if I killed you first, and then went after those two sweet-looking girls of yours? How would that make you feel?"

I opened my mouth, but words caught in my throat. It finally, truly sank in—some vamps still had humanity left inside, and if this was accurate, what else didn't we know about monsters? "How are you even possible?" I asked, distracted by the thought of what we'd missed all these years.

"There's so much you don't know, hunter, but you won't live long enough to find out." He used his knee to press down hard on my core, against the exact same spot I'd bruised when one of the vamps sent me flying across the dairy floor. I drew in a breath as the pain ricocheted from my abdominals all the way up to my throat. Bile followed the agony, stinging and sour. His free hand pulled at my chin, exposing my neck. His fangs extended further as he positioned himself to press down into my artery.

The faint moan of the hood bending came from behind him. Without a second to spare, I saw the glint of a blade as Jac skewered the vamp, the tip inches away from my own chest. Jac pulled him backward. His feet flipped up and landed on the dashboard. Before he could react, Jac sliced his head clean off. It rolled down and over the other side of the car. Blood sprayed everywhere, like a sprinkler system. Jac stood on the hood, machete shining in the moonlight as she twirled it around in her hands. Blood dripped from the steel.

"Thought you could use the assist. You know, since you decided to talk the vamp to death instead of staking him?" Jac's free hand went to her hip.

I peeled my blood-soaked shirt away from my skin. "Very funny," I said coughing up a mixture of bile and saliva and revoltingly swallowing it. I opened the car door and found a shivering Pepper leaning against the front tire.

"You killed his wife and brother. That's why he was so mad," she said in between chattering lips. The rain had lessened, but the chill in the air puckered my skin.

My eyes widened. "How do you know that?"

"I told you I could help." Tears fell down her face.

I tilted my head in disbelief. Did she mean . . .

"I can hear the undead people talk."

Jac gasped as she jumped down from the hood, a look of surprised understanding gracing her face. "Pepper, you're a psychic?"

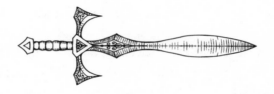

15

LIAM

My sister, Pepper, and I didn't even make it past the foyer of the Davis home before we were bombarded with questions from Dad, Sheriff Davis, and Olivia, wondering what had happened.

But words ceased to exist the second I announced that Pepper had supernatural abilities.

Dad's forehead crinkled and his lips twisted into the same horrified expression he'd donned when he found out there were no remains of my mom. Sheriff Davis's gaze volleyed between Pepper and our family, as if he could put the pieces together if he stared long enough. Olivia's cheeks flushed and grew more inflamed the longer she stayed silent.

Apparently, the combination of all three of us covered in blood mixed with hearing that your daughter and sibling could read vampire minds took a moment to process. And Jac looked like she had for the last ninety minutes: like she was sucking on a lemon, lips pursed and chin dimpled.

We'd heard of psychics like Pepper, but we'd never met one before. Doc and his nieces were the closest hunters we knew with abilities, and theirs were far inferior to Pepper's. Who knows what Pepper could do and had done? We'd just entered a whole new supernatural world. And the youngest Davis girl sat front and center.

Pepper broke the tension. "I still don't understand what the big deal is." She fastened her hands to her hips and rolled her eyes. From her nonchalant attitude, you'd think we just revealed she got an ankle tattoo rather than secret paranormal powers.

Ignoring her, Dad asked, "Are you sure?" His intense stare met mine, and I nodded in confirmation. Her knowledge about the vamp's anger confirmed it. From the moment I met Pepper, I'd had a strange feeling she belonged in our crazy world, and now I knew why.

"Trust me, I know how it sounds, but she's a psychic. She heard their thoughts," I told them, pulling at my now crusted long sleeve. My body ached in places I didn't even know existed.

Sheriff Davis and Olivia stared blankly at me until Olivia's angry voice crushed their silence. "I can't believe you took her on a hunt. How incredibly irresponsible!" She waved her hand in my face. "She's *fourteen* and, unlike *your* sister, completely untrained and ignorant of your unearthly world. She could have been hurt or worse, killed." She pointed at Pepper's blood-soaked shoulders. "And look at her! She looks like she fought in a war zone." Her gaze volleyed between Jac and me before she jabbed her finger in my face. "And you two look even worse!"

Fire ignited in my core. "Stop pointing that thing in my direction." I batted at her hand. "We didn't take her anywhere. She smuggled herself into the back of the Bronco and then followed us into the vamp nest." To be that quiet for such a long period of time impressed me, but I wasn't about to admit that now.

Olivia crossed her arms over her chest. "Well, then. What an advanced child she must be if the badass Liam Hunter didn't even know he was being followed," Olivia chastised, her voice dripping with sarcasm. "Maybe you're not as skilled at your job as you think."

"Livy," Sheriff Davis said, his voice firm. "I'm upset too, but to place blame right now would be counterproductive. The most important thing is that Pepper is home and unharmed." He turned to Pepper, who scowled at Olivia with narrowed eyes as her father scanned her body for the umpteenth time, confirming she was all in one piece.

"Is it? She left a regular teenager and now she is a psychic, for dead people?" Olivia huffed. "What will this family bring into our lives next?"

I stepped forward into Olivia's personal space. Jac grabbed my bicep, attempting to pull me back.

"What *we* are bringing into *your* life?" I tapped her on the head. "Do you have marbles bouncing around in that brain of yours? Maybe that's why you're failing science."

Jac tugged a little harder, and I retreated a step backward, satisfied by the crestfallen look on Olivia's face. Sheriff Davis bristled. Guess he didn't know she was bombing classes.

"We didn't bring anything to your doorstep. We are here to help." I pointed to Pepper. "And she's not a freak, which is exactly how you are treating her right now. She has a gift. She can hear what the revenants are thinking. There aren't a lot of people out there that have those abilities."

Pepper's frown flipped as she stood a little straighter. She tucked a blue strand behind her ear.

"What did you hear the vamp say?" Dad asked her.

Pepper gazed down at the tiled floor and played with her chipped black nails. Given the look she gave the vamp woman who had her by the shoulders, I started to think she heard a lot more than just one vamp's thoughts.

Her voice came out shaky at first. "He was mad at Liam and Jac because they killed his brother and wife back at the nest. He was out getting supplies."

"Supplies?" Dad flashed me a questioning look.

"Yeah, we've got to talk," I said, remembering the far too cohesive discussion I'd had with Mr. Tall, Dark, and Fangsome.

Dad agreed. "Well, it sounds like a lot of excitement for one evening. Why don't we all get"—his gaze traveled over the three of us before finishing—"cleaned up and situated?" He stepped to the side, and I could see all our suitcases and belongings behind him. "I've checked us out of the motel. We will take up residence here. Jac, you're sleeping in Olivia's room on the air mattress, especially since the ghost has appeared in there twice. Liam, you have the guest room across the hall from the bathroom that's in between Olivia and Pepper's rooms. Doc's shipment came in, there's a syringe in your suitcase." Dad looked me over. "Use it." He grabbed his suitcase, the largest of the group. "I'll be in the basement. The house's perimeter is lined with salt. We are all safe. Now, it's been a long evening. Let's get some rest."

I grabbed my backpack and duffel bag and walked up the stairs, deliberately ignoring Olivia as she glared in my direction. To think that just hours ago, I looked forward to seeing her again. At this point, I just wanted to strangle her.

I threw my bags on the bed, letting out an involuntary groan. Even that minor exertion caused my wounds to flare with unexpected new pain. I removed my leather jacket and hung it on the back of the door. I'd clean that tomorrow. Then I peeled my shirt and jeans from my skin, throwing them both into the trash can by the bed. I pulled out a pair of mesh shorts from my duffel and stepped into the legs. More grunts followed from even that slight movement. My body felt like it had collided with the Bronco. Visions of the mangled frame and missing windshield replayed in my head. My chest heaved as I managed to take a deep breath.

I walked over to the full-length mirror and eyed how close my opponents had come to success in orchestrating my demise. Puncture wounds at my wrist had dried and left crusted blood where it coagulated. Black-and-blue marks had already started to form, covering the rippling muscles in my stomach, leading all the way up to my shoulder. An outline of a hand in deep reds and purples covered my right side, reminding me of where the Suit Vamp had clutched me. Then my mind drifted to the bloody handprint on Pepper's shoulder. Her role in all of this had to mean more. My gut growled with worried instincts as I replayed the facts.

First, she had the patches on her bag of all the schools that had been attacked by the ghost; now we find out she has supernatural abilities that far exceed anyone we'd met before. Not to mention she barely flinched in the face of eminent threats. I still hadn't told anyone about the school patches. I had hoped to ask Pepper in private, but now I wondered if she would even tell me the truth.

Gathering my thoughts and my toothbrush, I ducked out of the guest room and made my way to the bathroom. I nearly ran right into Olivia. I sucked in a sharp breath as my eyes traveled from her painted toes up her bare legs, causing my whole body to physically respond. She had on a long T-shirt down to her mid-thighs with a cat and a rainbow on it. I scrunched up my nose as I read the words "So Meowgical" on the front.

"Nice top." I laughed uncomfortably.

"Shut up!"

I crossed my arms. "Still mad I see."

Her eyes roamed my body, stopping at my exposed chest and abdominal muscles. I swore her knee buckled an inch. Her hand snapped to her dropped jaw as she took in my destroyed physique.

"Cranky ungrateful girls first." I waved at her to proceed.

She dropped her hand, offering me a mocking half smile. "If I'm cranky, it's because you almost got my sister killed." She walked into the bathroom, tipping her chin higher. "I'm much more chipper when my sister is safe."

I followed, caring less about her privacy than about my own righteous anger. "You're kidding, right?"

Olivia opened the toothpaste and pressed a glob onto her brush. "I can't believe she was in a vampire nest." She shook her head. "I don't even know what that is, but the thought of her being their food—or worse, being turned into one of them—kills me, literally breaks my insides."

She pointed the tube of toothpaste at me. "And it looks like whatever it was broke your outsides." She stuck the toothbrush into her mouth before I could read if there was sympathy in her tone or only anger.

As she vigorously brushed her teeth, I regrouped. Maybe I needed a new strategy. Although she accused us of things outside our control, I hadn't given her much room for acceptance. In the span of three weeks, she'd learned there's an entire supernatural world and a ghost haunting her room and killing at her school; and she lived next to a town known for Angel of Death killings. And the cherry on top of this nightmare: Her sister had faced mortal danger in a vamp nest. That's a lot for anyone to swallow.

I gently grabbed her by the elbows, causing her to stop her furious assault on her incisors.

"I know it's scary." I gave her joints a squeeze. "I'm sorry about Pepper. I would never put your sister in danger intentionally." I drew my mouth upwards into a lopsided grin that I hoped she'd find endearing. "Ya know, she's pretty stealthy."

She pulled out of my grasp to spit in the sink. The slight jolt as she moved caused me to groan.

Her eyes widened when she saw me falter. "Are you okay?" She reached for my stomach then pulled her hands back. "I'm sorry." She stared at the marks along my ribs. "You look like raw meat. How did they . . ." She couldn't finish her sentence. Instead, she took a deep breath. "I have something that will help. Stay here."

She returned holding a tub of something that smelled floral and grassy. "What is that?" I asked, watching her use two fingers to swab the top of the balm.

"It's my own healing blend." She lathered it between her hands, creating a soap-like consistency.

"Is that why you have all those crystals and stones? Do they all have a purpose?" I asked, remembering the first day in her room and what I thought was a rock collection scattered across her floor.

"Yes. Crystals, stones, balms, ointments. I use them all. I like to . . ." She paused, looking upward. "I don't know exactly. It's strangely second nature for me to want to heal things. I've tried several different recipes, and this one right here"—she showed me the inside of the tub; it was colorless, almost emollient-like—"is made of crushed shungite stone, witch hazel, arnica, and vitamin K. I've used it on every scrape and cut Pepper has ever had. Your swelling will be gone by tomorrow, and the wounds should be mended as well. It's very powerful." She rubbed her palm over my chest and down my center landing right above the elastic of my shorts. The way she touched me with such care and precision drove my insides mad. Her fingers danced along the ripples of my torso. My heart rate picked up speed.

"Olivia," I said. My timbre dropped into a deep baritone.

Her hands paused right above my belly button, and the rush of blood downward pushed me to act. I grabbed her wrist. "Olivia," I warned in a deeper, gruff voice.

Her big hazel eyes gazed up at me. "Why do you always call me by my full name when everyone else calls me Liv or Livy?" she asked, her words as husky as mine.

I placed my hand on her face and gently rubbed my thumb across her cheekbone. Pulling half her bottom lip into her mouth, she sucked in a breath, looking everywhere but at me. I couldn't tell her it was because I chose a name for her that was mine and mine alone. I couldn't admit that from the moment I met her, I knew I wanted her. So instead, I looked down, unsure of what was happening between us, and studied her mouth. One minute she was using it to curse me out, the next she was teasing me with it.

"Olivia?" I said for a third time, now asking for her permission.

Our eyes met, and I dipped my head. I crashed my lips against hers. I had no idea what this was between us, but I wasn't going to fight it.

I could taste the faint hint of mint as she opened her mouth wider, inviting me in. Her warm tongue ran along mine, and my whole body ignited. My hands moved to her hips and pressed into her side. I lifted her onto the sink. Her legs spread, and I moved in between them, stroking my hands along her bare thighs. I cupped her ass in my hands and pulled her closer to my body. Her T-shirt pressed against the balm on my chest, gluing us together.

I drew away from her, and she whimpered at the loss of contact.

"Liam," she breathed as I moved from her mouth to her jawbone to her neck, kissing her like my life depended on it. I gripped her hair, pulling her head back, and trailed kisses along her collarbone, my breath quickly falling in sync with hers. I moved back up to her mouth and slid my tongue inside.

My mind was no longer in charge, and the sensation of touching Olivia took over completely.

My hands slid to the hem of her shirt. I balled the material in my hand and gripped. I lifted it past her stomach, ready to take her right there on the counter, when a voice in the doorway caused me to stop.

"Hmmm, am I interrupting?"

Olivia instantly pushed me and jumped off the sink, pulling her T-shirt down as far as she could. I groaned as she connected with my sore body.

Pepper smirked at us from the hallway.

"Liam needed balm, and I was trying to . . ." Olivia couldn't spit out her lie fast enough. Her lips, swollen from our kisses, were a deep pink that matched her flushed cheeks. She smoothed her hair with her hand.

"You thought mouth-to-mouth was how to apply your healing balm?" Pepper crossed her arms over her polka dot-patterned robe. "Extremely happy that's not how you use it on me when I'm hurt." She tightened the green sash around her waist.

I smirked in Pepper's direction, then glanced back at Olivia, waiting for her response.

"Yes, well, of course . . . I mean, I wasn't . . . well, what I am trying to say . . ." Olivia stumbled on her words.

I rolled my eyes, having had enough of the babbling chatter. "She's fourteen, Olivia. She's not stupid." Turning to Pepper, I continued: "We were making out, and you'll be glad to know she didn't punch me like I'd expected." I rubbed my jaw. "All my teeth are still intact."

"Nice," Pepper said moving into the bathroom and high-fiving me along her way. "Told ya!"

Olivia's cheeks burned a darker shade as she crossed her arms over her kitty rainbow shirt. "You two spoke about this?"

"Yeah. It's like so obvious you like him," Pepper said, rolling her eyes. She grabbed her toothbrush from the cabinet and applied toothpaste. In between brushing, she said, "Don't need to be psychic to know that one."

Olivia practically growled and stormed out of the bathroom. I laughed and winked at Pepper. She winked back. I mussed her hair like I do to Jac's and walked out of the bathroom. I followed Olivia into her room, dumbfounded by her anger. But when I entered, Olivia was holding her cell phone, her hands shaking uncontrollably and her face paler than any ghost I'd ever seen.

I peered over at Jac. She had stopped unpacking her clothes and was staring at Olivia with the same concerned face.

"What? What is it?" I tilted my head, looking back and forth between both girls.

Olivia swallowed, her whole body trembling. Afraid she might drop her phone, I hurried to her side and grabbed it.

"Nurse Daryl, from the first hanging two years ago"—her voice quavered—"she's not a victim or the vengeful spirit . . ."

My head snapped up when I read the text highlighted on her phone.

"*She* was the Angel of Death serial killer!"

16

OLIVIA

I stared at my phone and reread Kevin Archer's text over and over again. On shaky legs, I lowered myself down onto the bed next to Jac. Liam paced. I thought he'd be pleased to learn we'd gone to the hospital to investigate. Instead, the volume of his scolding grew as the disjointed lecture rambled on. Within five minutes, my room was filled with all the members of the Hunter and Davis families.

"Pepper, go to bed," Dad said, pointing at the door after Liam caught him up on the situation. The dark circles under my dad's eyes were even more profound than usual.

Pepper stomped her feet a couple times but finally left the room.

"Let me get this straight," Dad said as he pulled out my desk chair and sat down, straddling the backrest with his arms crossed over the top. Agent Hunter hovered over him, still in suit pants but with only a white undershirt on. "You went to the hospital with Dustin and Jessica to see if you could find a nurse serial killer and the woman you thought was the victim or witness to the victims turned out to be the killer?"

When Dad put it like that, it sounded more foolish than we thought at the time.

"And you got Kevin Archer to do your dirty work?" My dad's voice rose as he pinched the arc of his nose. "Do you know how illegal what he did was? How did you convince him to even go along with this hare-brained idea?"

I crossed one of my legs over the other, causing my long shirt to ride up my thigh. Before I could answer, Liam blurted out, "Would you put some pants on!"

Dad, Agent Hunter, and Jac all looked at him with curious stares. But he wasn't fazed by their judgment. I bristled, then stood up stiffly and grabbed a pair of folded sweatpants from the top of my dresser. Everyone turned away as I slipped into them and sat back on the bed. Despite the interruption, my dad looked somewhat grateful for Liam's demand.

"Better?" I asked Liam with a bitter edge to my tone. He ignored me and leaned against the dresser.

"As I was asking, how in the world did you get your childhood babysitter to go along with this?" Dad leaned forward, his eyes intense as they bore into me.

"It's a long story," I said, actively relaxing my shoulders as I sat back against the headboard. "But he owed us a favor. And we collected."

"And what did he find out?" Agent Hunter's voice caused goose pimples to dance along my forearms. The man's large stature wasn't the only intimidating factor. He played FBI agent better than anyone on television.

My palms had started to sweat under his cross-examination.

"While in Nurse Daryl's care, eight women in the maternity ward died. She was never fired, but they did finally ask her to leave. It was all kept off the books." I took a deep breath. "The hospital did a good job of erasing the information so they wouldn't get sued."

"There were eight cases?" Dad stood, exploding from his chair. His eyebrows rose in alarm. "Are you . . ." He paused, shaking his head. I was about to ask him if he was all right, but he pulled himself together and asked, "Did Kevin give you names?" He held up his finger. "Also illegal!" Dad's shoulders rose, almost touching his earlobes.

"No. He found this all out from a co-worker who was working at the hospital when this took place. About twelve years ago," I answered.

Dad's shoulders dropped, seemingly relieved. I watched Liam and Agent Hunter share a look I didn't understand. I couldn't be sure, but I suspected it had to do with the file they were hiding from my dad.

"We need those names," Jac said, unaware of her father and brother's silent exchange. I looked down at my phone. I had seventeen unanswered messages from Dustin and Jessica wondering where I was and if I saw the information Kevin sent.

Agent Hunter placed his hand on my father's shoulder. "You and I can look into this tomorrow. Let's give these kids a good night's sleep." He gave my dad a gentle squeeze. "Everyone is safe for now, and we have a starting point."

Liam left first, without even meeting my eyes, let alone saying good night. My dad and Agent Hunter followed. Jac checked the salt outline in the room before lying down on the blow-up air mattress. She pulled the covers up to her chin and yawned. "Never thought I'd see the day my brother acted so wound up over a girl. That pants comment?" Jac let out a low whistle. "That was new." She rolled over, facing the other way. "Night, Liv."

After a fitful sleep, I woke the next morning to see a Ford Focus in the driveway. Apparently, Agent Hunter and Liam towed the Bronco and picked up a rental, all before the rest of us even had breakfast. As I made my way into the kitchen, I saw Liam at the coffeepot, chatting with his dad while Jac and Pepper ate cereal at the kitchen table and fought over the prize at the bottom of the box. My dad sat in the living room with the local news on, his favorite blue coffee mug in his hand per his usual routine. If I had been anyone else, I'd have thought we'd all have lived together since forever. It appeared so . . . normal.

Liam looked at his watch. Oddly, it matched the one Jac wore. "We're gonna be late." He pointed at the door. "Let's go, girls."

We loaded ourselves into the Ford, a far cry from the Bronco, but this time our seating arrangements changed. Jac jumped into the backseat next to Pepper. No one seemed to notice or make a big deal that she left the front seat open for me. Given the way Liam acted last night, I thought he might have considered our kiss a mistake. He barely even acknowledged me this morning.

As we pulled into the school parking lot, I saw Jessica and Dustin getting out of the Volkswagen. I wanted to hide, but I knew eventually they'd find out the Hunters were staying with us. Better to face the music now than later.

We got out of the car and were headed toward school when Liam spoke. "Buddy system today." He pointed at all of us. "That goes for everyone here. You understand?"

Pepper nodded without protest, causing my mouth to drop to the floor. My sister compliant? Who was this teenager?

Ahead of us, Jessica turned slightly and caught my eye. "Hey," she said, running backward to meet up with me. Dustin followed in her wake. "We texted you all night. You never answered." She glared at Liam, who nodded to Jac and Pepper to continue walking. Funny how Pepper never chose to listen to me, but for Liam Hunter, I think my sister would jump off the Leo Frigo Memorial Bridge.

Unfazed by an obedient Pepper, Jessica pulled her bookbag higher on her shoulder. "You know, about the thing." Jessica's rapid eye blinking worked against her attempt to be discreet.

I motioned with my head to Liam. "He knows. They all know."

Dustin patted Liam on the back. "What's up, man?"

Liam nodded.

"Who's all?" Dustin frowned.

"My dad, her dad, and my sister," Liam answered, threading his fingers into mine. The scab on his knuckles brushed against my skin, his touch rough but sweet. He rubbed his thumb over the top of my hand as if he had done it a thousand times.

Dustin and Jessica's eyes fell immediately to our locked hands. Right then and there, I wanted to curl up into a tiny ball of self-conscious energy, but the hopeless romantic part inside of me screamed out with joy. *Yes.* Somewhere deep down inside, I wanted Liam Hunter whether I'd admit it out loud or not.

"Next time, do not do anything like that without me," Liam cautioned all of us.

"Are we, like, part of the team now?" Dustin asked, throwing his bulky arm over Liam's shoulder as the four of us walked toward school. A welcome warm breeze caressed my chilled cheeks as the front doors opened.

Liam laughed. "Dude, this is not a team you want to be on. I promise."

We arrived at my locker, and Liam leaned into my ear and spoke low. "Nothing by yourself today. Promise me." I quickly agreed, and then he kissed my cheek and released my hand. He and Dustin took off down the hallway while I just stared at the back of his head.

Jessica's voice broke my trance. "Seriously, I saw you yesterday, and now?" She waved between where I stood and where Liam just was. "What happens at the Davis house in one evening?"

"It's . . ."

"If you say it's complicated, I'm going to hit you over the head." Jessica looped her arm through mine and dragged me toward homeroom, making it clear there were no hard feelings, just pure curiosity. "Okay, I admit, he's hot, and if I was into guys maybe my ovaries would cloud my judgment too. But what in the world changed since yesterday? Are you guys together? Are you still staying with them? I need details."

I shook my head. There were too many things I couldn't explain.

The bell rang, saving me from my best friend's interest. We took our seats, and I gave Jessica a small smile. She huffed but left the questions alone for the rest of the period.

The school day passed without incident. Liam didn't make any more physical touches or passes, but everywhere I looked, he appeared. The buddy system was no joke. He stayed glued to me like peanut butter on jelly all day. Jessica and Dustin both noticed, but it's not like I could explain the supernatural world to them. Sure, they knew about the Angel of Death killings, but they still had no idea how that might be a danger to me, or school nurses.

Once the last period ended, Jac, Pepper, and Liam met me at my locker.

The four of us had proceeded to walk out to the parking lot when Pepper jolted past us, running to the car in a full sprint. She looked over her shoulder and screamed, "Shotgun!"

I smiled. Figured that little shit would want to sit next to her new hero. I turned to smile at Liam, but instead of finding Pepper's actions funny, he stopped dead in his tracks. His ears perked up as if he heard something. An exhaust popped, and I twisted, following his line of sight. A powder-blue minivan with no windows and something dark covering the front windshield came out of nowhere, speeding through the parking lot toward Pepper. Liam broke into a run. Jac and I followed but couldn't match his pace.

"Pepper!" Liam screamed. She stopped, confusion washing over her face.

The van, however, didn't stop. The engine's roar split the air as the vehicle sped up, coming within inches of Pepper's body. Liam threw himself between her and the front fender, taking the impact on his shoulder and blocking the blow to Pepper.

I gasped, pressing my palms into my eyes. What I thought happened, couldn't have really happened, could it? Liam should be dead. Pepper should be dead. I opened my eyes and instead of their bodies lying on the pavement, I saw the van jerk backward. A human-sized dent formed in the grill of the vehicle.

"Liam!" Jac yelled, rushing over to her brother.

"Pepper!" I screamed, chasing after Jac.

Liam glared in the direction of the reversing van, swerving all over the parking lot. Students jumped out of its way, while some of the cars drove up onto the grass to avoid collision.

Liam's hands encircled Pepper's face. "Are you okay?" he asked. His breath released in short gasps, but he seemed unharmed.

"I don't . . . I don't understand." Pepper's voice wavered.

Liam hugged her to his chest. "I know." His chin rested on her head. He squeezed his eyes shut. "I don't either." When they reopened, I saw something in Liam's eyes I never would have expected. Fear.

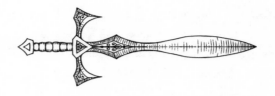

17

LIAM

I held Pepper to my chest while watching the powder-blue minivan's retreat. The blacked-out windshield made it impossible to see inside. Was the driver targeting Pepper or looking for us? Was it human or a monster? The van swerved backward, causing students to steer their cars out of the way to avoid an accident. It hit the main road, spun around, and fled in the direction it had come from.

Holding Pepper in one arm and extracting my phone from my pocket with the other, I dialed Doc. On the sixth ring his voice mail picked up. "Doc, it's me. You need to get to Falkville Falls, Wisconsin, and meet us at the Davis residence as soon as possible." I hung up, knowing he didn't need any more information than that to find us.

Now parked on the sidewalk, Jessica's Volkswagen had been one of the cars that veered out of the collision path. The doors flew open, and Dustin and Jessica rushed over to us.

"Dude, did that car hit you?" Dustin's eyes enlarged. They scanned my body, Dustin clearly having a hard time believing I survived the impact.

"I'm fine," I grumbled.

Olivia nudged me out of the way and grabbed Pepper by the shoulders. Her gaze skimmed over her, searching for injuries.

Pepper wiggled out of her embrace. "I'm okay." She tucked strands of fallen blue hair behind her ear. "I swear. I'm okay."

Olivia's gaze shifted to me, her eyes searching and assessing my body. Aside from a tear on the sleeve of my leather jacket, I remained in one piece. She shook her head. "I can't believe you are both . . ." Her voice wavered, and she couldn't finish her thought.

Jac held the phone to her ear, probably on with Dad.

A large hand grabbed my shoulder. "Liam, buddy, you sure you're okay?" Dustin asked, his pupils dilated. "Do you need to go to the hospital? Do you have any injuries?"

"I'm fine. I'd check on her, though." I pointed to a seemingly paralyzed Jessica, who looked like she might pass out from a lack of oxygen. Her mouth was agape and her face had lost all color. "We need to get home. Now!" I ordered, turning toward the girls.

The bottoms of Olivia's eyelids were filled with moisture, and her trembling hands had found their way back onto Pepper's shoulders. She mouthed *thank you* to me and proceeded to walk Pepper to the rental car.

Jac, Pepper, and Olivia got in and waited for me to climb into the driver's side.

I took one last look at where the van had come from. Questionable thoughts raced through my mind. I surveyed the rest of the parking lot. Not many students witnessed what happened, thankfully, but a couple here and there stared at me with unease. All I could hope for was their innate ability to form denial, the belief that no human could stop a van with the force of their body.

We drove in silence for most of the way home.

Fear, rage, and guilt all ate at me from the inside. How was I going to protect the Davis family when I didn't even truly understand what was going on? What if we hadn't been all together this afternoon? I knew it went against the promise we made to each other, but I couldn't help it—I blurted out, "Watches, Jac. Make them." I caught her eye in the rearview mirror.

"Liam." Jac's facial muscles softened as she held her ground against my command. "We can't and you know it."

"I don't care. Make them," I barked.

We argued back and forth while Olivia and Pepper just gaped in silence. When Jac first made the app, Dad had sat us down and given a speech that Jac was hinting to now. Eventually, we'd want to get watches for everyone we ever cared about, but we couldn't be in a million places at the same time. Our hunter's mission was to kill monsters, and if we saved humans along the way, that was a bonus. But it would be impossible to save every person we'd meet. Having outsiders wear watches that tracked their heart rates and locations would be counterproductive for our line of work. We couldn't be on a hunt worried about why Doc or another hunter or anyone else for that matter had an accelerated heart rate, because it would distract us from the current threat. At the time, my father's rule made sense.

In theory, I agreed with it. But seeing how quickly we'd almost lost Pepper, I changed my mind.

We came to a red light. I turned in my seat. "I don't care what the rule is, was, whatever. You make them tonight and you give them to the girls. End of story!"

Jac's lips thinned into a straight line, and she tensed her jaw.

For the rest of the ride, the only sound came from the hum of the small car's engine. Quiet and foreign. So unlike the familiar sounds of Mom's Bronco.

When I opened the door to the Davis house, I expected my dad and Sheriff Davis to be waiting, ready to grill us about the van. But what I saw caused my mouth to drop open.

My father was pointing a gun at Sheriff Davis.

"Dad?" I extended my arms out wide, holding the girls behind me.

"This can be real easy, or it can be hard." Dad directed his words to Sheriff Davis.

"Dad!" Olivia shrieked, lunging toward him. I grabbed her by the arm and pulled her back. Like hell, I'd let her get in front of my father's weapon.

Pepper's mouth fell open a solid two inches, as did Jac's. Both were transfixed.

"Let go of me!" Olivia pulled on my arm, but I refused to let her go.

"What the hell is going on?" I asked my father, now gripping Olivia with both hands as she squirmed to get free.

"Matt and I were having a chat, and I caught him in a lie." Dad didn't take his eyes off his mark as he spoke. "A rather big lie." He tilted his head to the side, signaling me to get into position.

I knew what he wanted, but it took me a second before I did it. Releasing Olivia, I grabbed the revolver I had holstered behind my back and held it on Matt. "Jac, grab Sheriff Davis's firearm, please." I kept my pistol directed at the sheriff and moved to his other side. The couch was sandwiched between Dad, Sheriff Davis, and me, a perfect place to keep an eye on the girls. "Olivia, Pepper, couch." I motioned to the cushions.

Jac retrieved the revolver from Sheriff Davis's holster, donning an apologetic grimace and aimed it at him. The three of us surrounded him and the girls. There was no escape, not without one of them being shot.

"Why are you doing this?" Olivia asked. Her pained face searched the room for answers as she moved toward the sofa. None of us connected with her stare. Pepper's lips twisted as she rolled her eyes. She plopped onto the couch, flinging her bookbag on the recliner and kicked up her heels as if this happened every day.

"Matt erased some files today linking him to Joanne Daryl and the murders," Dad answered.

I *knew* there was a connection.

Sheriff Davis held his hands up higher. "It's not what you think."

Olivia twisted in her seat. "Dad, tell them you had nothing to do with her," Olivia pleaded, pulling Pepper closer. Pepper pushed her away. "Or any murders."

Sheriff Davis gestured to my father. "If you let them go upstairs or outside, anywhere but here, I'll tell you everything."

Without giving my dad a chance to answer, I used my gun barrel to gesture a no. "Not gonna happen." There was no way I'd let Olivia or Pepper out of my sight, and I sure as hell wasn't going to lie to them later once we got Sheriff Davis's admission. "They stay. So, if I were you, I'd spit it out. Now!"

The corners of Sheriff Davis's lips tilted downward. "Joanne Daryl was my wife's attending nurse during her pregnancy with Pepper." Sheriff Davis's eyes filled with moisture. He swallowed before continuing. "I had no idea back then Patricia's death could be a murder. None!" He elevated the last word, causing Olivia to jump. "When I asked the hospital for more information, something that would bring me peace and closure, they blew me off and said sometimes these things just happen." He shook his head. "Years later, one of my officers lost his wife after she had given birth, and I started to put two and two together. Same hospital, same attending nurse, same inconclusive death. Too similar for it to be a coincidence."

"Dad," Olivia breathed.

He ignored Olivia's surprised and saddened tone and continued: "We investigated it, searched as many cases as we could, picking apart each mother's death, but we never had enough to even hold Daryl for more than twenty-four hours. Eventually, the department made me close the investigation, but the hospital did ask her to leave quietly. I thought that would be enough."

"Eight mothers died including Mom!" Olivia stood. She popped her head directly between her father and I, forcing me to lower my weapon.

"I didn't know," Sheriff Davis pleaded, looking directly at Olivia. "It wasn't until the Feds uncovered another case with a woman a town over named Rena . . ."

Olivia gasped. "Rena Mayers."

Sheriff Davis's eyes widened. "How do you know that?"

Olivia's stare volleyed between her father and me. "Liam found an article about her and shared it with me." She stayed laser focused on her dad. "Why didn't you arrest Joanne Daryl then?"

Matt shook his head. "Because by the time the Rena Mayers case unfolded, Joanne Daryl had hung herself to death."

Dad lowered his gun and gestured for Jac to do the same. Jac didn't hand Sheriff Davis back his revolver. Instead, she walked over to Dad and gave it to him.

Smart girl.

"I'm sorry," Sheriff Davis said turning to his daughters. "I should have told you."

Olivia stood and walked over to her father and threw her arms around him. Pepper stood and grabbed her bag. "Whatever! Can I go upstairs now?"

Everyone in the room yelled, "No!" at practically the same time.

Pepper huffed and flung herself back into her seat. Well, that was freaking odd. Had I found out my mother had been murdered, I would have been falling apart like Olivia. Pepper acted like it was old news. I attempted to address Pepper, but Olivia cut me off.

"I think you should leave." Olivia's gaze traveled to me, Jac, and then my father. "All of you."

"No," Sheriff Davis said. "We need their help."

"But Dad," Olivia stammered. "They held guns to your head!"

Before Matt could respond, the doorbell rang. Pepper jumped up and jogged to the door, throwing it open. We'd be discussing security protocols after this. Dad and I raised our weapons back up and pointed to the entrance to the foyer.

"Jackson, Jacqueline, William!" Doc shouted from the archway to the living room.

Pepper's wide grin twitched.

Doc traveled into the room. His gaze lobbed between us. "Put your bloody armaments away." He crossed his arms. "What in the world have you gotten into this time?" He pointedly stared me down. "No explanation, just a panicked message. I'd have thought everything went all to pot." He handed Pepper his worn leather briefcase and cane. "Be a love and hold on to these." He patted her on the head. Instead of refusing, she giggled, taking them from him.

Doc unbuttoned his fitted jacket, revealing a brownish-red cardigan sweater fastened with more buttons than all my jackets combined. It matched his maroon turban and bow tie.

"Well, don't just stand there, Poppet!" He waved his arms and Jac came running. She flung her arms around him. "That's my girl."

"We missed you," she said pressing her face into his chest.

"There, there, missed you too." He removed his coat and handed it to Pepper. This time she crinkled her nose. Her piercing wiggled.

Dad hugged Doc next and I followed, allowing the first happy smile to grace my face in the last twenty-four hours.

Dad kept his hand on Doc's shoulder. "This is Matt Davis and his daughters, Olivia and Pepper," Dad said, introducing the Davis family to the one and only Doc.

Only Olivia appeared to be holding a grudge. Her hands clenched into fists at her side, and she nodded.

Doc peered at Olivia and stroked his long gray beard. "I'm completely gobsmacked." He placed one hand at his heart. "In all my years." He walked over to her and peered down at her hands. "May I?"

Olivia looked at her father, who tipped his chin in agreement. She scrunched up her brows, but she held out her palms.

Doc grabbed her hands and enfolded them between his. "Brilliant. Just brilliant, I tell you." He turned to the rest of us. "You didn't tell me this was smashing good news." His eyes found me. "I thought I'd be walking into a barmy tragedy, the way William sounded."

William, Pepper mouthed.

I rolled my eyes. Liam was short for William in England, and Doc had a thing against using nicknames. Said it was "bloody boorish."

"This isn't great news, Doc." Dad crossed his arms.

Doc raised a brow. "A healer in our line of work?" He turned Olivia's hand over and kissed the top of it. His eyes locked onto her ring finger. "I see you are wearing an EMF protection stone." He looked over his shoulder at Dad. "I'm sure your EMF readings in this house were askew. The poppet probably didn't even know she was subduing them."

Well, that made more sense. Every time Jac tried to get a reading in Olivia's room, it showed no sign of a spirit. The stones scattered all over her floor unknowingly protected against detection from electromagnetic fields. No wonder it suppressed our reader.

Doc released her hand. "A healer is good news no matter what. I haven't heard of a natural healer with your powers in some time. You radiate green and blue auras."

All our mouths dropped open except for Olivia's, whose lips crinkled. "This is crazy. You are all crazy." She looked up at her father. "They should go."

"It makes sense," I said stepping forward and ignoring Olivia's meltdown. "Your room looks like a rock museum. You create ointments and balms. The salve you rubbed on my body has almost completely healed my bruises and cuts from yesterday's attack." I rubbed my chin. "And I took a van to my shoulder today without feeling one twinge of pain. No matter how powerful our serum is, something else kept me safe."

"You were hit by a van?" Dad's eyes traveled from my head to my toes and back up again. "And you're okay?"

I waved him off. "Yeah, I'm fine."

Olivia's fists balled at her side. "I don't believe it," she argued. "You sound like a madman."

"Fine. Don't believe us." I ignored her anger and pivoted back toward Doc, pointing at the other Davis sibling. "It's her we called you about. She's a psychic."

18

OLIVIA

Anger bubbled up within me. This man's claim about my "healing aura" sounded absurd, but I'd worry about that later. Right now, my attention shifted to Pepper. We'd just learned the truth about our mother's homicide. She didn't need any additional stress. Although given her relaxed posture, she seemed unfazed by all of it.

She showed zero reaction to the news of Mom's murder—a death she'd once blamed herself for. And she barely had a response to the accusation that she was some kind of psychic, which I wasn't entirely convinced of. It's not like Pepper had appeared clairvoyant or intuitive or anything.

Doc followed my gaze and turned to my sister. She scoffed, putting her hands on her hips as she locked eyes with him in defiance. "Yea, I'm some kind of dead-person psychic," she said, rolling her eyes in Doc's direction.

The older man laughed. "Well, Poppet, you are most certainly more than just that. You are a connection to the past, a voice for the unheard, and a conduit for the revenants' answers." He curled the bottom hairs of his long beard in between his fingers. "But how powerful you are and how potentially dangerous—well, that I do not know." A curious smile played in his eyes, but his mouth was set in a serious line as he pondered the thought.

"It's not Poppet. It's Pepper." My teenage sister crossed her arms, clearly not attuned to English slang.

Doc, Liam, and Dad chuckled. "Of course, love, of course," Doc replied, appeasing her. He went over to my sister. He lifted Pepper's chin, and she let him look into her eyes. "Who have you been speaking to in another realm, dear child?" His words were tender, curious.

My nose crinkled as Pepper shook her head out of his grasp.

"No one." Her eyes slid to the floor as she avoided eye contact with Doc.

"Pepper," Dad warned. "What aren't you telling us?" The creases around his eyes looked deeper and more noticeable than usual.

"Nothing," she said. She grabbed her backpack off the chair and pivoted back around, staring us down. "I have homework. If they"—she motioned to the Hunter family—"are going to stay and not put a gun to our heads, can I be excused?" Her glare challenged someone to stop her.

Dad's eyes widened.

"I don't see why not. But Pepper love, denying the truth will never change the facts. The sooner you admit them, the sooner I can help you," Doc said, fixing his turban. "If you are as powerful as your sister, you may have some abilities that can cause you harm if you don't learn how to control them."

Agent Hunter moved forward. The glint in his eyes held promise he'd get Pepper to talk, but Doc lifted his pointer finger, silencing Agent Hunter. "We will be ready to listen when you are ready to talk."

Pepper took a breath, narrowed her eyes, and then huffed in response as she walked up the steps to her bedroom.

Doc turned to my father. "Let me know where I can rest my head. I'm knackered. My luggage is on the porch. Do you mind helping me bring the lot in?"

Dad drew in a calming breath and then nodded, seemingly eager to have a task he could perform that took him out of the uncomfortable emotional temperature of the room. Casting an assuring look at me, he followed Doc outside.

"I'm going upstairs," Liam announced. His shoulders tensed while throwing a questioning look at his sister. "Jac, do you mind?"

His sister exchanged a glance with Agent Hunter and then tilted her head toward her brother. "Coming." She walked after him, and the two disappeared up the steps, presumably into Liam's temporary room.

Anger, confusion, and sadness weighed on my chest, constricting my breath. I needed a break from the Hunter family and my own. My father's admission left little room for closure. It felt like I'd lost my mother all over again. With a sigh, I followed Liam and Jac up the stairs. I had meant to head straight to my own bedroom, but instead I found myself lingering in the hallway by Liam's barely open bedroom door, willing my ears to hear the conversation on the other side.

Was I really that desperate to know what they were saying that I would eavesdrop?

The answer was obvious: Absolutely.

These two had a bond completely different from my own sibling relationship. And considering they weren't just family but practically co-workers, I wondered if this particular discussion covered personal or professional subjects, or both. Stopping inches from the door, I strained to catch their words while trying to keep quiet. Breathing was a way louder activity than I could afford. I barely allowed the air to be swallowed up into my lungs for fear they would hear.

"Liam, I really don't want to fight about this," Jac said.

"Great. Then don't. Make the watches, give them to the Davis sisters, and everything will be right as rain." Liam's voice rose an octave, faking a cheerful cadence.

Jac paused before heaving a sigh. "Listen, for the first time in a long time"—another pause—"Scratch that. Maybe for the first time ever, I can see you have real feelings for a girl, and it's not just the normal I-must-save-everyone Liam reacting here. It's an I'm-in-love Liam responding."

I swallowed a gasp and instead took in a short breath. Was Jac talking about *me*? Well, I guess. Who else could she be talking about? But was she serious? Liam didn't love me. Maybe he liked making out with me, but love? Was Jac the one who got hit by the van?

"Jacqueline, now you're the crazy one."

Agreed.

"Are you reading those romance novels Dad hates again?" Liam's chuckle sounded forced. He continued: "I do not love Olivia. Sure, I'm happy sticking my tongue down her throat, but when am I not making out with a girl on a hunt?"

Heat rushed through my veins. *What a complete ass!* Good to confirm, Liam Hunter was a player. That's a fun fact I could have done without. Silence followed, and I wondered if they had stopped talking. I pressed my ear against the door, and I heard Liam's voice pick back up. "Honestly, I don't think I'll ever love anyone, so it's better if we don't revisit that theory again."

My heart splintered as I heard Liam say those words. Sure, I wasn't in love with Liam Hunter either. Well, at least I didn't think I was. But to hear him say he never thinks he could love like that . . . how broken was he?

"Hmm, if that's the case and I've misread this whole thing, then why the watches?" Jac's voice grew in volume, causing me to step back. Was she moving closer to the door or just speaking louder? I couldn't tell.

"Just make the watches," Liam said, trying to end their conversation.

The creak of bedsprings alerted me to movement. Maybe he rolled over or sat up, but regardless, I'd bet my life it was intended to end the conversation.

Jac laughed loudly, like a full belly laugh. "You may be my big brother, but hell am I more mature." Her footsteps sounded, one, two, and then they stopped. "I'll set up the watches and give them to Olivia and Pepper, but when Dad finds out, don't be upset when he confiscates them." Jac's voice quieted, forcing me to take a step closer again. "I'm sorry, Liam. While you won't admit how you feel about that girl, I'm not stupid. Let me remind you, when we find out what spirit is haunting the school and lay it to permanent rest, we will leave this town and you will leave Olivia. So, make peace with what you need to, now. Because the wristwatches will come with us, and I'd hate for the watch to be taken along with her heart." Two more steps. "If you care for her at all, you'll end it sooner than later. Find someone else to make out with. You've never had any problems finding a volunteer before."

My top lip curled. I didn't want him to find someone else. Stupid or not, I wanted Liam Hunter, even if I currently ran hot with rage after he held a gun to my father's head. I shifted my weight from leg to leg, waiting for Liam to say something, anything. I stupidly hoped he'd say something warm. Something like; *I don't want to make out with anyone else. She means more to me than I said.* But silence lingered on the other side of the door.

I counted in my head how long before Liam answered. Twenty whole seconds.

"Fine." His one-word response came out gruff.

My hands covered my mouth. A part of my heart hardened at that one word: *fine.* He'd proved his motives behind his gestures, small or large, were just for entertainment. Nothing between us meant anything significant to him. A sharp pain pricked my throat, making it hard to swallow.

I hadn't even thought about what would happen after the mission. They were leaving eventually, and if I allowed one more sliver of my heart to go to that boy, he'd end up taking it with him.

"Get some rest. I don't think tomorrow's going to be any better than today," Jac said.

A laugh burst from Liam. "When have we had a good day? A hunter doesn't get the pleasure."

"Touché."

Jac strode out of Liam's room and almost rammed into me. I didn't even hear her footsteps coming but I did see the door when it came right up to my nose.

We both froze.

I frowned while Jac offered an apologetic smile. Then I braced for her outing me to Liam but instead, she walked past me into our shared bedroom not saying one word. My jaw slacked. I couldn't understand it. Why not just tell Liam I knew the truth about him not caring, and then this charade would be over? Or why not address me in the hallway for eavesdropping like a creeper?

She just left me alone with my feelings.

Pepper's low voice interrupted my twisted thoughts. It resembled her sleep talking in the middle of the night. Had that girl really managed to pass out and take a nap already? After all this excitement? A small part of me grew annoyed at her. I don't know how I'd manage to sleep at a time like this.

I stepped up to Pepper's bedroom door, which was plastered with signs that said things like "Keep Out" and "Beware of Dog." Not that we ever had a dog. I think she thought if she hung the sign, the dog might come later. I leaned my ear closer, fully embracing that I was now the type of person who listened through doorways.

"But they think you are . . . No, of course not! It's just that they know I'm . . ." Pepper whispered as usual, but it didn't sound like sleep talk. It sounded like she was . . . Was she having a conversation? With whom? Liam and Jac were in their rooms, and everyone else was still downstairs.

Unsure what I'd find, I eased the door open ever so slightly, trying to get a look. Pepper sat on her bed, staring into the darkened corner. A slight flash of light flickered in the outline of a woman. I threw open the door, startling Pepper as my knees buckled underneath me. A figure cloaked in shadows vanished for a split second and then rematerialized, its translucent eyes intent on Pepper. I knew that visage.

My throat constricted, but I managed to form a single word. "Mom?"

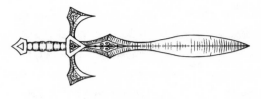

19

LIAM

Olivia screamed.

I jumped from the bed like it had burst into flames as her piercing voice echoed from the room across the hall. Jac and I almost collided as we rushed through Pepper's door. Amid my excitement, I didn't grab my revolver. Hell, nor a shirt. Dressed in only my gym shorts, I barreled into the room unprepared. Elastic waistlines weren't meant for holding weapons anyway.

Olivia's shoulders were hunched. Her hands covered her mouth as she sat on her knees just inside the entrance. My initial instinct to move toward her fractured when an impossibly blinding light flashed in the air. The brightness forced my eyes to close for a split second and seared the insides of my eyelids. I blinked them open, adjusting to the radiance silhouetting Pepper. Her blue hair glowed appearing neon like. Splotches danced in my vision before it completely settled. A spirit. How could it break the salt barrier?

That's when I saw it.

Someone had kicked the protective border away, smearing the tiny grains across the room. And since the salt hadn't been anywhere near normal foot traffic, that left only Pepper as the culprit. Olivia's hands clutched her chest, and tears streamed down her face as she stared at the translucent figure of a woman who looked extremely familiar. She bore Pepper's cheekbones, jawline—just older, with more creases around her eyes, lips, and neck. Her long reddish-brown hair contrasted with Pepper's artificial blue.

I reached out to touch Olivia but remembered what Jac had warned. *Treat this professionally.*

"Olivia?" I held up my hands. Her gaze moved back and forth from me to the ghost. "It's okay," I cautioned, but I had no idea if that was true.

For the time being, the spirit hovered in the air just over Pepper's shoulder. She—it—appeared calm, and Pepper's stance looked protective of the supernatural being. Clearly, she was Team Ghost right now.

"Olivia," Jac said, waving her closer to the door. I could tell from her tone that she shared my reservations.

Olivia stood and inched toward my sister as Dad, Doc, and Sheriff Davis pushed their way inside. Sheriff Davis fell to his knees at the same time my dad cursed.

"Patricia," Sheriff Davis whispered. His hands clutched his face.

Dad, Doc, and I all exchanged looks of concern. Patricia Davis. Matt's wife. Olivia and Pepper's mom. *This wouldn't be difficult.* I rolled my eyes. Why couldn't any of these hunts be easy? Just once?

"She's not trying to hurt anyone," Pepper fiercely explained. "Momma wants to help." Pepper glared at Jac and me. "And she'd prefer it if you didn't shoot her!"

"That seems fair," I said, nodding to Pepper. Not like I had a weapon anyway. If I had been armed, I wouldn't be speaking, I'd be shooting. The spirit would have been blasted several times already. "But you need to be honest with us and tell us what's going on."

The spirit pointed to Doc, and his eyes widened. A wave of understanding settled into my stomach. Doc hadn't explained his abilities yet to the Davis family. Unlike Pepper, who could hear the revenant, Doc could foresee them. He had the power of premonition, a vital gift to Hunterland. Visions appeared in dreams or through a technique called spirit-drawing. Sometimes he'd just start sketching a person or a place he'd never even known existed. If the information was concrete enough, he'd call us to take care of what he saw, but sometimes it would be too late before he fully understood what his visions were trying to articulate.

"Bloody hell," Doc whispered. "She's the woman from my last drawing. The one in the hospital gown with the bruises around her neck." In a quieter voice he asked my father, "Jackson, was she strangled?"

Sheriff Davis answered from the floor, his voice distant. "She couldn't breathe. She clutched her own throat so hard with her fingers, she left marks. She struggled, desperate for air."

Olivia left Jac's side and dropped to the ground, throwing her arms around her father. It took everything inside of me not to reach out to her and comfort her. The two of them sobbed and rocked each other. Seeing your mother and wife as a ghost wasn't an everyday occurrence. And since spirits couldn't talk to the living, they wouldn't be able to communicate.

"She's the one killing school nurses," Jac said, her tone neutral.

Pepper flailed her arms. "No, she's not. She hasn't killed any of the nurses. It's not her." Pepper glanced back at her mother, who dipped her head as if to tell her to continue. "It's one of the other victims. Momma can only go where I go." Pepper lifted the necklace with her mother's wedding band. "So, I take her everywhere with me so she can get a better look at the suspects. And we think we've figured out who it is."

"Pepper." Sheriff Davis's voice broke. "Why didn't you come to me?" He lifted himself and Olivia off the ground, keeping his arms wrapped firmly around her. His bloodshot eyes barely left his transparent wife. "You're too young to solve a murder investigation, and you should have . . ." He stopped. I imagined formulating criticism on how your teenage daughter should have turned to you when she started talking to her dead mother and trying to solve a mysterious murder case was a hard sentence to spit out.

"Who is it?" Dad asked, moving in front of the Davis family as a protective measure. Spirits, especially feisty ones who had been roaming freely for some time since their death, could be violent and even worse, unpredictable. And although Patricia Davis showed no signs of ill will, she had been dead for fourteen years, making it unlikely she had much of her humanity left.

"Billy Lyons's mother, Jody Lyons. She was killed around the same time Momma was, by Joanne Daryl, and Momma has seen her at the schools Billy and I spray graffiti on." Pepper fastened her hands to her hips.

"Has your mother seen her commit the crimes?" Dad continued.

"Not all of them, but most. If you burn Jody's bones, won't that confirm it?" Pepper begged. "There will be no more dead nurses."

"Yes, it would be telling," Doc answered. "Pepper, can you ask your mom to leave us?" Doc's question was a test. If the spirit listened to Pepper, then at least we knew she wasn't taking revenge out on any of us and that she trusted Pepper. It afforded us a measurement of their relationship.

Pepper looked at her mother and within a second, she disappeared.

"No," Matt and Olivia both said. They weren't ready to see the ghost of their loved one go just yet.

Dad walked over to Matt and pulled him out of the room. Jac offered her hand to Olivia, and they retreated along with our fathers. I didn't have to be present to know the speech they were both receiving. We would have to incinerate the wedding band and put Patricia Davis's spirit to rest. Since she had been cremated— something we had discovered during our preliminary research— the object had been the spirit's tether to our world. I worried about Pepper though. She already knew everything, and she had from the start, yet she'd hidden it all from us. How cooperative was she going to be?

Doc and I exchanged a knowing look as we approached Pepper.

"You're a tough little bugger," Doc said messing with Pepper's unruly blue hair the way I did Jac's. "It was dangerous to chase after another spirit." Doc lifted Pepper's chin. "They can be aggressive, you know."

Surprise washed over my face as Pepper nodded in agreement. "Has your mother ever been violent with you?" I asked.

Pepper glanced down but didn't shake Doc's hand away like she did earlier.

"She didn't mean to." Pepper's voice faltered. "She's protective." Pepper's gaze reached mine. "And she *really* doesn't like being shot at."

I chuckled. "Well, that makes sense, but you know the longer she's in our world and not put to rest, the more dangerous she can become."

Pepper unhooked her necklace and draped it around her hand. She reached out to Doc. "I'll miss her," she said handing the last piece of her mother over. To send Patricia's spirit to its final resting place, Doc had to melt the gold wedding band down. "She's changed since she came to me two years ago. I know she wouldn't want to be like Jody Lyons. Not really."

I wrapped my arm around Pepper. "You are one tough cookie." She crashed her face against my chest and cried. I smoothed her hair down her back, resting my chin on her head. "Your mom would be so proud, kiddo."

Dad walked into the room and summoned me. "You and Jac are on graveyard duty. Go burn the bones. Jody Lyons is buried in Falkville Falls Cemetery."

I released Pepper and kissed her forehead. "You did the right thing," I said, encouraging her bravery. Not all people let go of their loved ones with such understanding.

I hurried to get dressed, grabbing my newly patched-up leather jacket. I poked my head into Olivia's room to retrieve Jac. I thought she'd be ready to go, but instead I found her standing rigid, arguing with Olivia.

"Absolutely not," Jac barked, threading her arms through her coat. By the tone in her voice, I'd bet she had said this multiple times and stubborn Olivia refused to hear it.

"What's the problem?" I asked from the doorway. I leaned my shoulder against the frame.

Jac pointed at Olivia. "She wants to come." Jac's inflamed face was beet red as she slipped on her leather gloves—gloves that were once mine. The oversized fingers always made me laugh, but she refused to get her own pair dirty when we had grave duty.

I shrugged. "Fine. Let her."

"What!" both Jac and Olivia asked in tandem.

I motioned for the two girls to follow. "It's a dig, burn, and rebury job. If she wants to come and see how it's done, let her. We don't have time to argue. According to social media, Billy Lyons, the Art Beat King, or whatever his stupid name is, has planned another school defacing this evening. So, let's get what we need, pack the rental, and go."

When we arrived at the cemetery, I asked Jac to grab the gasoline, salt, and one of the shovels from the trunk and to head to the grave without us. I needed to clear the air with Olivia. Jac shot me a pointed glare that spoke volumes, but she followed the instructions anyway. She grabbed the items and proceeded to the burial site.

"We need to talk." I leaned against the car.

Olivia crossed her arms as she glared in my direction, her hazel eyes churning a storm gray. "So, talk."

I didn't expect her to make this an easy conversation. After aiming a gun at her father's head and alerting her we'd have to kill her mother's spirit, I assumed she'd harbor some ill feelings toward us, especially me.

"I know how hard this must be. You lost your mom when you were young, and it must feel like you are reliving it now."

Before I could continue, Olivia cut me off.

"Like you even care." She huffed.

"I do care." I stepped forward, mentally reminding myself not to touch her. "Too much," I mumbled. I ran my hands through my hair, busying them with anything but her. "Listen, my mom was killed by a werewolf pack. They tore her body so badly, all we found were bits of skin and nothing else. We never got to bury her." Against my better judgment, I grabbed Olivia by the shoulders. I pulled her in front of me, making sure I kept her at an arm's distance. "I would be losing my mind if we had to bury her memory again. I'm haunted every day over what happened when she died."

Olivia's eyes softened. "I'm sorry," she whispered.

"Thank you," I said, and I meant it. I rubbed her arms, appreciative of her coat sleeves for being the barrier between our skin. "But I'm not asking for your sorrow. I'm just letting you know I am fully aware of the pain you are going through, and I wish I could take it all away."

Olivia broke our embrace. "I'm more worried about my dad, you know, the man you held at gunpoint." She straightened her spine. "So, let's burn the spirit who's caused this mess and then go home and put my mother to rest. Okay?"

I agreed, knowing not to push my luck. I wanted to address more, but she'd already turned her back on me and started to walk after Jac. My gaze traveled the length of her, memorizing every curve and edge of her body, taking the moment to secretly soak her in. I inhaled a deep breath, letting the air cool my insides. We'd be leaving soon, and I'd have to let her go.

On my exhale, I grabbed the second shovel and walked behind Olivia in the direction of the grave.

When we reached Jac, beads of sweat dotted her face, hair clinging to her chin and neck. She swung the pick side, breaking up the snow-covered soil and devouring the ground. We dug for over an hour before we hit the coffin, six feet deep. Drenched in my own perspiration,

I wiped my forehead. I used the sharp end of the shovel to pry open the top. A decayed body lay in the satin-lined casket.

"Ew!" Olivia covered her nose with her jacket while peering into the opening. The putrid smell hadn't affected me for years. "Now what?"

"Can you pour the salt can over the body?" Jac asked, pulling herself up and out of the grave to stand next to Olivia. I followed her path, digging my foot into the indentation Jac made with her own boots.

As Olivia deposited the salt, Jac sprayed the gasoline. I lit the match and threw it into the hole. We watched as the body and silk lining of the coffin went up in flames. Firelight danced across our faces, and for perhaps the hundredth time, I could only imagine how macabre the scene would have looked to anyone else, but to me it was beautiful and peaceful.

The way closure should be.

"It's sad but kind of serene," Olivia said. I shook as I heard her mirror my thoughts.

Illuminated by the spouting blaze, I watched the tears streak down her cheeks. Her jaw twitched as if she was clenching her teeth to keep her mouth shut. Knowing we'd be doing this to her mother next couldn't have been easy.

But something told me she knew it was the right thing to do. What I didn't tell her was while we were gone, Doc was already melting the wedding band and clearing the salt lines from the house. By the time we made it home, Patricia Davis would be at rest and the Davis family would go back to normal. Well, as normal as one could be after finding out monsters existed.

Olivia turned to Jac and I. "So that's it? No nurse will die tomorrow at Danbury High?"

Jac shook her head. "No. They are safe."

Olivia's nose crinkled. "I still don't understand one thing. Why did the spirit kill Mr. Bailey? He's not a nurse or related to health care at all. Do you think the ghost started targeting other teachers?"

Both Jac's and my mouth dropped. How could we be so stupid? Pepper told us her mother had changed. She was adamant she hadn't killed the nurses, but she never said her mother hadn't killed *anyone*.

Which meant if Patricia Davis knew Doc was about to put her spirit to rest, there was no telling what she might do.

20

PEPPER

I knew I messed up, but I couldn't risk it. They'd have thought badly of Momma, and she was just protecting me. Once they laid her to rest, I'd tell them about Mr. Bailey. I mean, I still hadn't told them the truth about the vampire's nest either, but I didn't want to hurt the Hunter family. They'd showed me more kindness in the last month than anyone else I'd ever met. I didn't have a lot of friends. I found it difficult to make them when spirits hovered around me whispering all the time. My ears bled some nights from the constant chatter. Momma protected me. She made the spirits go away.

I climbed into bed, grateful that no nurse would die tomorrow and that Billy's mom would finally find peace. More selfishly, I was thankful I could stop stealing for Billy and his crew. Could stop pretending to be their friend. My eyes fell on my backpack, and the sequence of patches from all the high schools we'd tagged stared back at me. *Badges of honor,* Billy called them; symbols of being part of his crew. I hated them. I wasn't even any good at painting graffiti. The only reason Billy kept me around was because I stole the supplies they needed for their masterpieces. I excelled at stealth.

I rolled my eyes and silently groaned at the thought of Billy's artwork as "masterpieces." Dumbass Dustin was right. They were complete crap. But I needed to leave my tag behind for Momma to be able to roam the school for a couple hours after I left. A spirit could exist in the same place their object once was for a short period of time but after that, they'd return to exactly where their object was located.

I pulled the covers up to my chin as I closed my eyes.

A startling white light flashed, brilliant and soundless. Momma had returned.

I jackknifed up in bed, and the breath in my chest hitched. "Momma," I said bringing the covers up to my neck. "I thought we talked about you going away for the night. Jody Lyons is being put to rest now. You don't need to worry."

I am worried, baby girl. Her comforting voice rang through my head as she floated across my comforter and sat cross-legged at my feet. *That old man lied to you, sweetie. He lied to me!*

I scrunched up my nose at her accusation of Doc. I liked him. More than I'd have expected to. He was kind and funny with his head wrap and cane and sweater with all the buttons.

He said he had a vision of me with marks on my neck, but he also had a vision of Mr. Bailey's death. I saw it in his notebook. She pulled her knees up to her chest, exposing her feet from under the hem of the hospital gown she always appeared in. Her toes, covered in black grime, wiggled. *He knows the truth,* she whispered.

I released the blanket and lunged forward. "It was an accident. He'll understand. You were protecting me. It's okay, Momma. Everything is going to be okay," I lied. I knew she was losing her grip on humanity. She had never acted like this before. It's why I gave Doc the necklace in the first place. I didn't think I could trust her anymore, not as much as I wanted to.

Speaking of which, how was Momma here? I had assumed Doc would have melted the ring down by now.

Momma stood from the bed. *He'll take me away from you. He tried once already, holding the ring over a crucible.* Her eyes narrowed in on me. *I wondered how he got it.* She shrugged. *He must be dealt with.* She floated to the door. Her head swiveled back in my direction while her body remained forward. *I love you, my Peppermint Patty.* My namesake.

Momma had told me why Daddy called me Pepper. On their first date, Dad's nerves got the best of him, and he ate a whole bag of peppermint patties. Momma said he tasted like chocolate and mint, her favorite combination. Hence the nickname.

I jumped out of bed. I couldn't let her leave. I had to stop whatever Momma planned to do. Suddenly, she turned and held her palm up toward me, blasting me back into the wall. I hit my head hard and tumbled down.

My eyes fluttered shut, and everything around me went dark.

I woke to Dad cradling me in his arms. "Pepper, can you hear me?" In my groggy haze, I heard him repeat the question. I groaned. A dull ache throbbed on the back of my head. I reached for it and touched a golf-ball-size bump.

"Doc!" My eyes opened wider taking in my surroundings. "She's going after Doc," I said, as Momma's threat tumbled back into my memory.

Dad stood carefully, lifting me up with him. "Who's going after Doc?"

"Momma," I said regaining my footing on the carpeted floor. I glanced around the room, hoping to spot a trace of her still here, but there was nothing.

Without a word, I darted out my bedroom door and down the stairs, careful to hold onto the banister as I took the steps two at a time. Dad followed, hot on my trail, calling after me. I flung open the basement door and continued my descent, coming to a halt at the bottom of the staircase.

Just around the corner, Agent Hunter lay unconscious amid the remains of a broken shelf of old tools. Blood pooled under his head. His long black hair clung to his face in what I could only hope was sweat.

"No!" I yelled as I watched the spectral form of my mother lift Doc's body up with one hand, her translucent fingers curled around his throat. His face had turned a shade of purplish red, nearly matching his turban. His long beard was draped over her forearm.

"Patricia," Dad yelled behind me. "Let him go!"

She faltered at the sound of Dad's voice, losing her grip. Doc dropped to the floor, his body wracked with coughing.

She whirled toward us, her eyes pinched, her jaw strained. Any signs of humanity I once saw had disappeared. She held up her palm in my father's direction showing no remorse, no love. I realized in my gut that she hadn't been herself for a while now. A wave of force erupted from the angry spirit's hand, blasting Dad backward. He hit the bottom of the stairs with a thud.

Without wasting any time, she aimed her palm toward me. I moved and dived behind an old leather couch beside the staircase. She instead blasted a plastic tub filled with my old Barbie dolls. Heads flew through the air.

"Pepper! Dad!" Livy yelled from the top of the staircase. I could hear her boots against the wooden steps.

"Doc! Dad!" Jac's voice followed as well as two more sets of footsteps.

"No!" I screamed from behind the couch. "Stay back. She'll hurt you!" But before Momma could injure another person I cared about, I heard a loud bang, and my heart stilled.

21

OLIVIA

Liam held a shotgun like he did the first day I met him. He'd blasted the spirit of my mother with his rock-salt bullets right where she stood. She'd vanished in a flash, but it would be just a matter of time before she came back. We only had moments to spare.

I rushed to Dad's side. "Wake up!" I grabbed him by the shoulders and shook him. He moaned in response: a good sign. "Get up. We have to get you out of here." I struggled to put his arm around my shoulders. Using all my energy, I pushed into my heels and hauled him upright. He swayed slightly on his feet but steadied himself against me. Pepper rushed to our side and slipped his other arm over her shoulders. I was relieved to see she appeared unscathed.

"I'm okay," Dad breathed. His eyes fluttered, barely staying open. I glanced back at Liam. His nostrils flared as his gaze landed on his own father whose head laid in a red puddle.

Jac and Doc pushed through the rubble to get to Agent Hunter. Although Liam's attention stayed on his dad, he didn't release his hold on his weapon. His family threw aside tools and pieces of shattered pressboard shelving. Once Agent Hunter's upper body was freed, Doc gripped under his arms and pulled the large man's body out. Jac and Doc lifted him and brought him over to the couch. He groaned, moving slightly. A bruised face surrounded his nearly closed, swollen eye.

"Get him out of here," Liam ordered, holding his shotgun up in the air and moving around the room in anticipation of our mother popping up again. "I thought you melted the ring. And why is all the salt cleared from the house?" Liam asked Doc, who was propping Agent Hunter up against his shoulder.

Bruises peppered Doc's neck, but other than that, he looked okay. "Bloody hell, of course I melted the ring. It was the first thing I attended to after you left. Then I cleared out the salt barrier." He wiped his sweat-covered forehead with his sleeve.

"It must be something else," Liam said, looking from Dad, to Pepper, to me. "Do you have any other objects of hers on yourself?"

Pepper shook her head, and I followed with the same motion. "The ring was all we had," I confirmed.

Dad held up his hand, twisting his wrist back and forth. The promise bracelet Mom made him in high school. How could I have forgotten?

Through puffs of breath, he tried to speak. "She weaved in parts of her . . ." Dad trailed off, unable to finish his sentence. A bright light appeared, and our spirit mother formed.

Within a heartbeat, multiple explosions shot from her hands, each hitting a new target. Doc, Agent Hunter, Dad, and Jac all fell to the ground. Pepper jumped out of the way and did a somersault to dodge the blast.

Liam pulled the trigger, but the spirit reacted quickly and moved out of the way, causing the rock-salt bullet to hit the cement wall. Dust and chunks of brick crumbled to the ground. The enraged spirit whipped around the room and positioned herself behind a wobbly Pepper. She grabbed her, using her forearm to cut the oxygen flow to my sister's throat.

"Don't hurt her," I breathed. Tears welled in my eyes at the sight of my baby sister in pain at the hands of a twisted reflection of our mother.

Pepper's body shook as she began to speak. "She said to tell the boy to put down the gun, or she will kill me," she stammered, her words barely audible through her tears.

Liam moved forward, and the insane spirit's grip tightened.

"Stop!" I yelled at Liam. His eyes darkened, but he froze. I blinked away my own tears as my breath escaped in short gasps. "Please, please, don't hurt her." I sucked in as much air as I could as the knot in my throat grew bigger. "She's your daughter," I pleaded. How could she want to hurt Pepper? Was she so far from being human that she couldn't even remember her own children?

Liam bent down and laid the gun on the concrete floor. "Listen to Olivia. You don't want to hurt Pepper." He held up his hands as he stood and retreated from his weapon.

Mom laughed, but there was no sound. She bobbed her head as if she wanted Pepper to translate.

Streaks of mascara stained Pepper's cheeks. "She said that's ironic, coming from you."

Liam tilted his head. "And how's that?"

I silently begged him with my eyes not to pick a fight with the angry spirit using my sister as a bargaining chip, but I trusted him. Maybe more than I should. I moved closer to my father, thankful for Liam's distraction.

Pepper wheezed for air as she answered Liam. "She thinks it's funny that you don't want her to hurt me when you will end up hurting us all when you leave. She says she won't hurt us because she'll never leave. She'll stay with us forever."

I bent down to the fallen body of my father, his breath shallow. My fingers looped around the bracelet my mom had made with a lock of her hair, and I ripped it off Dad's wrist. I gripped it tightly in my palm. I didn't have anything to burn it with, but I knew Liam did. He had slipped the matches into his pocket back at the cemetery. If I could get it to him and distract the spirit, I could save us.

I drew in a breath and moved toward the boy that had changed my world forever. "Even when Liam leaves, he won't break our hearts because he would never hurt us," I said, knowing Liam needed to hear this as much as, if not more than, the vengeful spirit. "Real love is sacrificing yourself for another, and Liam's done that, for all of us." My eye caught Liam's as I moved even closer to him. "I know you care about us. I know you would do anything to protect us." I grabbed his hand and pushed the bracelet into his palm, directing my next words to only him. "And I know you have to leave so you can protect others like us because that's who you are." I paused and swallowed. "And I would never change you." His hand curled around the woven material as he gave me a knowing squeeze. His eyes glistened with understanding as my own throat choked. "And I know you will always be here." I pressed my other hand over my heart.

I turned back and faced the spirit, blocking Liam from her line of sight. She held her free palm out to blast me. I stood strong, knowing that whatever happened next, Liam would save my sister.

I could feel the heat behind me as Liam set the bracelet on fire. The spirit closed her fist and reopened it, holding her palm to me.

"It doesn't have to be this way. We could live forever together. I could be your Momma for the rest of your life and beyond," my mother said, no longer in Pepper's voice but her own. The vocals were shaky, but I could understand them. Pepper looked up at her with wide eyes.

My hands balled into fists by my side. "You are *not* my mother!"

Her feet were engulfed by flames. She broke her grasp on Pepper. My sister rolled to the side as fire spread up the spirit's opaque legs, then to her torso. But before it could reach her hand, a blast of force escaped.

Air exploded from my lungs, and a sharp pain thrust my chest backward. My eyes squeezed shut. My body was jostled painfully with each impact as I hit the floor and skid into the shelf that housed our

Christmas ornaments. Through the noise of broken glass and shattered statues, I heard Pepper scream my name. She could breathe. She was free. A warmth spread to my heart at the sound of her voice. My nostrils stung, and a foreign metallic taste formed in my mouth. I tried to spit it up, but it stuck to my tongue. Blood dripped down my lips and chin.

And as suddenly as it began, everything went dark and silent.

22

OLIVIA

I rested next to Pepper in my bed, smoothing stray strands of hair away from her forehead as she lay in my arms. After I woke from my mother's blast, my little sister refused to leave my side. Now, exhausted from all we'd been through, and content knowing we were all safe, she finally slept soundly.

I hadn't realized how strong and brave Pepper was until now. All the secrets she held from us. Whether she felt like it was for our own good or hers, I can't imagine what that had done to her insides. No wonder these last two years had been so rough. The acting out, the attitude, the resentment, the loud music in the middle of the day, being wrapped up in Billy Lyon's crew; it finally all made sense.

My gaze lifted to a sleeping Liam in the recliner next to my bed. His relaxed features made him appear peaceful—so different from his normal hard exterior. Although he'd avoided physical harm from my mom's spectral wrath, he'd carried the stress from the ordeal. Exhaustion won the battle, and he fell into a deep sleep.

Liam had refused to leave my room even after Dad demanded it. Too tired and worn out, my father had conceded. It was obvious Liam cared about us, and although his family would be leaving soon, I had no doubt he would check in from time to time to make sure we were okay.

I certainly wasn't happy about how complicated things were between us. It may have seemed like Liam was just after one thing. Maybe that's because his job was too serious, and he needed to let off steam. I could understand that, on some level. I just wasn't going to be the outlet for him to use and leave behind.

Morning came, waking me up from the troubled sleep I'd suffered. At some point, Pepper must have woken and left. I looked around the room and didn't see Liam either. Slipping out of bed, I walked into the hallway and followed the noise of conversation down the stairs.

The scene in the kitchen unsettled me just like the first time I woke to the Hunters in our house. Liam sat at the kitchen table with Jac and Pepper, all three shoveling food in their mouths. This time, pancakes, eggs, bacon, a bowl of cut fruit, several ketchup bottles, and orange juice were spread across the table. Doc had on a green apron that said, "I love sleep—It's like a time machine to breakfast!" He hummed a tune I didn't recognize while pouring coffee into Liam's mug—my mug, actually. I grimaced as I watched him sip from my purple-and-orange Falkville Falls Tiger cup as if he owned the place. It wasn't the first time he seemed to think he was welcome to take my things without asking.

My dad and Agent Hunter sat in the living room with the local news on. The reporter was speaking about an incident at Danbury High.

"Another school, another wall defaced," the reporter's voice relayed. "We have several leads including students from Falkville Falls High school. At this time, the authorities are not releasing names but are hopeful the vandalizations will be stopped."

I scanned everyone's faces to see what types of injuries surfaced from yesterday. Doc had a couple of marks under his chin. I had a balm that would clear his bruises up by tomorrow. Jac had a cut above her left eye matching the one her father had across his forehead. His right eye was swollen as well. The ointment I used on Liam the other night would be perfect for those. Dad and Pepper seemed intact, but I knew Pepper incurred a bump on the back of her head and bruising on her neck from where the spirit had held her. I'd ice that later if she'd let me. And Dad—well his ache wasn't something I could mend. Seeing my mother as a violent spirit had to hurt in places I couldn't even begin to understand, let alone heal.

Liam was the first to look up and acknowledge me. "Have a nice rest?" His mouth quirked up in a half smile.

I crossed my arms, causing my shirt to rise. "How are you all dressed already?" I asked releasing my arms to my side and pulling down on my hem.

Pepper stood and took her empty plate over to the sink. To my surprise, she began washing it off. My mouth must have dropped open at least two inches. "We've got school," she said over her shoulder at me. "You better change."

"School?" My brow raised. "Aren't you in pain? Shouldn't you rest?" I looked around at everyone else. "Shouldn't we all rest?"

Pepper shrugged. "I'm fine. Nothing that won't heal."

Dad and Agent Hunter placed their cups next to the sink. Dad, dressed in his police uniform, and Agent Hunter, in his pretend FBI suit, looked at the clock. "We'd better get on the road," he said.

"If Pepper's fine, then school it is. Jack and I have work," Dad said, patting me on the back. "We can chat later. I know yesterday was rough, but we can't let you kids miss school."

I took a step back, feeling like I'd entered the twilight zone. My ghost of a mother had just tried to evaporate all of us. You'd think this would get us out of school for a day. Not because I wanted to play hooky or whatever, I just thought we should address the aftereffects of the incident.

Jac took the leftover food to where Pepper was hunched over, loading the dishwasher. I rubbed my eyes as if the vision wasn't real. Pepper washing dishes? Dad insisting we go to school like nothing happened? I knew the Hunters and Doc were used to this insanity, but my family? This was a first.

I gaped at Pepper.

"Doc said he will help me with my powers, but only if I do chores," Pepper said, sticking her tongue out at Doc, who faced the opposite direction.

"I saw that," he said, taking a bite of his pancakes. "Beware. I have eyes in the back of my head."

Liam took another sip of coffee before handing his cup—my cup—to Pepper. "Seriously, I think he does." He turned and looked at me. The slight lift in his lips was the only clue I knew the next sentence was at my expense. "While I love the bare-legged Olivia, I'd rethink pants before jumping into the Bronco for school." He winked.

"Liam," Agent Hunter warned. My dad glared at Liam, who stared at my legs.

"I can't be the only one who thinks she needs to put on more clothes," Liam said, gesturing with his head to my father.

"Go get dressed, honey," Dad said.

Minutes later, we all barreled into the newly repaired and detailed Bronco in the driveway. The ride was filled with small talk. No one addressed what had happened the night before. No one even mentioned Mom.

The rest of the day felt like I was looking through a foggy window. Nothing felt real, and all my interactions seemed fuzzy and convoluted. Maybe this was me processing everything we'd just gone through.

Morning came and went, and when I arrived at lunch, Dustin, Jessica, Jac, Pepper, and Liam were already seated. I hadn't remembered Pepper and Jac having the same lunch hour as us. Regardless, I threaded my legs through the bench next to Jessica, seating myself across from Liam.

"How was your night?" Jessica asked. "You never called me back. You've been pretty distracted lately." She glared in Liam's direction. "You're acting like I'm dead or something."

I shook my head. "What? No, of course not." I swallowed. "There's just been a lot going on recently." I paused, realizing I hadn't given a real apology. "Sorry I disappeared."

"So, what's up with you two?" Dustin asked, cutting into the conversation. He waved his hand between Liam and me.

"Nothing," I said staring at my food, but just like this morning, I had zero appetite. Something wasn't right. I didn't eat as much as Pepper, but I'd never skip two meals.

Liam acted as if he couldn't hear us. He poured a blob of ketchup on his ham-and-cheese sandwich, then closed it up and took a big bite. A red drop oozed from the bread and landed on his plate. He continued eating, more focused on the lost condiment than the conversation.

"I'm not hungry," I said and stood. I walked out of the cafeteria and straight for the Bronco. I had no idea why or what I would even do once I got there. Liam had the keys. Hell, I didn't even grab my winter coat, yet for some reason I wasn't cold.

When I turned around, Liam was standing less than a foot away. "Why are you running from me?" he asked, tilting his head to one side. He closed the distance between us. "Do I make you nervous?" Ever so slowly, he used one hand to gently grip my chin and angle my head to the side, exposing my neck. My eyes widened as I stepped back, hitting my rear on the side of the truck. Although I should have been running from him, my own desire trapped me.

He placed his other hand above me and against the car, lowering his head to mine, breathing in and out. Warm air caressed my collarbone.

"Don't you want me?" Not waiting for a response, he pressed his lips against my neck, then behind my ear as he nuzzled in closer.

I tipped my head back, giving him further access to my body. I wasn't even thinking anymore. My eyelids shut as he placed another lingering kiss against my chin and then at the crook of my lips. His breath bathed my face.

Things had changed so quickly, I wasn't even processing what was happening. One moment he was ignoring me in the cafeteria and the next, drawing a line of kisses across my upper body.

My throat became dry, making it hard to speak. I opened my eyes a fraction to stare into Liam's blue irises.

Blue. Powder blue.

The image came out of nowhere. I pushed Liam out of the way and ran into the middle of the parking lot. The powder-blue van veered straight for me. I screamed as the front grill closed in on me. The driver wore what looked like a full bodysuit covering everything but his face. His irises flashed red, his mouth covered in crimson gore, and fangs protruded down his lips. The tires screeched, and everything went dark.

23

LIAM

Olivia's cries woke me up in the recliner. Pepper screamed along with her sister. Couldn't we get through one night without shouting? That thought seemed impossible.

I went over to Pepper, the closer of the two. "It's okay." I placed my hand cautiously on her shoulder. "It's okay," I repeated. Turning my gaze to Olivia, I said, "I think you were having a nightmare. You had a rough night with your mother's spirit. It happens. But you're okay. You're safe."

Olivia's gaze darted all over the room, like a bouncy ball ricocheting off the walls. Her chest rose and fell in wild succession. "No, no. That's not it," she yelled between ragged breaths. Her eyes finally settled on me. Her tongue brushed over her lips. Gathering herself together, she continued: "Doc, I need to talk to Doc. Now!"

"I'm right here, love," Doc said rushing into the room. Spots of black and blue dotted his neck, nearly matching the color of his silk button-down pajamas. Worry set in the creases around the eyes of Dad and Sheriff Davis, who trailed behind him. Jac didn't come running from her nest on the guest-room floor, but that was no surprise. Dad had given her a sedative. Someone around here needed to rest. With all the night terrors we were experiencing lately, I wondered if I'd ever see the REM cycle again.

Olivia pressed her palms into her eyes. "I . . . I think . . ." She shook her head. "How do you know if you have the power of premonition?"

Doc smoothed out his beard. "You're a healer, my dear, so I guess this wouldn't be too far from . . ." Doc exchanged a look with my dad. "What would make you say that? What do you think you saw?"

A trembling Olivia looked down. She idly played with her ring, rubbing the smooth amethyst stone. Pepper grabbed her hand and held it in hers. It was the first time I'd seen Pepper show affection and concern for her sister, and I wondered if Momma Ghost had helped to unite them.

"I dreamed we all woke up and had breakfast together." She gazed at Pepper. "You did the dishes."

Pepper's lips twitched. "Yeah, definitely a dream, not a premonition."

"Pepper," Sheriff Davis warned.

She held her hands up. "Just saying, I don't do the dishes. Not my thing."

Olivia glared at Pepper. "Anyway, Dad made us go to school with Liam and Jac. The whole day seemed blurry until . . ."

Doc pulled Olivia's desk chair up next to Olivia's side of the bed and sat. Sheriff Davis hovered like a helicopter over Doc's shoulder. His drawn face and sunken eyes spoke volumes to his physical and mental fatigue. I wasn't sure how much more this man could take.

Dad, considerably banged up, kept himself stationed at the door. The gash on his head started from his swollen right eye and continued into his hairline. I'd hoped he would inject himself with more serum to speed up the healing process, but it didn't look like he had yet.

"When did it start coming into focus?" Doc placed his hand on Olivia's knee, and I had to stop my instinctive reaction to smack it away.

Was it so wrong that I wanted to be the only person to console her? Touch her? I internally sighed. *Get it together, Hunter!*

"Well, Liam and I . . ." she looked up at her dad, then Doc. "Do the details matter?"

"Yes, they do." Doc squeezed her knee. I moved forward protectively. I had no idea where I was going or what I could do to help, but I wanted to subdue her fright. She had already been through so much.

"Liam and I were sort of . . . kissing," she mumbled, biting her lower lip.

I burst out laughing. "We were making out and that's why you screamed?" My gaze traveled to my father, who rolled his one good eye and then to Doc, who looked mildly concerned. I avoided Sheriff Davis for fear he wouldn't be too happy his daughter had dreamed of kissing me. "Did you scream because it was amazing or because we need to work on our moves?" I waggled my brow, but Olivia didn't share in my humor. Her cheeks reddened, and she glowered at me. I lifted my hands up, and then spoke in a more serious tone. "Okay, okay, we can talk details later, but you thought this was newsworthy and Doc needed to know?" From the sounds of it, Olivia just had a dream. Welcome to real life.

Olivia stood, nearly knocking into Doc. Her curled hands flanked her body. "No, you jerk. And it wasn't like it was anything to write home about."

I always left my customers satisfied, and by the moans she emitted in the bathroom the other night, I'd say she'd leave a five-star review. I went to object, but she held up her hand, silencing me.

"Anyway, it went directly from that to me running into the parking lot like Pepper had, and the powder-blue van drove toward me." She crossed her arms over her chest. "But in my vision, I saw the driver."

"Who was it?" Doc asked. He slid his chair back to give Olivia room.

"A vampire. And he was coming for us," Olivia said. "All of us."

Definitely not what I expected her to say.

My chin dropped to my chest. Looks like we weren't leaving Falkville Falls yet. "Okay, so maybe it's one of the two that got away from the vamp nest the other night," I offered. "Maybe they followed us back here?"

How else would they have known where we were?

"How am I seeing this?" Olivia asked. She directed the question to Doc, but her gaze focused on the glow of the dark stars plastered across her ceiling.

Doc stood. "I have no idea, but that is exactly how the visions have come to me in the past." He smiled. "Although I can honestly say I have never snogged William in my premonitions."

Olivia's lips twisted. "Thanks." She huffed. "Very comforting."

Sheriff Davis straightened his shoulders. "I think it's safe to say you should go to your room now," he said glaring at me. "You are no longer needed here."

I held my hands up in defense. "You realize it was just a dream."

Sheriff Davis crossed his arms and narrowed his eyes. "And why do I feel like this 'dream' is somewhat relatable to reality?"

"Fair point," I said, holding my finger up high. "Guest room it is." I turned to face Pepper. "You okay? Can you handle taking care of your big sister?"

Pepper smiled. "I'm okay, and are you kidding? I've got this." She high-fived me. "Hey Liam." She paused, staring down at the comforter. When she looked up, she had a twinkle in her eyes. "I always wanted a big brother." She sat up on her knees and threw her arms around my waist. Her small head with crazy blue hair clung to my shirt.

A knot in my throat formed and by the looks of Sheriff Davis and Olivia, they felt it too. Pepper was a hard nut to crack, and it appeared I was able to wiggle my way into her heart. Something I didn't take too lightly.

"Can I stay with you?" Pepper asked Olivia. She plopped back down on the bed.

Olivia smiled. "Of course, I'd really like that." She climbed under the covers and nestled next to Olivia.

After a fitful night's sleep, morning came. The whole family gathered downstairs to eat one of Doc's famous breakfast buffets. He never skimped on what he considered to be the most important meal of the day. You could count on him making so much food that you'd eat the rest for dinner. Today was no different. Fluffy pancakes, bacon, and scrambled eggs sat in the middle, while cut-up fruit, orange juice, and coffee surrounded the main meal. Everyone had come down early except Olivia.

The six of us sat at the table.

"Should we discuss last night?" Sheriff Davis asked. His right arm held up his head while his left cradled his coffee mug.

"It would be for the best," Dad answered. "My kids are used to this bizarre world, but I'm sure you all have questions."

"I don't," Pepper said through bites of her pancakes. "Momma told me everything two years ago. I've had a lot of time to process."

Doc chuckled under his breath. "Well, that is good news. What about what she did to your family yesterday? To you? Do you want to talk about that?"

Pepper took a sip of orange juice wiping the pulp that lingered on her bottom lip away.

"She wasn't Momma anymore. I understand that. I'm happy I got to meet her, for a little while, anyway, before she went batshit."

Doc smiled at Pepper the same way he did at us, like a loving uncle. "Well, she did what any spirit ends up doing that stays too long in a world that isn't theirs anymore. She lost most of her humanity. But she did love you, Pepper," Doc said.

"I know. She told me all the time. That's the part I'll hold on to."

"And what you two accomplished by uncovering Jody Lyons as the spirit serial killer was remarkable. You saved others from unnecessary deaths. You know that, right?"

"Yeah, we crushed it."

Doc placed his hand on top of Pepper's. "You certainly did, Poppet." Pepper wiggled her nose as he released her hand. I don't think she completely understood the poppet terminology, but at least this time she didn't correct him. "Do you want to talk about Olivia?"

"You mean her badass superpower?" Pepper said. Her eyes lit up.

Jac snorted. "I hope she feels that way."

"Doubtful," I mumbled.

"It is a superpower," Doc added.

"Nah, I'm good. Now we both have one. I'd feel badly if I was always cooler than her," Pepper said stuffing another piece of bacon in her mouth while trying to hide her smirk behind her food.

Doc grabbed the napkin in front of him and dabbed it to his lips. "Sheriff, anything you'd like to get off your chest? Are you feeling okay? I know you took a couple of ghost hits like Jackson. It's not until day two you really start to feel the aches."

"I'll live," Sheriff Davis said. He leaned in closer. "Maybe in private I'd like to ask some more questions, but in due time. I'm still processing." He placed his hand on Pepper's shoulder. "But I'm very proud of my girl and how she handled everything." He looked behind him to the stairs leading to the second floor. "I'm proud of both my girls."

Pepper's smile widened. "Can we go to school?" she asked grabbing some of the fruit and placing it on her plate. This was after she'd devoured four pancakes, three slices of bacon, and two scoops of eggs.

Sheriff Davis exchanged a look with Dad. "Sure, if that's what you want."

Pepper jumped up from the table and cleared her plates.

"Dishes, love, they don't wash themselves," Doc motioned for Pepper to go to the sink.

"I'll help," Jac said, meeting Pepper's amused gaze. Jac had been rather quiet this morning. It normally took her a day to come out of the sedative, but Dad knew she needed to get a good night's sleep. We had all been burning the candle at both ends. It was only a matter of time before our exhaustion would affect our ability to hunt.

The four of us men sat at the table talking in hushed voices. "Maybe Olivia should stay home. If she has another ability and doesn't know how to use it . . ." I trailed off, more worried than anyone else. I stabbed my eggs and dipped them into the blob of ketchup on my plate. "Well, isn't that dangerous? What are the odds she's a healer and has the power of premonition?"

Doc grabbed a slice of bacon with his fork and dipped it into my ketchup. I glared at his utensil. "You have enough ketchup to feed everyone in this house for a year. I'm helping you not waste a good condiment." I moved my plate out of reach in case he went for round two. Ketchup was life.

Doc shook his head. "Anyway, back to Olivia. It's not very rare at all. If she's blessed with abilities, it would make sense she has multiple." He chewed his last piece of bacon. "Her mind has expanded to a fuller potential, which all humans could achieve if not for the common barriers that Olivia lacks. She just chooses to use more of her brain at one time. The only danger would lie in suppressing it. Who knows how long she's been having these visions, not knowing what they were? She's probably experienced strong waves of déjà vu, misinterpreting events as something she's experienced before, rather than something she's envisioned. It's very common if you don't know what you are looking for."

"What can I do to help my daughters?" Sheriff Davis asked, his voice heavy with concern. "It seems they both have these . . ." His brow rose in a silent question.

"We call them abilities," Dad answered, leaning back in his chair. "And they are gifts."

"Are these vampires targeting them because of it?" the sheriff asked, pouring more coffee into his cup. The dark circles under his eyes warned of an impending burnout. The spry cop we met a month ago now looked a shell of his former self. He seemed ready to crash, and

I worried he was one supernatural encounter away from a psychotic break.

"Honestly, I'd guess they are after us, not your daughters, but I'm not sure." Dad downed the rest of his coffee. "Any chance we can drive to the station outside the nest site the kids located and ask some questions? Maybe the local sheriff knows something useful."

Sheriff Davis nodded, shoulders coming back to life. "Yeah, let me just call in and tell my guys I'll be out of the precinct today." I got the feeling this man needed to keep busy. He and Dad had more in common than I think either would admit.

Fully dressed in jeans and a sweater, Olivia walked into the kitchen carrying tubs of balm. Her eyes widened, taking in the boys' roundtable meeting and Jac and Pepper huddled at the sink. No doubt she was reliving her dream from the night before.

"You want coffee?" I asked. Olivia stared at the stupid tiger paw on my purple-and-orange mug.

"Olivia, do you want to talk about last night?" Doc asked as I stood and grabbed her a cup from the cabinet. Her gaze traveled the room, and mine followed, paying more attention to her reactions than to pouring the coffee.

Olivia shook her head. "I just . . . it's so weird." She gestured around the kitchen. "Some of this is the same as my vision and some of it is different."

Doc pulled out a chair. "That's how it is."

Olivia sat at the table, placing the healing balms in a neat line.

"It's not exactly what happens—it's more of an idea of what could happen. Premonitions can be altered," said Doc. I handed her the coffee black, just the way she liked it, and she nodded her thanks. "You don't have to go to school today. Pepper wants to, so Liam will go with her, but Jac and I can stay home with you," Doc added. "It's a lot to process."

"No, I want to go," Olivia said. She pushed one of the containers to Doc. "This will help with the bruising on your neck. The marks will be gone by tonight." She pushed the second one toward my father. "This is the one I used on Liam." I smirked, thinking back to the night she lathered me up. "It'll heal the gashes and acts as a barrier to new pain. It'll wear off after your skin is completely healed." She bowed her head. "I'm sorry my mom hurt you and your family."

Dad accepted the ointment. "Do not be sorry. Bruises and scrapes will heal. What you endured in your encounter with your mother will take longer to mend." He dabbed the salve along his forehead and swollen eye. "Give yourself time."

"Are you okay?" I asked, remembering how her mother had blasted her. She didn't have visible marks, but that didn't mean she'd escaped unharmed. "Maybe you should use some of that stuff too."

Her hands fluttered at her chest but quickly dropped to her lap. "I'm fine."

Fine was never a good sign.

Soon after, we piled into the newly fixed Bronco. Olivia cut in front of Jac to jump in the backseat with Pepper. I acted as if I hadn't noticed and wasn't bothered by it, but I did and was. I pulled out of the driveway as Jac unzipped her bag. She plucked out two watches like ours and twisted in her seat.

"Put these on, for protection," she said handing them out. "It'll alert us if your heart rate or pulse spikes past the norm." She showed them the app on her own watch. "We can touch this, and your location will ping to our phones."

I watched Olivia's face in the rearview mirror as she threaded the band and fastened it to her wrist. Heavy lids hooded sad eyes. I couldn't gauge if the watch made her feel secure or like a prisoner, but I hoped the former.

Jac patted Olivia's knee. "If the vamp van comes back and we aren't around, this will help us know you are in danger, and we can find you."

"I like it," Pepper said, holding it up to show me. "It's like Batman's watch."

I smiled, catching her eyes in the mirror. "Cooler than Batman. More like a *Total Recall* watch, the Arnold Schwarzenegger version. The remake was lame."

Pepper wiggled her nose, clearly unfamiliar with the movie.

"That was a holographic watch," Olivia said, twisting her wrist to admire the new accessory. "Completely different."

I laughed. "Fair enough, but just as cool."

The whole day passed without a hitch, a welcome change to our usual chaos. At the end of the day, I met Olivia by her locker for a planned rendezvous with Jac and Pepper.

I reached for her elbow. "Are you okay?"

Her gaze lingered where my hand touched her skin. "Are we ever going to talk about the elephant in the room?" she asked, plucking her arm from my grasp.

I leaned up against the lockers. "And what's that?"

Olivia slammed her locker shut. "You. Me. Us?"

My lips curled into an impish grin. "There's an us?" I clutched at my heart. "Do tell. Are we going steady?"

Olivia smiled, a real smile. Then she smacked my shoulder. "I hate you."

I leaned into her personal space. "Oh, on the contrary, Olivia Davis. I think you like me."

Her smile suddenly dissolved into a straight line. "I heard you, ya know."

My brow rose.

"Talking to Jac that night . . . You're not really looking for anything real. You just wanted to make out or something?" Olivia's eyes left mine and found the floor. "I guess I'm just another girl."

I lifted her chin with a hooked finger.

"You are not just another girl. Not even close." I released a deep sigh. "But we're leaving soon, and I care too much about you to do anything that will ruin our . . ." I huffed through my nose, unsure how to finish that sentence.

Olivia nodded her understanding.

"Friends?" I asked, even though I wanted nothing of the sort.

She shrugged. "Sure. Why not?"

Pepper coughed, startling Olivia, but I'd heard her and Jac approach a second before. "Are we interrupting another make-out session?"

I caught Pepper in a pretend headlock. "You said you always wanted a big brother." I mussed her already tousled blue hair. Pepper giggled, struggling to get free.

The four of us walked out to the car, radars on high alert for the powder-blue minivan. We made it safely inside the Bronco, and as we started to pull out, Olivia waved to Jessica and Dustin, who'd just walked out of school. Jessica picked up a light jog toward the car, smiling.

I heard it before I saw it. The engine revved.

Olivia screamed as Dustin sprinted for Jessica, but the powder-blue van sped up. It slammed into her with an awful *thwack*, tossing her clear across the parking lot. Her head bounced off the cement walkway as she landed, rolling with legs and arms twisted at unnatural angles. Tires squealed as the van swerved over the curb and onto the main road. Olivia pushed open her door and flung herself from the vehicle.

"Don't!" I yelled, charging out of the driver's side. I slid across the hood, grabbing Olivia's forearm before she could get too far. She struggled to break free, but I pulled her into my arms. Her teary eyes found mine, glossy pupils swirling with hope. With questions. But she didn't want to hear my answers. I bit the inside of my cheek, knowing the horrible reality but unable to confirm it aloud.

Jessica was dead.

24

OLIVIA

There were moments you wish you could forget, erase from your memory forever, and the last forty-eight hours qualified as mine.

First, the spectral wrath of my mother, and now . . .

The ambulance and cop cars had left the scene, and yet I still couldn't wrap my head around Jessica's death. Why would the vamps go after her? Were they using her to provoke us? Or was it a freak accident, and she happened to be the one in the wrong place at the wrong time?

I continued to shiver beneath the blanket one of Dad's deputies had wrapped around me. The paramedics called it shock, said I needed to regulate my body heat, but this chill blew in from the gaping hole of loss in my chest that no amount of bedding could fill. The surrounding conversations became background noise as I lost focus. The clamor in my head even drowned out Dustin's anguished cries. I had known something like this would happen. I could have prevented it, but I didn't. And now my best friend was dead.

I felt an arm lift me from the back of the police car and embrace me in warmth. The smell of spices and cinnamon told me it was Dad. I realized then that I had been exchanged between several hands in the last half hour. First Liam's arms, then Jac's, then another officer, who'd assisted me into his cruiser's backseat, where the vehicle's dry heat could blast my face. It wasn't until Dad wrapped me in his arms that the memories surged back.

"Let's go home," he said softly. It took three unsteady heartbeats for the words to click together into any semblance of meaning.

Instead of riding in the Bronco with Jac, Liam, and Pepper, I got into the backseat of Dad's truck. Agent Hunter rode in the passenger seat. The two of them discussed the vamp hit-and-run while I sat in silence. Apparently, my dad had sent his patrol officers to canvas the area in search of the vehicle and ordered them to not engage but rather alert him the second they found it.

But at the end of the day, we knew they'd find nothing, and Jessica's family wouldn't get the closure they needed.

The closure they deserved.

As we entered our gated community, Agent Hunter turned to face me and spoke matter-of-factly. "It's not your fault."

"Why would she think it was her fault?" my dad barked, his tone as sharp as his glare.

"Those with her abilities often do, and they drive themselves mad, convinced they could have stopped events using fragments of the visions that only make sense after the fact," Agent Hunter countered.

He was right. I had replayed my vision the whole afternoon, picking through minute moments and forming a hundred if-onlys. What could I have done differently? How could I have saved Jessica? How could I have the power of premonition and yet feel so powerless?

"Now you're just putting ideas in her head," Dad argued. He turned the wheel, making a right onto our road. The treelined streets became one green blur. "She had nothing to do with Jessica's death."

My body seized at her name.

"Whatever or whoever hit her had nothing to do with Olivia," Dad went on.

"Stop!" It was the first word I'd said in hours. "Just stop." I wiped away the free-falling tears as I caught my father's concerned look in the rearview mirror. "He's right, Dad. All I've been doing is trying to figure out how I could have stopped this." My dad went to speak, but I cut him off. "I know what you are going to say. I don't want to hear it. This burden is mine, and I'm not ready to give it up just yet." I pressed my shoulder into the leather seat and returned bleary eyes to the window, fuzzing the evergreens. I lost my best friend because I couldn't see a clear-enough picture in my dreams; I'd be damned if I saw one now.

As soon as we parked, I shot out of the car. I walked through the front door and strode straight up to my room. I didn't need a dark sky to hear the call of my mattress. I dug into my dresser, absently pulling out a long shirt. Peter Pan was screen printed across the chest, and the back sported a list of names. I stuffed it back into the drawer before Jessica's name could leap out at me. We'd worked as backstage crew for the musical in seventh grade, and we all got T-shirts way too big for us. I couldn't bear to see her name right now, for fear it would summon her voice at my ear, asking, "Why, Olivia? Why didn't you help?" I retrieved something plain pink, changed, and crawled into bed.

The door opened and closed several times throughout the evening. At one point, voices drifted through it, wondering if they should wake me up for dinner, if they thought I needed to talk, if I should get professional help.

I tossed through a restless sleep for hours, half dreams plaguing me with fuzzy memories of my best friend, many right here in this very room. I saw slumber parties and study sessions; I relived hugging Jessica when she came out to me; I leaned in close on the bed, smiling behind my hand as she told me all about Tiffany and realizing how much she mattered to her.

Oh God. Tiffany. The choking grip of anxiety yanked me from sleep. Would Dustin call her? Should I? I didn't think I could handle that, not right now.

I checked the clock. It was almost midnight; not the time to call anyway. I got up and trekked into the bathroom, careful not to bump into anything in the dark. I combed my hair and brushed my teeth. The cold tile stung the bottoms of my feet. I spat, then wiped my mouth on the hand towel. Bent over the countertop, the memory of its cool pressure against my skin and Liam's warm, urgent kisses hit me like a blinding light, a revelation. I wanted to get lost in him. I wanted to forget.

I peered around the corner, checking that the coast was clear before I strode to his bedroom and opened the door. Tomorrow I might regret this, but for now, I needed Liam. I slunk across the room to his bed and sat on the edge. The mattress dipped beneath me, and he shot up, gun in hand. I swallowed a scream and instead squeaked, "It's me!"

I ducked away from the barrel of the handgun pointed at my temple.

"Olivia?" He clicked the safety back on and returned the gun to the end table. "What are you doing in here?" He sat up straighter, rubbing his eyes. "Are you all right? More dreams?"

"No. I just . . . can I lie with you?" I asked, my gut tightening at the realization that he might reject me. I needed more than anything in this world right now to be shielded, to be loved, even if it was temporary, even if it meant nothing.

After a moment of silence, he said yes. I slipped my legs under the covers and pressed my back into his torso. He groaned, scooting his waist away but keeping his bare chest against me. The heat of his body engulfed me while his arms encircled my torso. His warm breath bathed my skin as he whispered, "You know this is killing me, right?"

I flipped around, my face inches from his. "Why? Can't friends cuddle?"

"Olivia," he cautioned in a gruff voice. "Listen, today was a rough one, rougher than most I've ever—"

I didn't want to talk. I didn't want him to talk. I wanted a distraction. Without another thought, I pressed my lips against his. At first, he stilled—a statue, unmoving and rigid. I pulled back enough to move my lips from his mouth to his ear, and his chin lifted toward my touch. I trailed kisses down his neck and along his collarbone until he coaxed my face back up, so we stared at each other, nose to nose.

"I don't think this is a good idea," he whispered even as his arms pulled me closer.

I gripped the nape of his neck and crushed my mouth against his again, as if I could force those unwanted words back inside. This time, he surrendered, kissing me in return. I slipped my tongue over his bottom lip, past his teeth, and made it dance as I rocked my body against him. A groan slipped out of my mouth as his hands trailed down my spine and over my butt. At first, his cupped hands were firm and unyielding, but then, as if coming to his senses, he released me. He regained control of the kiss and softened it, willing my body to conform to his and slow down.

As his lips molded to mine, I let go of all the pain I had trapped inside over Jessica's death, my mother's vengeful spirit, and even the fact that Liam would be skipping town soon. With each tender kiss, more stress released: the threat of vamps out for our blood, the weight of my abilities as a healer, the crushing responsibility of my power of premonition. All of it a distant memory as Liam's fingers played along my body. Like a musician, he found the rhythm to my deepest desires.

He tilted his head to change the pressure of the kiss, walking his hands back up my spine and under my shirt. Tiny goosebumps tingled on my skin at his gentle touch. My fingers threaded through his thick hair as his hands moved their way to my rib cage. I let out another groan, louder than the first, in anticipation of where they were headed.

Instead, Liam retreated. One of his hands slid up my bare arm and cupped the side of my face, gently pulling me away.

"Olivia." His voice was husky. "You're not in the right frame of mind—"

I didn't let him finish. I pressed my lips back onto his. His other hand tightened against my waist, surrendering to my request. He deepened the kiss as his thumb slid under my chin, demanding I obey his movements. I wrapped my legs around his, entangling our limbs, and my pulse went wild.

"I want you," I whispered. "Now."

Before he could respond, the bedroom door flew open, startling both of us. The hallway light outlined Jac and Agent Hunter, standing breathless at the rug's edge. The floor lamp flicked on, and I squinted in the intense brightness.

"What in the world? Liam!" Agent Hunter hissed. "Are you looking to get shot by Matt?"

Jac shushed him. "Dad!"

Liam started laughing and pointing at my watch. "First rule of a watch that monitors your heart rate: Never wear it while hooking up."

I smacked Liam across the chest, mortified. "You could have warned me." I checked his wrist. No watch.

"You jumped into my bed in a pitch-black room while I was sleeping. You think my first thoughts were to check for your watch?"

Agent Hunter ran a hand down his face. "I think you should—"

"We will just sleep, okay?" Liam interrupted, sharing a look with his father. "A hunter's promise." Surprisingly, Agent Hunter turned and left the room, mumbling something under his breath as he vanished down the hall.

Jac's face faltered for a quick second before she regained control. Whatever she was thinking, she covered it up fast. "She better be out of your bed before Pepper wakes." Jac held her hands up. "Just saying, that one will not keep this a secret." Her finger waggled between Liam and me. "I'm done warning you both. Try not to make me an aunt this year, okay?"

Liam chuckled and pulled me back into his arms. "We won't. Thanks for the lecture, Jacqueline."

Jac gave him the finger, then switched off the light.

I squirmed under Liam's hold.

"What are you doing? I should get back to my room."

Liam threw a leg over me. "No. You came in here tonight because you needed me. Let me be there for you." He hugged me tighter. "Just to hold you."

My head rested in the nape of his neck as he stroked my hair. And without any warning, I started to cry. With the barrier of distraction gone, the weight of Jessica's death crushed my heart.

"I've got you." He kissed my temple. "I'll always have you."

I don't know how long I lay there sobbing, but the tears eventually subsided. Sleep took me soon after.

I woke in a vivid dreamland. I didn't recognize the area. Darkness surrounded me, and a damp chill crept up my spine. The vamp from the van stood between towering, empty milk tanks. I recognized him right away by his bone structure, blood-soaked incisors, and bloodshot irises. He spoke to someone I couldn't see but who sounded familiar. I closed my eyes and listened closer, and that's when I recognized Pepper.

"I couldn't tell them. I couldn't hurt them like that," Pepper said through sighs. "Once they find out about her, they'll be crushed."

She knew him. Another voice spoke, its tone smooth and saccharine, almost like a lullaby. "Child, they must be told. We need their help. They and only they can hunt her. You have no choice. If you care for them, tell them."

I widened my eyes, peering into the dark, willing it to open up to me, to brighten. An image zoomed out at me—old scaffolding and abandoned crates, with something cloth-like hanging above. Pepper spoke again, more clearly.

"They're coming, right behind me. What do you want me to do?"

She warned them? Why? The vamp had just opened his mouth to respond when I felt cold water splash my face.

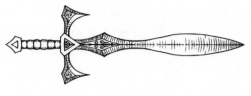

25

LIAM

Ice-cold water doused my face and bare chest, and I jumped, forgetting Olivia was in my arms. Pepper stood over me, smiling like a fool. She looked back and forth between us as she shook the cup, getting out the last few drops for good measure. Her blue hair stuck up like Cindy Lou Who from the Dr. Seuss book Jac used to make me read to her before bed.

"You two are gonna be in soooo much trouble if Dad finds out," she said, cheek twitching from a poorly suppressed grin. "How dumb are you?"

I couldn't help but laugh, but Olivia's cheeks flared fire-engine red. She wriggled deeper beneath the covers, resting her head against my stomach—her breath a little too close to my waistband for comfort.

"Pepper, can you leave please?" The comforter muffled her voice.

"And chance Dad kicking out the Hunters because you're hormonal? Nope!" She crossed her arms over her pj's. "Definitely not leaving without you."

Footsteps sounded outside the door, and Sheriff Davis's voice boomed, "Pepper, did you run the washer without detergent again?"

Pepper shrugged. "It's easier to forget than you'd think."

I patted Olivia's sheet-covered head. "I think you should probably walk out with Pepper, so it looks like you both came in here together to harass me." Plus, I'd prefer she move her head away from the goods, especially with her little sister in the room.

Olivia pulled the covers down as I sat up. Her eyes narrowed on me, coaxing out a broader smile. I kissed her nose, and she playfully smacked my face. Her lips twitched, hiding her grin.

"Okay, lovebirds, can we get moving?" Pepper tapped her foot.

Olivia scrambled away, letting the covers fall back onto me. I reached out and caught her wrist.

"Hey," I whispered. "It's okay to be sad. One day at a time."

I knew Olivia blamed herself for Jessica's death. Hell, *I* blamed myself. After talking with Dad and Doc last night, we decided it was time to hunt. Thankfully, today was Saturday. We had forty-eight hours to give those bastards what they deserved.

And I guess after that was done . . . I pushed that thought down. Way down.

Olivia and Pepper left, passing my dad as he walked in.

"Good morning, ladies," he said with a slight dip of his chin.

Olivia's head dropped, her face inflamed. Pepper waved hello.

"I hope Doc made us breakfast," she cooed through her Cheshire-cat smile.

"He did. Waffles with fresh cream and homemade berry compote await."

Pepper took off down the hall. That girl had a one-track mind, and that track always led to food.

Dad shook his head. I wasn't sure if it was for Pepper or the fact that I'd petitioned for Olivia to stay in my room last night against his better judgment.

I stood and grabbed a T-shirt from the desk chair and slipped it over my head.

Feeling his eyes boring into my back, I said, "Oh, come on. You know I didn't do anything." I motioned after Olivia. "She needed someone to comfort her. That's all I did."

Dad rolled the desk chair toward him for a sit. "I hope that's all you did, because, Liam . . ."

I held my hand up. "I know, Dad. We're leaving soon."

His eyes softened. "I am sorry. She's a sweet girl. And I wish—"

I waved him off. A speech about romance from my aloof father was the last thing I wanted to hear right now. I wanted revenge and a plan.

"What did you really come in here to talk about?"

Dad nodded to show his respect for my personal life before switching gears. "So, tell me. You had a conversation with one of these vamps. A real one, like you would with a human?"

With all that had transpired, Dad and I still hadn't discussed the details of what happened at the nest. "It was the weirdest thing." I studied a corner of the ceiling, remembering the way Pepper had reacted to the woman vamp's clawed hands on her shoulders. "I think Pepper knows more than she told us. There was a moment when one of the vamps held her hostage, but now that I think about it, maybe she wasn't forced anywhere. Maybe Pepper was trying to . . ." I shook my head to displace the malformed thoughts like ghosts in an attic. None made perfect sense. Nothing about that night did. "I don't know what I saw, but the vamp who attacked our car wasn't a slobbering mess. He was well-spoken, believe it or not."

"Doc and I looked back through the lore, and we found something interesting. When the Origins were born, they communicated like humans and didn't suffer from bloodlust."

"You think this is an Origin?" I shook my head. No way that guy was one of the first three purebred vamps. He'd spoken like a young prep, not an ancient immortal. "I don't think that's who we're dealing with."

Dad shrugged. "It's all we could muster up to explain what happened. We'll keep looking." He started toward the door. "Tonight, we hunt. And we're taking Doc, Jac, Sheriff Davis, and Pepper."

I stepped back, certain I had misheard. "Excuse me?"

Dad pivoted. "You heard me."

"What about Olivia?" My heart rate kicked up a notch.

"She can choose."

"Dad," I growled. My fingers curled, sending heat through my flexed forearms.

He turned and lifted a brow. "I never stopped your mother from joining a hunt. If you care for Olivia the way I think you do, you'll give her the same choice. She belongs in this world more than you're willing to admit."

I sucked in a breath. The mention of Mom punched me in the gut. Dad never spoke about her, and now he was using her against me. I knew they met when he was young—both of them were kids of hunters. They'd grown up in the same world. Of course she chose the hunter's life. It was all she'd ever known, all she'd ever trained for. Just like us.

Olivia was different. She wasn't born to danger and death; she was thrust into it, and I'd be damned if I didn't protect her from it.

I changed into a pair of jeans and headed downstairs to breakfast, thoughts of my mother remaining on my mind.

———— • • ————

"This dance is getting old," Olivia said, stating her case in the middle of the kitchen. All seven of us were gathered around the center island discussing tonight's hunt.

"She's not going," I repeated for maybe the twentieth time. Sheriff Davis also wanted Pepper to stay home, but we needed her. She could speak to the vamps. She could hear what they were thinking, and we needed that leverage.

"I'm going, and that's final." Olivia's hands clung to her hips. "If you think I am letting my fourteen-year-old sister go on a vamp hunt without me, you are out of your ever-living mind, Liam Hunter."

"You're not even trained!" I yelled. Her stubbornness sent me off the Richter scale.

"Neither is she," Olivia countered, jabbing a finger at Pepper.

"Listen you two, bickering isn't getting us anywhere. I realize this isn't ideal," Doc said, rubbing the bridge of his nose. He pivoted toward Olivia. "Poppet, I'd rather you and your sister stay home as well, but we need Pepper. If you feel like you cannot stay here without her, then we will protect you out there."

I stepped forward, thumping a finger down on the island. "She just lost her mother for the second time, and not even twenty-four hours later, she watched her best friend die. She doesn't need to be exposed to any more brutality. She's not going," I spat. Doc might have run things from the inside, but he rarely attended hunts. He was in no position to put Olivia in danger. Hunterland be damned, for all I cared.

Olivia grabbed my forearm. "I'm not sure who made you the boss of me, but you don't have the right to make decisions that affect my family."

I ripped free of her clutch. "Okay then." I gritted my teeth, turning to her father. "Can you, in good conscience, let Olivia go to a vamp nest when there are no guarantees she doesn't end up their next meal? Would you like to live with the fact that another family member died on your watch?"

Sheriff Davis flinched as if I had slapped him.

"Liam," Dad cautioned.

"That was too far," Jac added.

I spun to face my sister, ignoring my father. "Was it? We'll have to watch Pepper like hawks. It'll take all of us to protect her. We have no idea how many vamps are in the nest, but we're going to bring two untrained humans into the fray? You don't think that's irresponsible?"

"It's not your decision." Dad came to Olivia's defense, using the same tactic he'd thrown at me in my bedroom. "Matt, if you don't want your daughters, and I mean both of them, to accompany us on this hunt, I understand." He placed his arm around Pepper's shoulder. "We could really use her help, but it's not our choice. Not Liam's or mine. It's something the three of you need to decide."

I clenched my teeth. I was wound so tightly, I almost flipped Sheriff Davis over my head when he laid a steady hand between my shoulder blades.

"I know you care about Olivia and Pepper," he said. "And I understand your anger, more than you will ever know. In many ways, I agree with you, but it's important my daughters get to make their own decisions, and I need to support that." His eyes closed briefly. "They both can go."

Olivia jutted her chin in my direction as if to say, *I'm going whether you like it or not*, and marched upstairs to change.

"We leave in thirty minutes," Dad announced. "And Liam, you'd better get on the same page if you really care about that girl. Quit pissing her off, because you may be the only reason she comes out of this alive."

26

OLIVIA

My anger at Liam flared hot enough to burn my own face. Who the hell did he think he was, acting like the judge and jury of my life decisions? He was worse than an overbearing boyfriend. He was a helicopter mom on steroids.

I slammed my dresser drawers shut, shaking my healing stones. Some toppled over, and a few rolled off the edge. I tossed my decorative pillows one by one at the closet door. The thin wood rattled with each collision.

"Not sure the room did anything to deserve this kind of abuse," Jac said, leaning against the door frame. She cocked a hand on her petite hip, giving me a knowing scowl. "Is it safe to come in or will I be the next victim?"

"How do *you* deal with him?" I yelled, thrusting an accusatory finger at her chest.

Jac smiled sweetly. "Normally, I'd be all female power and right behind you telling you how awful he's being." She held up a finger. "But you're not thinking with a clear head."

My mouth dropped a good two inches. "Are you serious? You're taking his egotistical side?"

Jac's manicured fingernails tapped along her crossed forearms. I wondered when she had time to get them done. After all we'd dealt with, my nails were just chipped paint.

"Listen, Liam didn't handle that well downstairs, but he's only trying to protect you. He's right about your lack of training adding to the challenge of this mission. We've already got to watch out for Pepper, your father, and even Doc. The three of them have never gone up against a nest, but they all have something you don't, and that's the difference." She sighed at my offended scoff. "Doc knows our world and all the lore he reads makes his insights valuable. Hell, he practically runs Hunterland. Your dad is a police officer and knows how to handle himself in bad situations. And Pepper can hear what the monsters are thinking. While you might have kickass premeditative powers, you do not have any specific talents to help you survive in the field. Bringing you is an added risk with little to no benefit."

She walked in and picked up the fallen heart-shaped pillow. She looked at it a moment, then clutched it to her chest as if making a point.

"My brother doesn't act like this over just any girl. It's not his MO, and for once, he's not speaking from ego." She shook her head with an eye roll that had no bite. "Sure, he cares about saving the world, and he puts unnecessary pressure on himself to make a difference." She sat on the edge of my bed and crossed her legs. Her eyes filled with an emotion I couldn't quite understand—worry, possibly. "But I think Liam would sacrifice the world if it meant keeping *you* safe." She held my gaze as if waiting for that to sink in.

"Your brother can't stand me half the time," I grumbled. "I doubt he'd put me before the world, or anyone else for that matter."

Jac lifted her brow. "Really? Because last night when he used our hunter's promise, he sure showed more care than he ever had before."

"Hunter's promise?" I crinkled my nose.

"For us, the words *hunter's promise* go beyond their dictionary definition. In our family, it's a specific oath. We don't use it often, and when we do, it means no matter what, the other family member cannot inter-fere. And he used it last night with our dad to comfort you."

I crinkled my forehead. "I don't really understand."

Jac shook her head and stood, offering the pillow to me to put back on my bed. "The last person in our family to use it was my mother. When the werewolf infected her, she said, 'Stay back. A hunter's prom-ise.'" Jac swallowed, and now I clutched the heart pillow. "She was tell-ing us to leave her, and we did. That's how far that oath goes."

I opened my mouth but couldn't form words. I didn't know how to respond to something so personal and heart-wrenching. Nothing any-one said about my mother could truly take the sting out either.

"She knew there wasn't anything we could do the second she was bitten. So instead, she made us leave so that we wouldn't fall victim to the same fate." Jac's throat visibly tightened. "They tore her to shreds. When Dad and Liam went back to retrieve her body, all that was left were scraps of her skin." A tear slipped from her eye. "We never even got to bury her." She took in a deep breath and regained control. "That was my first hunt, and I *was* trained."

Jac's sorrowful eyes motioned to my closet. "You need to dress in all black for tonight, so you blend into the background." And with that, she walked out of the room, leaving me with her words swirling around in my head and weighing down my heart.

Maybe I was wrong to go all high and mighty on Liam. I'd forgot-ten all that he'd lost, hadn't considered what the fear of losing someone else he cared about might do to him. Sure, I wanted to protect my little sister, but Jac and Liam were right: I had no special abilities or extra training to do so.

I changed into a black turtleneck, dark jeans, and a pair of hiking boots. There was something I had to do before we left, and I needed Doc's help to get it done.

I walked down the basement steps, slowly releasing a trapped breath. Less than two days ago, the ghost of my mother tried to choke me to death down here. My eyes surveyed the room, taking note of the Hunters' thorough cleanup job. Everything was either thrown out or put back in order. No broken glass or shelving. No blood or burn marks from the fire. No reminder of what happened down here. I couldn't decide if that made me feel better or worse. Like we just shoved everything under a throw rug and walked away.

Doc sat at his makeshift desk, which was really just a folding table, stool, and laptop. He had on a high-necked black sweater and his maroon turban.

"What can I do for you, Poppet?" he asked, never taking his eyes off the screen. The blue light reflected off his reading glasses.

I walked over to where he was typing away and spotted a sketch pad.

"Are these drawings of your visions?" I asked. Without thinking, I picked it up and flipped through the pages. The third sketch caught my eye—a portrait of a woman, maybe in her late thirties. One of the most breathtakingly beautiful people I'd ever seen. She had long curly hair, wild ravenous eyes, and a figure . . . whoa, did she have a figure. But she also had extended canine teeth that looked as sharp as the vamp fangs I saw in my dream but more animalistic.

"She's a werewolf, a shapeshifter," Doc said, answering my unspoken question. "Do you recognize her? Any dreams of someone like this?" Concern dug creases around his mouth, and his eyes swam with something troublesome, something I couldn't quite put my finger on.

I shook my head. Something about her tugged at my memories, yet I couldn't recall a vision. I looked closer. Her cheekbones and eye structure were familiar, but I couldn't place them. "I don't think so, but her eyes . . . what color are they?"

"Ah yes, her eyes, as blue as a sapphires," Doc said. His face slackened into a sad frown. "So, what can I do you for?" He changed the subject, holding out his hand for the sketch pad.

"It's about Pepper," I said, closing the book and giving it back.

I rubbed my onyx bracelet. The black gemstone provided strength and stamina, both emotional and physical, especially during times of stress, confusion, or grief. And boy, did I have all of that and more. I hoped it would balance my intense feelings as well as help protect me this evening.

My eyes rose to find Doc's.

"I had another dream, and well . . ." How was I going to explain that it seemed like Pepper was working with the vamps? I knew that wasn't true, but I'd seen it for a reason. Maybe I'd misinterpreted something. This hunt sounded dangerous, though, so I thought I should inform Doc. I believed out of all people, he wouldn't jump to conclusions, and he'd have the best chance of unraveling my vision before villainizing Pepper.

When I was done explaining what I'd seen, he said, "It really could be anything. You didn't see much. She could have been talking to one of us, and you mixed the vampire exchange with our own conversation." He tapped his chin. "I don't think it's worth mentioning to the others when I'm not even sure what it's warning against. But this place you describe, now that could be helpful." He stood and removed his reading glasses, putting them back in a thin brown case. "It seems as if your visions paint clear background pictures, but the details are often mangled. Something we will work on over time. Let's tell the others what you saw. But leave the Pepper part out until you understand a little more. If you have another bout, let me know."

Checking his screen one last time, Doc shut his laptop, and the two of us headed back upstairs.

The Hunters were gearing up in the living room. Liam, dressed in a black long-sleeved shirt, black jeans, and his leather jacket, strapped a gun to his ankle and sheathed a machete to his side. Next, he concealed the gun that he slept with in his waistband at the small of his back, then threw a satchel over his shoulder. Wooden points peeked out at the top. He looked badass, and my stupid heart skipped a beat.

"Locked and loaded. Jac?" Liam asked with a twinkle in his eye. This was where he shone, fighting monsters.

"All set." Jac winked. She wore a similar outfit, but hers better resembled a catsuit, tight like a second skin. Liam threw another stake-filled satchel toward my dad. He caught the bag and placed the strap over his head, letting the weapons hang at his side.

"Guns with silver bullets will stun them," said Liam. "But to slay them, you'll have to behead them or stake them in the heart. Don't hesitate. Turn them to ash the first chance you get."

Dad nodded, looking "sharp," as he always said, in his police uniform.

"Olivia, why don't you tell the group what you saw in your latest vision?" Doc suggested. "Olivia may have seen an important location in her sleep last night," he explained.

Agent Hunter's eyebrows raised. "Excellent. Please do. Every detail matters." He fixed his weapons to the harness crisscrossing his chest, equipped with several holsters for knives and stakes.

I swallowed. "It was cold, damp, and dark." I closed my eyes, concentrating on each detail.

Liam grumbled. "That's helpful."

"William, let her finish," Doc snapped.

I opened my eyes and narrowed them on Liam. "The vamp from the van was standing between these huge, empty milk tanks on some sort of landing. I saw another person by some old scaffolding and abandoned crates, but I couldn't get a good look, just heard his voice. Smooth, almost charming." I swallowed, quickly diverting my eyes away from Liam to Agent Hunter, who was threading his arms through a leather jacket resembling Liam's. "Before the vision cut out, I saw swaths of cloth hanging above me, but then it started to get blurry, and I couldn't see anything else."

Jac's and Liam's eyes went wide. "They're in the same vamp nest?" Jac asked, incredulous.

"That's too easy." The blatant disbelief in Liam's eyes stung more than I'd care to admit.

"Vamps are cocky bastards," Agent Hunter said. "They probably assumed we'd never look in the same place twice. I'm not too surprised. Plus, when Matt and I visited the local sheriff the other day, he mentioned more 'animal killings' in that area. So, it's got to be close to there, regardless. It's a starting point." He whirled his finger in the air. "Load up the cars. Let's go hunting." He pointed at me. "Olivia, you ride with Liam in the Bronco. You two take the drive to work out whatever you have going on. Pepper, Jac, you babysit."

Liam stormed out of the front door, leaving me in his dust. Pepper and Jac chuckled as we followed his path.

The car ride was eerily quiet for almost sixty minutes before anyone spoke.

"Can't you two make out again or something so this can be over?" Pepper whined from the backseat.

Liam ignored her, keeping his keen eyes fixed on the dark, winding back roads. It wasn't until I saw his white-knuckled grip on the wheel that I realized her suggestion had affected him.

I shook my head, remembering what Jac told me. After a few meditative breaths, I gave the white flag approach a shot. "I'm sorry," I conceded.

Liam looked at me like I had ten heads. "Sorry for what?" He risked taking his eyes off the poorly lit road for a hot second to gauge my expression, like he expected me to slash his throat.

"For not acknowledging that your asshole display was just you trying to keep me safe. Because you care." I smiled wide. I wasn't going to go that soft on him. He'd still acted like a jerk.

His lips wavered, and he pressed them together to repress laughter or maybe a grin. "Asshole display, huh?" His death grip eased, and he allowed his right forearm to rest on the center console between us. "Kind of a weak apology, but I'll take it." He reached his hand out, silently asking for mine.

My breath hitched as I interlocked our fingers. This boy was going to be the death of me. Well, if a vengeful spirit or vampire didn't get me first.

"Will you promise to stay by my side and do exactly what I say no matter what?" I heard the desperation tightening his throat, rasping the words. Saw it when he took his eyes off the road and traced them over my lips before focusing back on the street.

"Yes. I promise." I squeezed his hand. I wasn't taking the danger of the mission lightly. I needed him to understand he had my full cooperation. All I cared about was the safety of my family.

"Do you promise to book it back to the car with your dad and sister if we're outnumbered?" This time, he kept his gaze straight.

Staying around wouldn't do anything to help. My lack of monster experience and fighting skills would only put them at a disadvantage. "I promise," I said squeezing his hand again, but he wasn't done.

"Do you promise that even if something happens to your father or Pepper, you will listen to me and allow us to protect them? Even if that means you have to run away without them?"

A harder question, for sure. I bit the fingernails of my free hand. I didn't think I could promise that. The whole reason I'd insisted on coming was to protect Pepper.

My nosey sister leaned in between us and placed her hand on top of ours. "Livy, promise him! You can't do anything stupid. No matter what I do or what happens to me. No matter what it might look like in there when they tell the Hunters what they know. You have to listen to Liam."

With a squeal of brakes that gave off the scent of burnt rubber, Liam swerved off the road and threw the car into park. He twisted in his seat and faced Pepper, his brows pinched together. "Pepper, what do you mean? What do you know?"

But it was too late. Pepper had flung herself back and flipped open the car door. The last words she breathed as she jumped out were, "I'm sorry."

With that, she disappeared into the woods.

27

PEPPER

I ran like hell. The second we'd turned onto the dirt road leading to the vamp nest, a voice in my head had told me to get out of the car and hurry toward the abandoned building. The First of Three was coming for the Hunter family, and there'd be no stopping him.

A shortcut, said the smooth voice of a man I hadn't met yet. I breathed heavily, sneakers smacking the hard ground. My thighs burned, and my stomach growled with hunger pains.

You're almost there, child. Keep going straight ahead.

The van wasn't supposed to hit anyone. The vamp driving had been instructed to convey a message to me, but his sanity wavered because of the bloodthirst. His steering skills sucked. Hard to keep your hands at ten and two when you were fighting off inner demons. I'd stopped in the parking lot that day because the vamp's voice in my head had startled me. I didn't have a clue what I'd heard. Sure, spirits found me in my sleep, but Momma stopped that years ago. So, when it happened at school, it took a minute to collect myself. I'd never even heard Liam call my name. Nothing registered until he took the brunt of the van's hit, protecting me from its idiot driver.

Hard right, through the two crooked trees.

And then poor Jessica . . . It was my fault. The van was back for me, to remind me I had a message to deliver to the Hunters. He never meant to kill Jessica, but he also didn't care that he had. The only sadness I'd sensed in him was for the lost meal, regret that the sunlight would fry him if he tried to retrieve her body.

One more right turn and you are there.

I sprinted toward the trees. I had to make it there before the others. The first time I heard the voice in my head, I hadn't understood why. The second time, I'd ignored it. But tonight, I'd take action.

The abandoned warehouse loomed ahead, decrepit and tilted a fraction, like an old giant with a bad back.

Go through the back entrance. Stop at the milk tanks. I'll meet you there. I'm looking forward to it.

I pushed open the warehouse's back door, and movement in the rafters led my eye to the impossibly tall man pacing on a beam between two pillars. I craned my neck to take him in, three-piece suit and all. His skin, smooth like polished stone, sparkled in the moonlight coming through the rotted openings in the ceiling.

"Patricia Davis, I presume," he purred through a smirk, his tenor voice putting me in a dreamlike state where the world took on soft, blurred edges and my head wanted to droop.

Between ragged breaths, I answered. "Yes, that's me." I glanced back at the door, willing it to stay closed. "They're here. They're coming. What do you want me to do? Please don't hurt anyone." I blurted everything out at once.

"Wonderful," he said, hands together as if in prayer. "I don't want to hurt them at all, dear psychic. Quite the opposite. I need their help." The tall, dark man narrowed his black eyes.

"Why was that vamp looking for me at school?" My lungs still stung like frostbite from the icy air I'd gulped while running, but I wanted— needed—answers.

"I have need of your services. I still do. I never meant for that neanderthal to hurt anyone." He shook his head. "He's on the verge of permanently becoming a lesser vampire. Such a disappointment." He flicked a speck from his lapel. "Never mind that now. Let me properly introduce myself. You may call me Reginald. I am the First of Three. We are called the Origins. It is nice to meet you, Patricia Davis." He lowered his head in deference.

Did that mean I needed to kneel or something? I started to, dipping one knee, then thought better of it. Reginald's lips appeared to twitch. Was he holding back laughter?

"You do not need to kneel, dear child, but I do appreciate the thought." He lifted his chin and smiled. "I apologize for the burden bestowed upon you. I know my message for the Hunter family is a hard one to deliver." He gazed up to the open sky. "The world is a cruel and unjust place."

I agreed. Thoughts of Momma and the others who'd fallen victim at those hospitals crossed my mind. I pitied Billy Lyons's mother, Jody, enslaved by a single-minded thought that all nurses were evil because one had killed her. I wondered if maybe the Hunter family harbored a similar mindset toward vampires. Maybe those like Reginald were good.

"I had hoped it wouldn't come to this," Reginald said, glancing over my head.

The metal side door clanged against the concrete wall. My family—both blood and newly found—barreled into the room. They looked straight at me at first, not noticing the large man in the rafters.

"Pepper!" Livy cried. Liam held her back, one arm hugging her to him, as his eyes darted to Reginald. With his free hand, he unsheathed his weapon and pointed it at the vampire. Only a muscle twitched in Agent Hunter's jaw, but the rest of the group—my dad, Jac, and Doc—staggered back and gaped in varied states of wonder at the towering vampire.

"Bloody hell, you're an—" Doc started to say.

Reginald cut him off with a bow. "I am an Origin, yes. The First of Three born of our witch mother by the power of divine Grecian magic. Genevieve and young Delphi are my sisters."

Doc's mouth opened so wide I was afraid he'd catch flies. It was entirely possible; this place was disgusting.

"Patricia is a gifted child. She meant no harm, running off and scaring you like that. It was my wish that she arrive prior to you." He scanned his audience. "I had intended to have more time with her."

"Pepper, come here." Dad beckoned me.

Reginald gestured for me to go, and I hurried into Dad's arms.

"It's okay. He's not here to hurt anyone. He wants to speak to the Hunters, that's all," I assured them.

When I had followed Liam and Jac into the vamp nest a few days ago, Magda—the vamp woman—explained that her master, one of the Origins, was looking for the Hunter family. She tasked me with arranging the meeting. I couldn't bear to tell them what she'd told me, so I ignored it. A lot of good that did. I almost got hit by a car, and Jessica died.

Liam released Livy and bent down to my level. My sister leaned in and examined my arms and face for marks.

Liam held my hand. "I know this is hard to understand, but he's a bad guy. You cannot trust him, no matter how charming he seems. It's one of his gifts as an Origin."

I shrank from his hold and then placed a hand on his shoulder. "Just let him tell you what's going on first. Please." I knew Reginald needed to tell the Hunter family his story. Someone had to, before they found out about it in a worse way.

"We will listen," Agent Hunter said, motioning for Liam to lower his weapon. "But only if you answer some of our questions first."

"I'd be glad to." Reginald sat on the beam, agile as a cat. The shine of his polished shoes reflected the moon as he crossed his legs, heels dangling in midair. He waved for Agent Hunter to proceed.

"Why can some vamps talk, while others act like slobbering idiots?"

Reginald chuckled, bouncing his broad shoulders. "By that brilliant question, I'd wager you are not aware of our first and most precious rule. Not to kill a single human by draining their blood."

The Hunters wore matching incredulous glares. Magda had made the same claim, that feeding on people ate away their humanity.

"That's impossible," Agent Hunter said loudly, taking a step forward.

"Settle please." Reginald put his finger in his ear and wiggled it back and forth. "My old ears are sensitive, and this, friend, is a gentlemen's conversation. To answer your question, it's part of the curse. The only way we can safely drink from a human is if they consent. The only situations that allow killing a human are matters of self-defense or through consent. If we kill for bloodthirst, it turns us into a monster. The more a vampire kills for pleasure, the more humanity they lose. And thus, the slobbering idiots, as you call them, are created. I have nothing to do with those filthy creatures." He held his chin high. "They give my kind a bad reputation. We had tried to rectify their existence ages ago. Although our means didn't necessarily adhere to our original plans."

Livy stepped forward, her eyes cold in the moonlight. "You shouldn't have the power to kill anyone, even if they consent." Liam wrapped his arm back around my sister, for which I was grateful. Sometimes she talked too much.

"That is your opinion. That would be like me telling your father he doesn't have the right to use the weapon attached to his hip to defend himself. Or a family that they cannot take a loved one off life support even when they are brain-dead."

"Not the point. You—" Liam muzzled Livy with a hand.

In the blink of an eye, Reginald was on his feet, chest puffed to display his full, imposing stature. He pinched the bridge of his nose. "As I was saying. We do not go around murdering. My sisters and I are very aware of the blessings and curses of our kind. We have servants, and they are consenting, of course. We can be very convincing when need be—one of dear Mother's blessings. But we do not keep prisoners or victims, regardless of your preconceptions." He pivoted toward Agent Hunter. "But back to your question. The farther removed the biter is from our bloodline, the more bloodthirsty the newly turned vamp will become and the less humanity he or she will have. And so on and so forth, ad nauseam. *Those* are your drooling fools who can't form words." He tutted. "So embarrassing. And sadly, in this era, there are more of them than us."

"You still feed off helpless, manipulated humans," Liam countered. "And that makes you a monster all the same."

"Your opinion of me, dear boy, is the least of my concerns." He waved off Liam's comment just as easily as he had the dust on his suit. "Now your father looks like a smart man. Jackson Hunter, I presume?"

Agent Hunter nodded.

"Back to business." He clapped his hands. "Patricia, darling, shall we bring in the drooling vamps so you can translate?"

I was struck for the first time by my importance. Before I could censor my thoughts, I blurted out, "You can't hear them, can you?"

Reginald pivoted with the speed of a striking viper, plowing a fist into the old milk tower, creating a huge dent in the metal exterior. His venomous growl vibrated through my body, making the hairs on my arms stand at attention. His fangs extended past his lips, dripping saliva onto the ground below. My body convulsed, and Dad cradled me in a shaky embrace, pulling me against his strong chest.

Note to self: Don't make the fancy ancient dude feel incompetent. Makes him cranky.

"I have many powers, child. Do not make me use them on you."

"Don't threaten my sister," Livy yelled.

Reginald jumped from the rafters, landing in a crouch in front of Livy. The foundations shook with the force of the impact. He stood, looking down his nose to meet her gaze. His breath pushed her hair back from her forehead.

"I do not kill humans to feed, but that doesn't mean I won't kill you because you've angered me. That is not part of our curse. I could easily snap your neck. Do you understand the difference?" His hand moved to brush stray hairs from her cheek, but Liam grabbed his wrist.

"Do not touch her," he growled.

Livy gulped, wide eyes on Reginald's sharp nails. My own breath ceased, waiting to see what happened next.

The vamp grinned. "A hunter, a healer, and a psychic. My, my, my, there should be a nursery rhyme about you three." The snarl in his voice smoothed to a purr when he addressed Livy. "I would never hurt Patricia."

I exhaled, somewhat relieved.

Reginald stared at me with what I could only describe as affection. "I think she's a special, beautiful child. She reminds me of my own daughter." His lashes lowered. "She was recently murdered."

Magda had told me the same thing the day we met. It was the story of his daughter's death that caused my silence. Tears welled in my eyes.

"Follow me," Reginald said.

Dad threaded his hand in mine like I was a toddler ready to cross the street. I welcomed the contact. Livy took my other hand. They used to swing me every couple of steps like this. I loved those walks. I wished for simpler times like that, when monsters didn't exist, and the power to speak to the undead lay dormant.

Liam came up behind me and ruffled my hair. "I'm still mad at you for running off, but you are the bravest girl I know." He leaned down and whispered in my ear, "Don't go near Reginald again. Stay with Olivia and your father. And if I tell you to run . . ."

I nodded. I'd run.

Agent Hunter, Jac, and Doc followed in line with Liam ahead of our family.

We entered the back corrals, where cloth shades hung from the ceiling. Twelve ravenous vamps crouched, ready to pounce, among the pens.

"Don't." Reginald lifted his palm, and like puppies, the wild vamps heeled.

These were the bad guys, the ones Reginald didn't like, but he needed to know what they knew.

Why is Master stopping us? They are hunters. Let's play with them first, then drink until they die.

I shivered. My eyes darted to each vamp, not knowing which one had spoken.

"What did they say?" Reginald asked. He must have seen the fear in my eyes because in secret he said, *Don't worry, my dear child, they cannot harm you while under my control.*

"They know they are hunters." I hesitated, cringing in apology to the Hunter family. "And they want to drink their blood." My tongue clashed clumsily against my teeth, saying those ugly words out loud.

Reginald rolled his eyes. "Ask them about the attacks, the details of where the last one occurred," he ordered. He crossed his arms, tapping his long, white nails against his bicep.

My ears perked up. "I can talk to them?"

Reginald softened when he turned to me. "Of course, my child, just like you have been doing with me."

I hadn't realized I was trading my own thoughts with him, just like Momma and me, but he was right. Doc and Agent Hunter exchanged a look I didn't understand. Maybe they'd already known more about my powers than I did.

Tell me about the attacks, I asked, having no idea if this would really work.

I wonder how your blood tastes?

I shook my head. "They want to know how my blood tastes. How do I get these idiots to focus?"

Reginald held his hand up and mimed turning a knob.

The vamps fell to their knees, crying out in pain. "Hopefully, that helps, Patricia."

The werewolf pack has been organizing! A strangled voice echoed in my head. *They are killing all the vamps in the Midwest, taking out nest after nest. The last we heard, they were in Chicago.*

Another chimed in, and my gaze darted around, unable to track who was speaking.

I was there. The North Park nest. We came here for safety. I'm hungry. Would you like to be my next meal?

"That worked," I said, stomach churning. "The pack was last seen in Chicago, North Park area, and they're taking out all the nests."

Agent Hunter motioned for me to return to Dad and Livy, behind his family. I gladly obliged.

"What does this have to do with us? To be frank, as hunters, we aren't going to stop people from killing your kind. Whoever's group this is, they're doing us a favor." Agent Hunter cracked his neck side to side.

Reginald twirled around, wearing a broad grin, his fangs on full display. "What if said people are a werewolf pack? I believe you regard them as monsters as well." He arched his perfectly shaped brows.

I braced for what came next as I squeezed Livy's hand. *Please don't hurt my new family.*

Reginald's lips pressed into a straight line. He heard me. "I'm so sorry, precious one," he said out loud. "I wish I could adhere to your request."

With a more serious countenance, he turned to Agent Hunter.

"Jackson, I need your help because you know the pack's Alpha better than anyone. The creature orchestrating this extinction of my kind is your wife, Veronica Hunter."

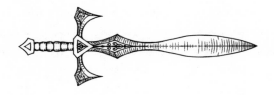

28

LIAM

White noise roared in my skull, so I only heard Mom's name echoing in the static.

Dad exploded. He lunged for Reginald, who skyrocketed to the top of a stack of crates in a single bound, too high for us to reach. Jac's face paled, whiter than the Wisconsin snow.

"Patricia was tasked with setting up this meeting a week ago, when she met one of my associates, but she failed," Reginald shot Pepper a sympathetic look, as if he understood her plight.

Guess we needed to have a serious sit-down with Pepper. She couldn't be so trusting of the revenants.

Reginald continued: "I tried my absolute best to relay the information without having to meet like this, in a place where you'd be at your most defensive. Your wife is dangerous. I need you as much as you need me."

The lying vamp leaped onto the ledge of a broken second-story windowsill. He looked left, toward a planned exit. Crouching, he steadied himself by holding the piping that ran above his head. Part of me wanted to shoot at it and send him crashing into the cement floor, but that wouldn't kill him, only put him closer to the Davises. I had to push my emotions aside, hard as it was.

"I don't believe you," Dad bellowed, fists curling and uncurling. Dad's restraint often astounded me, but other times it scared the shit out of me. Right now, sweat beaded my neck and palms.

The Origin's face fell. "Yes, you do, or at least you will when you think things through." He shook his head like a mourner at a wake. "I am sorry, for what it's worth. Take your time to process. I'll be in touch." He turned to Pepper. "Tell them the rest of Magda's story, my child."

"Okay."

"I leave you with a gift." He waved his hand, acknowledging the salivating vamps below. "Feel free to rid the world of these so-called slobbering idiots." And with that, he vanished, taking his powers over the other vamps with him. Free of his control, the twelve hissed, eyes glossy and bright with ravenous hunger.

"Get Pepper and Olivia back to the cars, now!" I yelled at Doc and Sheriff Davis. No one argued except Pepper.

"I can help," she contended.

"Now, Pepper," Olivia barked, snatching his sister's wrist. Her eyes were large as saucers but filled with steely determination. She'd fought to come on this hunt for this very reason. She yanked Pepper between her father and Doc.

Our eyes met for a brief moment and held for a heartbeat until she glanced over my shoulder, and horror marred her face.

"Go," I said.

Fear for her family won out. Olivia sprinted, dragging Pepper with her. I spun to face the oncoming vamp.

"Is it true, Dad?" Jac yelled.

"No!" he said, legs braced with a stake at the ready, forearm across his chest. "Origins lie to get what they want. It's who they are!"

I waved my machete in a figure eight motion. The moon glinted off the blade. True or not, now wasn't the time to discuss it. "Whatever he wants, he'll have to get in line." I tilted my head toward the slavering monsters creeping closer, fanning out like geese in flight. "Twelve against three. I'd say the odds aren't very fair."

Dad caught my eye. "Not feeling sympathy for them, are you?"

I threw my head back and laughed. "They'd need about a dozen more to make it even."

A young vamp couldn't contain himself and charged ahead of his flock.

"Less talking," Jac muttered, knocking back the vamp with her boot in his chest. I heard the metal stake in the heel spring free. "Maybe these spikes could be longer—get some kill shots instead of needling them like a pincushion."

"I'll work on it," Dad said knocking a vamp out of his way with a spinning fist that whacked the revenant's head into the wall.

Jac grabbed a wooden stake from her bag. Running as fast as she could, she charged the vamp as he slumped, taking him out with one downward thrust. "That's one," she called. Jac pivoted and impaled a sneaking predator in the heart. "That's two. You boys want to get in the game, or are you letting me have all the fun?" She wiped sweat off her forehead with her sweater sleeve.

Another vamp jumped higher than our heads, releasing a high-pitched scream. Dad tracked the motion and waited for him to descend, hard and fast. Dad crouched, freeing one of the stakes from his chest harness, and pierced the vamp's heart as he fell on top of him. "One for me." Dad straightened, covered in the falling ash. He brushed off the dust and unsheathed his machete.

Together, we forged our way into the thick of the remaining nine vamps. They fought smarter, forming a staggered wall to protect each other's backs. I collided with one, nicking his shoulder. Blood sprayed across my chest as the vamp roared and slashed out with his unhurt arm. Dad spun and chopped off the clawing appendage. "I had him," I muttered. I swung my machete around and took off his head. "One," I yelled.

"More like half," Jac said from somewhere behind me. "Dad totally helped."

Without taking my eyes off our opponents, I yelled back, "Bet you twenty bucks, I kill the most."

"Deal," Jac and Dad yelled at the same time.

I flung myself at another vamp, his mouth covered in congealed blood from a recent feeding. We'd have to check the grounds for victims later. My pulse surged with the thought of revenge. My boot connected with his throat, and the spike sank into his neck, sending him tumbling to the ground. Gore gushed along his collarbone and soaked through his ripped clothing. I grabbed one of my stakes and stabbed him in the heart. Dust settled into the pool of blood on the floor. "Two," I yelled.

"Three," Jac yelled, winded. We had taken half of the den out. With six more to go, I needed to get at least three more to win my bet.

I gripped my machete with two hands and stormed three advancing vamps. One jumped high, hurdling over my head, while the other two crouched into formation in front. A soft impact in the dirt alerted me to the jumper's landing. I was surrounded. So much for slobbering idiots.

"Kill," said the pair's female half. She pivoted on dirty bare feet and swung her fist into my abdomen.

The hit knocked the wind out of my diaphragm, sending me flying backward into the vamp behind me. He gripped my neck while the woman who'd hit me dislodged my weapon. Spots danced at the edge of my vision as he tried to choke me to death. The vamp woman clawed at my chest, shredding my shirt and gouging the skin beneath. The agony spiked fresh adrenaline, and my vision cleared. And that's when I saw it. I'd know it anywhere. It glistened on the vamp's middle finger, reflecting the moon. A sapphire, an emerald, a blue topaz, and a ruby—each of our birthstones—flanked a small diamond. Mom's engagement ring. She'd added Jac's and my stones when we were born.

Normally, fear would have kicked in. I'd lost my weapon, I was surrounded, and the vamp strangling me had the upper hand, but I wasn't afraid. Something dark, buried deep, snapped, seeing my mother's most valued possession.

Rage. Guilt. Revenge.

Reginald was right. Mom was alive. Either her ring was torn from her, or she'd given it to these creatures. A small part of me hoped she had relinquished it as a sign to us, but I knew how unhinged that sounded, how impossible and foolish. She was a werewolf, a monster, no longer my mother. And no childish wish on a star or a diamond ring could change her fate.

I tucked, releasing the vamp's headlock by flipping him over my shoulder. His back smacked the hard cement. I grabbed a stake from my bag and pierced his heart. Disturbing the revenant's dusty remains, I sent a roundhouse kick to the vamp woman wearing my mother's ring, bringing her to the ground next.

Wailing like a cat run over by a car, she released my weapon, and I dove for it. I gripped the handle and thrust upward, hitting the third vamp in the stomach. He keeled over as I stood. In one fell swoop, I sliced off his head.

Face to face with the final vamp, I smiled. Killing her would be not only justifiable but pleasurable. I brought up my machete and severed her arm. Blood spewed from the wound, wet thuds mingling with her screams. Ignoring her cries, I bent and sliced into her thigh and femur bone, taking off her leg. She went down hard on her remaining knee and fell backward.

I lowered myself to the ground as the blood pooled around us. Her candy-apple lips trembled against her coughing and her gurgled breaths. Her fangs retracted.

"This doesn't belong to you." I slipped the ring off her finger.

A small smile appeared on her paling face. "Kill," she said.

Unsure if that was her dying wish or what she wanted to do to me, and not giving a damn, I gripped the hilt of the weapon and drove it into her chest. Her heart exploded around it, and nothing but ash remained.

When I stood, I saw Jac and Dad looking at me like I had lost my damn mind. Both frozen. The ends of Jac's hair were crusted together in matted nests, her body covered in gore. But Dad's eyes held the weight of the world, fracturing his usual composure.

My heart thumped so loud, I could barely hear myself breathe, "Five." The ring burned in my hands.

"Four," Jac said, looking from Dad to me. Confusion washed over her face.

Dad didn't bother to say three. Instead, he stared at me, at the ring I twirled between my fingers. He knew.

Mom was alive.

29

OLIVIA

Listening to Pepper tell Veronica Hunter's story had the same groggy, surreal quality as waking up from a dream. I could have believed I'd fallen asleep on the living-room couch, reliving nonsensical imaginings from dreamland. Veronica had challenged and slaughtered her alpha to claim the pack for herself about four years ago—only a year after her first full-moon shift. Under her rule, her pack's new creed was to slaughter all monsters except werewolves. It almost sounded funny. She'd kept her hunter mission but made her new species the exception.

Veronica and her pack had taken out over twenty nests in the Midwest region and were making their way south. Unsure of exactly how many vamps that totaled, Reginald rounded up and approximated over a thousand. He might have been impressed with her tenacity, had his daughter not fallen victim to the raids.

"Magda said Reginald's biological daughter, Savannah, was a scholar going to night school for a degree in astrophysics. She, like her father, controlled her feedings for the purpose of survival, not bloodlust. According to Reginald, she was an upstanding citizen with a bright future," Pepper said.

"She was still a vampire," Jac said. She pressed her lips into a tight line. I squirmed, sitting that close to her blood-and-guts-covered clothes. Even her hair had entangled pieces of flesh, dangling like freakish ornaments.

Pepper shrugged. "Maybe they all aren't bad."

Liam's back tensed and his nostrils flared, but he stayed quiet.

Pepper continued: "Reginald has been following Veronica's movements for the last four years, but since she typically killed the lesser vamps, he and his sisters didn't concern themselves with stopping her. However, in the last few months, she started targeting 'his' vamps, as he calls them, which got his attention. Then the death of his daughter triggered him into action. I mean, I guess it would trigger anyone, right?" Pepper gazed around the room looking for confirmation.

Agent Hunter ran a hand over his head to grip his neck. "Yes, that would be a reason for an Origin to get involved." He dropped the hand to his thigh with an audible smack. "Continue."

"Reginald's problem is he can't ever get enough intel to figure out where she'll show up next, and he has no idea how to track her. But he knew you would. That's why he's been trying to find you."

"Anything else, Poppet?" Doc asked, massaging his temples as if he couldn't digest any further information.

"No." Pepper shook her head but avoided eye contact, her trademark tell.

She was holding something back.

Liam, disheveled and blood-covered, stood wordlessly and retreated upstairs to his room. Jac, equally covered in guts and gore, followed in his wake. Neither commented on their mother's story nor asked any questions. They moved like zombies, numb to the implications of Pepper's report.

My eyes tracked Liam out of sight around the upstairs banister. By the time I turned my attention back to the rest of the group, I had missed some crucial information.

Doc stroked his gray beard, shaking his head. "Jackson, you cannot go by yourself," he implored, eyes wide and wild. "It's not safe." He threw his hands into the air. "You don't even know what you're walking into. There are so many variables."

Agent Hunter swallowed, and I could see tension roiling in his shoulders. "I will not subject my kids to seeing their mother as a monster." His Adam's apple bobbed, betraying his stoic expression. "And I need to make sure it's true before I act. I have to go."

So, he was going after his wife. I sat up straighter, my insides churning like choppy waves.

"If Veronica is alive, I don't . . ." Agent Hunter cleared his throat. "Matt, this is asking a lot, but can my kids stay with you while I sort this out? They've got a good thing going here. They're doing well at school." He eyed me. "They've got real friends, a support system. It might be a solid change of pace."

Pepper and I inched to the edge of the couch, drawing Dad's eye. "If it's okay with my girls, it's okay with me."

"Yes," we said in unison.

My clammy palms pressed into my black jeans. We had never wanted them to leave in the first place. Of course, we didn't want them to have to stay for a reason like this, either. My heart broke for the Hunters. Having just laid the spirit of my mother to rest, I knew the turmoil and stabbing heartache of encountering a tainted version of the mother I'd adored. I wouldn't wish it on anyone, much less a family who faced hardship and death on an almost daily basis.

Dad turned to face Doc. "I was actually hoping you'd stay as well. We can turn the basement into a studio apartment and make it a more fitting long-term option. I'm not a contractor, but my guys and I can add a wall and a bathroom. It won't be much, but . . ."

Doc waved my father off. "Nonsense. It would be my pleasure. And we will cover the building costs. Hunterland has the funds intended for things of this nature." He looked at Agent Hunter. "Plus, I'd like to be with William and Jacqueline during this time. We can all operate from here, supporting your search, and work any local cases we may find as well."

Dad walked behind the couch to place his hands on Pepper's shoulders. "I think my daughters need help understanding and honing their new abilities." Dad brushed back Pepper's hair like he had in the days when he still helped us with our ponytails. "And what if Reginald comes back? I wouldn't be able to ward him off alone."

Doc nodded. "I've been mulling over an idea to do just that. I'll make a call and see if I can set it in motion."

"I'll go tell the kids," Agent Hunter said, standing like a mummy fresh from a coffin, shoulders hunched and feet dragging as if this afternoon had aged him a hundred years. "I will be leaving tonight. Doc, please make sure monthly funds are transferred into Matt's account to take care of Liam and Jac's living expenses."

Dad scrunched his eyebrows together and fidgeted. "Normally I'd fight you on redecorating my house or paying for extras, but thank you."

Dad and Agent Hunter reached out to shake hands, then pulled each other into a hug. I hadn't known my dad to make fast friends outside of his deputies, but apparently, he had found some common ground with Liam's father.

I wanted to give the Hunters some space to just . . . exist. So, instead of going upstairs to my room, I followed Doc into the basement.

"Questions, Poppet?" Doc peered over his shoulder, wearing a wry smile.

"Tons," I said. I held my finger up. "But more like a comment for now." I swallowed and paused. "I know who she is." After what transpired at the abandoned warehouse, it had all come together. I wouldn't necessarily call it a vision, but something clicked.

Doc lifted his brow.

I pointed at the sketch pad on his fold-out table next to him. "The beautiful shapeshifter woman is Veronica Hunter. You knew, didn't you?" My insides soured at the thought. I braced myself to stand my ground, no matter how he retorted or threatened or denied, but none came. He only sighed and walked to his makeshift desk, trailing his fingers over the pad's cover. So, he had known this whole time. How could he have kept it from Agent Hunter? Or had he? "Do the Hunters know about your vision?"

Doc shook his head. He took off his coat and hung it over the back of an old cloth recliner. "You'll soon realize, our visions . . . they aren't always the whole picture."

He sat on the stool at his computer. "I saw Veronica as a werewolf, but that was it, no background image, just white, blank space. I couldn't pinpoint a location, tell if she was dangerous or not, nothing to even indicate she was still alive. For all I knew, it was a dream of what could have been, not what she had become."

I picked up the sketchbook and flipped to the third page. The woman's smile, though it marked her as a werewolf, was not malicious or hungry, like the smiles of the vamps I'd encountered. She looked genuinely happy. Her eyes were the spitting image of Liam's, down to their shape, luster, and allure. "When did you have this vision?"

Doc's eyes glossed over. "Once the day I thought she died, and then the first night I arrived in Falkville Falls. I haven't seen her in my premonitions since."

"How is that possible?"

Doc gestured for me to sit in the recliner. "That's why I want to bring someone in to help us. We can't necessarily control our powers of premonition, but maybe with a little expert help, we can understand more."

I scrunched my nose.

"Visions aren't always black-and-white," he elaborated. "The future can change. Context and perspective can blight their clarity. For example, your vision of this evening. Was it correct?" He crossed his arms over his chest.

"Not all of it," I admitted. "The vamp who drove the van wasn't even there."

"Exactly. Maybe he was, right before we got there. Or maybe he only appeared because we received an explanation of why he was driving the van. When we believe we have a lead or know what's about to happen, we have to be careful how we communicate it to others. Once we do, it's like setting it in stone. It's hard to change other people's minds, even if we later learn more illuminating information and come to better understand what we saw. The vision of Veronica was something entirely new for me. No words, scenery, signs, nothing to provide context or surety."

"But it confirmed she was alive and a werewolf. Couldn't you at least have told them that? This whole time, they thought she was dead." Heat flared in the tops of my ears as I put myself in the Hunters' shoes. If it were me, I'd want to know. And I damn well knew that Liam would want the same.

Doc shook his head. "If I'd told Jackson that I had seen his wife as a werewolf, he'd have done exactly what he's doing now: leave his children to look for her. Jacqueline was nine when we lost Veronica, and William was fourteen. They had just started mourning their loving mother. I wasn't going to take their grieving father away as well, leaving them parentless all at once." His throat choked with emotion as he continued: "I made that choice not to deceive, but to protect."

I stood from my chair and walked over to Doc, placing my hand on his shoulder.

"I'm sorry." I squeezed. "I didn't think about it like that. I'm just trying to understand."

"Oh, Poppet, I know," Doc said, patting my hand. "If I could inform Jackson of more, I would, but until I get a clearer picture, it's my choice to keep it hidden from the family."

"I understand," I said. "Maybe I'd have done the same thing." I realized now that having to decipher what to share and what not to share would take time to master.

I left Doc to his work and headed back to my room. At the top of the landing, I heard Agent Hunter, Jac, and Liam arguing. I told myself not to eavesdrop again, but my feet were already tiptoeing closer to the slightly cracked door.

Holding my breath, I caught Liam's rush of words.

"I agree. Jac should stay. I'll pack, and we can get on the road tonight." It sounded like he was shoving items into a bag.

"Stop, son," Agent Hunter said, a gentle tone softening the command. "I need you to stay with Jac and the Davis girls. You are far too valuable to Doc here."

"I'm not letting you go by yourself, old man." Liam's voice faltered, on the brink of crumbling. "You'll need me if it's an entire pack, and if Mom is . . ."

A sob broke over the silence. A girl's cries. Jac's cries.

Liam never finished his sentence. His words were muffled as if someone had pulled him into a hug. Jac's sobs grew louder, and for a second, guilt made me half turn away. I needed to give this family the time alone they deserved. But Liam's voice glued me to my spot.

"Don't do this," Liam pleaded. "You can't face her alone."

Agent Hunter sighed heavily. "I won't do anything without telling you. And if I need you, I will call." There was a long pause. "But Liam, you need to stay here. Pepper is not safe. They will come for her."

I leaned in closer, forfeiting the Hunter family's privacy for the sake of my sister. Who would come for her? What did he mean? My heart pitter-pattered like a frightened mouse racing back to its hole. I'd thought we were past the danger. After all, Pepper had delivered Reginald's message, finally.

"I know," Liam admitted. "Doc will figure something out."

"It's more than that. She trusts them as if she's connected to them somehow. You need to stay here, go through Hunterland lore with Doc. Figure out what her powers can really do and why she's linked to the revenants." All gentleness had momentarily left Agent Hunter's voice.

These were orders. "I love you, kids," he said, voice cracking. "I always will. No matter what."

"Dad," Jac croaked. "Are you going to kill Mom?"

"Oh, Jacqueline, don't do that . . ."

I didn't stay around to hear the rest. Instead, I walked into Pepper's room. She sat on the bed with her tablet in her hand. The bright light shone ghostly blue on her smiling face. My heart sank into my chest. Who could smile like that at a time like this? A normal kid her age would be terrified. Hell, I was scared. "What are you doing?" I asked warily.

"Learning about my powers." She flipped the tablet over and tapped the screen with a nail. "Doc sent me some books about it. Cool, right?"

I couldn't return her enthusiasm. She had no idea the troubles that came along with her abilities. "Good night, Pepper. I love you."

"Love you," she said without looking up. I faltered on my way back toward the door. She hadn't uttered those words in almost three years. If my heart wasn't so heavy, I might have smiled.

Coming back into the hallway, I almost bumped into Agent Hunter. The remnants of his battle with the vamps still covered his clothing, face, and hair. His swollen and red eyes connected with mine.

"Take care of my son," he said, keeping his voice low. He glanced back at their door, where I'd been eavesdropping. "He'll need you, more than he'll ever admit." His shoulders dropped. "And you'll need him. He will protect your family from whatever monsters come your way. And there will be trouble."

I dipped my chin, acknowledging Agent Hunter's warning. Liam would protect us with everything he had and then some. I gently touched his forearm. "If you find her . . .?" I knew it wasn't right for me to ask, but I wanted to understand.

"When I find her," he said, as a muscle in his jaw twitched, "I'll kill her."

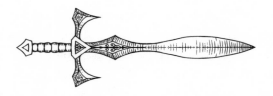

30

LIAM

The bedroom door opened. Without turning around, I knew her by the cadence of her footsteps. Unspoken words hung between us. Tired, beaten, and destroyed inside, I didn't have the energy for anything but a shower and sleep.

Olivia heaved a shaky breath and took another step. I turned to find her holding my father's watch. "Your dad wanted me to give this to you." As I took it, I clicked with my thumb on the app where his name would show his heart rate and location. The screen declared, "No data."

I placed it on the nightstand. Without catching Olivia's eye, I said, "I have to shower." As I passed, she grabbed for my fingers, and our pinkies hooked.

"I am so sorry," she whispered as we lingered there, neither looking at the other.

I nodded.

It was all I could do without breaking down.

The next day, Doc, Pepper, and I sat at the kitchen table in a grim mockery of our previous breakfasts together. My coffee settled poorly in my knotted stomach. Part of me, the little boy who missed his mother, had a sliver of hope that Dad would find Mom—my real mother. That she'd be the same. But the logical hunter part of my brain, the honest part, felt like I had been kicked in the balls. I knew Dad would kill her. She was a monster, after all.

Olivia, Jac, and Sheriff Davis—excuse me, Matt, as we were now supposed to call him—went out for household supplies like soap, toiletries, paper goods, and so on to accommodate the additional three bodies. I had no idea how long we'd be here. But the second Dad sent word he'd found Mom, I'd leave to meet him. I wouldn't let him do this alone.

Brewing questions from the last couple of days, especially from our encounter with the vampires, spun my head. "Pepper," I asked, suspicion narrowing my eyes, "what really happened between you and the vamp woman, Magda, when we first went to the nest?"

She was inhaling the ham, spinach, and cheese omelet with a side of hash browns Doc made for her. "What do you mean?" she asked between bites. "I told you everything yesterday."

I leaned forward, elbows on the table. "She wasn't holding you captive, was she?"

Pepper shook her head no. She cut an enormous bite from her hash browns slab and shoved it into her mouth.

"Then why the ruse?" I pressed, my brows furrowed. If she hadn't been holding her for ransom, what was the vamp doing with Pepper? And why had Pepper trusted her?

"She was trying to keep you safe. She just put her hands on my shoulders so you'd *think* she had me captive, but she stayed to make sure the vampires wouldn't hurt you. Like I said yesterday, she needed me to get a message to your family, and she had specific orders that your family be unharmed."

"What happened to her then? Why did she take her own life?"

"Magda had been living as a good vamp for a long time, until she ran out of blood." Pepper scrunched her nose like the words tasted coppery on her tongue. She scooped her fork under the eggs and wrapped the melted cheese around the prongs before taking another bite. "Most of the vamps at that nest were good once. But in desperation, they killed one human to feed, and then another, and I don't know. I guess that's how they become bad." Her eyes lit up. "Like spirits when they're here too long."

"Sure, just like spirits," I said sarcastically. I leaned back in my chair and shook my head. Pepper's reactions to the events of the last month were sometimes scarier than the revenants. Spirits and vamps had nothing in common except that they were monsters, and it was our job to kill them.

"Actually, Pepper, that's a great analogy," Doc interrupted. He kicked me under the table. "Tell us more."

Pepper sat up straighter and released her fork onto the plate, excitement sparkling in her eyes. "Magda was part of Reginald's clan. But she got addicted to feeding out of bloodlust. She was becoming too thirsty and couldn't speak as well as she once could."

Okay, now this was getting interesting. Tall, dark, and Fangsome hadn't been lying. There really was a lot we didn't know about vamps.

"Why did she care about us though? Who told her to keep us safe?"

"Her master. Reginald needs you alive to help him with your mom," Pepper said with sad eyes. "I'm sorry about that, by the way."

"It's okay," I said, and I meant it.

Pepper and Olivia had just gone through this same heartache with their mom. How could I fault her for wanting to save us from the same fate? But even though I understood, I'd wanted to strangle Pepper for her omissions off and on for the last twenty-four hours.

"Okay, so back to the original question. Why did she kill herself in the end?" I asked. None of this made any sense.

"Because she didn't like what she had become, and she didn't want to get any worse. She never wanted to be a lesser vampire. When she asked to be immortal, she hadn't signed up for bloodlust." Pepper took another bite of her eggs. Through a mouthful of food, she continued: "Plus, once she did what her master told her to do, he said she could die."

Doc and I exchanged a look. Pepper was in way over her head. What she'd really said was that Reginald used his powers of persuasion to force Magda to postpone her wishes until she found one of us. How long had she been looking? I knew Pepper didn't have the answer, but I wished I could find out. Then it made me wonder how many vamps out there were looking for us. How safe were we?

"Pepper, would you like to help me with a spell later?" Doc asked.

She popped up like a jack-in-the-box. "That is so cool. Yes, yes, yes!"

"Great. William, why don't you spend some time with Olivia today while Jacqueline and I teach Pepper a protection spell?"

I wanted to roll my eyes right out of my head. Doc couldn't be more obvious. But Pepper seemed unaware. He would be cloaking her from other revenants. For good reason too. Pepper believed anything they told her, like she was forged to them somehow.

I retreated to the family room to watch *Full Metal Jacket*, one of my faves. Getting lost in old movies, like the ones Mom used to watch, shut off grim reality for roughly two blissful hours.

The front door opened. Olivia, Jac, and Matt walked in with groceries.

"Hey." Olivia plopped on the couch beside me, dipping the cushion.

"Hey," I said, not taking my eyes off the screen.

Her intense gaze warmed the side of my head. She wanted to talk. "Jessica's funeral is tomorrow," she whispered. "It still doesn't feel real."

"I'm sorry," I said. I knew how hard all of this was on her and I wished I had more poetic words, but words are not my strong suit.

"I'm really sorry about . . ."

I glared at her, enraged by her pity. If she finished that sentence with "your mother," I was going to lose it. Already I struggled to breathe, my throat closing. Talking about my mother was off-limits.

Olivia read my face and started to stand. Before she could, I reached for her hand and pulled her back down. There were other ways to find comfort than talking.

"You ever see this movie before?" I asked.

She shook her head.

I folded her into my side, and she rested her cheek on my chest. Her breath warmed me. I inhaled her sage-and-vanilla scent as I slowly stroked her arm. "Good." I kissed the top of her head as my free hand slipped into hers. "I expect to have a lot of firsts with you, starting with *Full Metal Jacket*."

Olivia gazed up and smiled. It didn't reach her eyes, but it was a start.

Later that night, while everyone slept, I heard my door creak open. Light footsteps sounded across my floor.

"Should I be grabbing my gun?" I whispered, peeling one eye open. Olivia stood in a long T-shirt at the edge of my bed. Her glassy eyes shone in the moonlight from the window. Tears coated her cheeks.

I opened the covers, and she crawled in. Her body wrapped around mine, and she pressed her head under my chin. Her sobs vibrated my chest. We had found sanctuary in each other's arms in the last couple of weeks, and although I couldn't promise her any type of future, I could make the most of our present.

Tomorrow would be hard. It wasn't often a teenager buried their best friend. I kissed her forehead and stroked her back until our breaths mingled, and sleep found us both.

When the sunlight hit, my eyes fluttered open and nearly popped out of my head. Olivia was still curled in my arms, but Matt towered over us.

"Are you two out of your ever-living minds? Under my roof, with Pepper and Jacqueline in the house?" Matt's face burned fuchsia. "Are you trying my patience because you think I haven't endured enough?"

"Dad?" Olivia woke with a little inhale, head swiveling and eyes half-lidded, not recognizing where she was at first. Then she jumped. "Oh my God, Dad! What are you . . .?" She pulled the covers up to her chin.

"What am I?" Matt thundered.

I rubbed the sleep out of my eyes. *This is gonna be fun.* A good night's sleep was impossible to find in the Davis house. How motel beds filled with pointy springs could give me a better night's rest, I'd never understand. At least at extended stays I got some shut-eye.

Summoned by the commotion, Pepper and Jac ran into the room. Both girls stifled their laughter under their hands, and Olivia let out a groan, fingers covering her face.

"Get up, both of you," Matt yelled.

"Dad, can you give us a second?"

"Give *you* a second?" Matt raked his hair, looking to the ceiling like he might find restraint or some divine strength there.

A rogue chuckle escaped my mouth.

"This isn't funny," Olivia said, smacking my bare chest.

"Olivia, get up!"

Matt poked his finger at me. "And you, young man, are now living under my roof with my rules, and this"—Matt waved his hands—"is definitely on the list of nevers. You will sleep in your own bed."

"Technically, this is his bed," Pepper said, jumping onto the mattress and curling her legs underneath her. "Dad, you're acting so lame. Is it really a big deal?" She rolled her eyes. "It's not like this is the first time, anyway."

"Pepper!" Jac, Olivia, and I yelled.

31

OLIVIA

A month passed, and although Jessica's funeral would forever be one of my life's darkest, most painful moments, Dustin and I were starting to heal. Jac and Liam fell into a rhythm at school. Every day, little by little, they released some of their anger toward their father for leaving. He called and checked in every Tuesday and Friday evening like clockwork. For the first two weeks, Liam wouldn't talk to him, but last week, he took the phone from Jac and reported like a lieutenant to his sergeant about a possible monster case in the area, fifty miles south of Falkville Falls. I think it was his way of saying he missed him. He might not have been happy with Agent Hunter's decision to leave, but he could at least talk shop and move on.

Pepper soared on cloud nine. So far, Doc had succeeded in protecting her from spirits, dimming the voices in her head. Every day after school, they devoted two hours to reading lore on psychics, confident they'd find a more permanent form of protection than a simple spell. Pepper spent more time in the basement now with Doc than we had our entire lives. And every Saturday and Sunday, we'd have Hunterland classes, learning more about monsters, how to kill them, and what to look out for. I still didn't feel like I had anything significant to add, nothing like Pepper did. I hadn't had a vision since I dreamed about the abandoned warehouse, but Doc said he wasn't worried. At my age, I was still growing into my abilities.

Today, Dustin and I walked down the hallway, and as we cut through the main lobby, my gaze traveled to the ceiling. It was comforting to know I'd never have to come across another teacher hanging there. Yet, it didn't take away from the ache of Jessica's absence between us as we passed the spot where she and I had found Mr. Kline.

"What should we call the foundation?" Dustin asked. We'd begun work to start a charity in Jessica's name. Tiffany had been the one to initially suggest it, but because she lived so far away from Jessica's friends and family, she asked that we take the lead. I was grateful Dustin had been the one to tell her about the accident. Tiffany surprised us all with her strength and support.

"Maybe we could call it—" I yelped when I felt a squeeze on my left butt cheek. I spun. A grinning Liam stood behind me.

I cocked a hand to my hip, giving him a fake scowl. He pulled me into an embrace, arms around my waist.

"Can you two just get a room already and be done with it?" Dustin said, rolling his eyes. "You can cut the sexual tension in here with one of Liam's knives."

I pushed Dustin's shoulder, and he feigned a hurt expression.

"Your room or mine?" Liam said, rubbing his knuckles down my jawbone. Amusement danced behind his piercing blue eyes. In another week, he'd be living on the lower level. Dad had decided to turn his study into Liam's bedroom and give Jacqueline the guestroom upstairs so she didn't have to sleep on an air mattress anymore. I doubt a floor would keep Liam and I apart. Most nights, I'd sneak into his bed and then I'd leave in the morning before Dad woke up. We hadn't hooked up since that first night I'd crawled under his covers, but we had found comfort in each other's arms.

"You are so bad," I said, trying to wiggle out of his hug.

His gaze locked on my mouth, and my body seized. I instinctively nibbled my bottom lip, a too-frequent slip lately. He freed the lip with his thumb and ran the pad to the corner of my mouth, where he lingered.

"Why do you resist me?" He pulled me in tighter, playfully fighting my lame attempt to shed his warm, muscular arms.

A goofy grin tugged at the corners of my mouth. "Because we decided to go slow," I said, finally breaking free.

"There's no *we* in that. It's just *you!*" he teased.

I'd realized we had a pattern of hooking up when I was aching and avoiding reality. I didn't want Liam to just be a distraction. Eventually, I wanted more, but after everything that had happened, we both needed to slow it down.

"Literally, you two make me sick." Dustin jabbed his finger in his mouth, pretending to gag. "Pizza night like usual?"

It wasn't really a question, but I said yes anyway. It had become our Friday tradition. Doc would make us homemade pizza, new toppings every week. Pepper had deemed herself Doc's sous chef and helped at every meal. She had set the smoke alarm off twice, but hey, she wasn't vandalizing buildings anymore, so Dad and I were happy.

"Yeah, buddy. See you tonight," Liam said, patting Dustin's back. "I'm thinking *Lethal Weapon* as our movie choice."

"Oh, hell yeah! Eighties action movie theme." Dustin tossed his bag over his shoulder and started down the hallway.

As if we ever had any *other* theme.

Once Dustin was out of earshot, Liam leaned in. "You ready for this weekend?" He raised his brow.

Agent Hunter and my dad wanted Liam to start training Pepper and I in self-defense. They were both worried other monsters might target Pepper for her powers or that Reginald would return. Starting this weekend, we would be adding combat lessons to our weekly supernatural repertoire. To think, months ago, I'd walked down this hall and seen a dead teacher hanging from the ceiling and thought that would be the most disturbing encounter of my life. Now I'd be training to combat the things that go bump in the night.

"Not really," I groaned. More like dreading it, in fact. I'd used every excuse in the book to get out of gym class, and now I had somehow signed up for weekend workouts during my free time. Ew.

"Think of it as an excuse for me to put my hands all over your body," Liam's lips curved into a seductive grin.

I rolled my eyes in mock annoyance as I opened my locker. As I pulled out my science notebook, a girl's screech echoed down the hall. "William!" I peeked around my locker door.

As if in slow motion, Liam turned, and a beautiful girl with a waterfall of hazelnut curls and doe-ish green eyes jumped into his arms. She wrapped her smooth, dark legs around his waist and kissed his cheeks, forehead, chin, and nose as if making the sign of the cross. Not his lips, thankfully. To my freaking surprise, Liam laughed, accepting her peppering of pecks.

"Jazzy," he said, shock lacing his voice. He wasn't the only one surprised. My mouth hung open a good two inches. "What the hell are you doing here?" He spun with her in his arms.

Another squeal erupted, this time from Jac. She barreled down the hallway and threw her arms around Liam and the insanely pretty girl still in his embrace.

"I've missed you buggers." She had a British accent. *Great.* The perfect posh accessory to her sex appeal.

"We missed you," Jac screamed, jumping up and down. "I can't believe you're here!"

The British beauty caught my scornful stare from her elevated height. I willed Liam to put her down. "And who is this? She's a peng ting. Right up my alley." She cocked her head at me. "You single, love?" she asked, shooting me a cheeky wink, not unlike something I'd expect from Liam.

I stammered.

Liam chuckled as she slid down his body. *Finally!* "I don't think you play for the same team, but you can always try and change her mind." Liam leaned against the lockers. His gaze volleyed between us as he crossed his arms, stretching his T-shirt against his lithe muscles.

"Oh, bugger off, you daft wanker." Accent girl extended her hand. "It's Jaeleah, but my mates call me Jazzy." Her hungry eyes bored into me.

"Jazzy's part of Hunterland, like us," Jac explained with a knowing look I could have done without.

I relaxed slightly, knowing she was more into me than Liam and that she was a part of their world, but a twinge of jealousy still lingered in the pit of my stomach from their familiarity. I reached out and shook her hand.

"I'm Olivia, but my friends call me Liv or Livy." I squinted at Liam. "Except this one. For some reason, he calls me Olivia."

"Ahhhh, does he now?" Jazzy looked Liam up and down. Her nose twitched. "You got a thing for her, mate?"

A muscle ticked in Liam's jaw. Before he could answer or even play it off, another voice trickled down the hallway, stinging my ears.

"Well, well, William Hunter. How are you surviving without me?"

My gaze shifted over everyone's heads. If I'd thought Jazzy was pretty, this girl put her to shame. Gorgeous jade eyes stared right into Liam's as she swayed her curvaceous body like a strutting lioness. Her darker skin made her features pop as if highlighted by a real-life filter. Her black knee-high boots complemented her barely-there skirt, and her emerald shirt looked painted on.

Was this girl even real?

Jac grumbled, "I forgot you were a matching set."

Jazzy laughed and threw her arm around Jac. "I try at least once a day to forget myself, mate." She gave her a squeeze before letting go.

Like the Red Sea, Falkville Falls students parted the hallway for her grand entrance. Every eye stared, guys and girls alike, as she passed by.

A marching band could have struck up a tune in the corridor and she'd still command all the attention.

Liam's jaw tensed as he pressed his lips into a straight line, his eyes like daggers.

"Look what the cat dragged in." Jac's voice could cut glass. She crossed her hands over her winter-white sweater, her fingers tapping against her biceps. "Nicolina."

"Jacqueline, you look smashing, love. Finally filling out your tops, I see."

Jac glared in fuming silence.

Nicolina walked right up to Liam and ran her fingers through his hair, planting a chaste kiss on his lips. He grabbed her wrists, lowering them, and put space between their mouths. I wanted to high-five him, and more pressing, slap the crap out of her.

"We need to work on your hellos," he quipped. His mouth twisted, as if he was stifling harsher words. Both Hunter siblings were holding back. I wondered why.

"I don't know. I seem to recall you pinning my wrists above my head and rather enjoying it before. I'd say this is a good start, love. Shall we find a place to lie down or do you want to continue this upright?" she purred.

The blood drained from my face, pooling in my chest and clogging my arteries.

Liam smirked but said nothing. He released her hands and took a step back.

A pang of jealousy pinched my heart as a thousand questions assaulted me. Who was she? Where did she come from? And how did she know Liam? All were terrific starts, but I had plenty more.

Darkened eyes stared back at me beneath perfectly shaped brows puckered in disapproval. They were delicate, unlike her personality, and a shade or two darker than the curly hair falling off her shoulders. She cocked her hand on her hip, sporting a deep scowl.

"Who's this?" She pointed at me with her free hand.

I looked from her to Liam. Her gaze followed. The bravado I'd gained in the last several weeks deflated while hers seemed to kick up a notch with my unease. Her lips peeled upward, showcasing her pearly white teeth.

Nicolina laughed, breaking the tense moment. "You can put the claws away, love. Just 'cause he shagged you once doesn't mean he's yours." She flashed a wicked grin, lashes veiling lustful eyes. "If that were the case, he'd be mine a thousand times over." She turned to croon to Liam. "Over and over and over again."

My blood boiled.

"Knock it off, Nikki," Liam said. I couldn't be sure if he was defending me, him, or us. At this point, I was just happy we appeared to be on the same side.

"Oh, come on, mate, just having a little fun. I missed you," she cooed, feigning innocence.

To my surprise, Liam's face softened. "We missed you girls too. It's good to see you."

"That's my fella." She blew him a kiss.

Liam placed his hand on my lower back, steadying me. "Nikki, this is Olivia Davis." Liam turned his head toward me. "Olivia, this is Nikki, Jazzy's twin sister." He looked from one girl to the other. "They have nothing in common but their last name and their uncle—you call him Doc."

Jazzy winked.

Nikki rolled her eyes.

I nodded but kept quiet.

Liam asked Jazzy, "So, what's up? Why are you here?"

She looped arms with Jac and pulled her into her side. "Uncle Harold didn't tell you?" She appraised them both.

Liam lifted his brow as Jac shook her head.

"We're here to train the Davis girls," Jazzy said.

Nikki flipped her hair over her shoulder and shot me a conspiratorial smirk. "Welcome to Hunterland, Poppet. Hope you survive."

ACKNOWLEDGMENTS

First and foremost, I have to thank you, the reader, for picking up *Hunterland* and diving into this supernatural world. Without you, Liam and Olivia's story would not be heard. I must warn you though. Reading *Hunterland* may cause supernatural visitations, the need to stock up on rock salts and stakes, protective crystals, and stone purchases, an addiction to investigating unexplainable crime stories, and a craving for more *Hunterland* Lore. Just kidding. Or am I? But seriously, I am so grateful you have chosen to take this journey with me. Thank you from the bottom of my heart.

Secondly, I have to thank Jennifer Eaton who has taught me more about creative writing than anyone and has challenged my writing every step of the way. Jennifer, you are an incredible developmental editor and book coach. Thank you for all your feedback and unadulterated honesty.

Hannah Sandoval, I love that you come to the call of my notes when I scream help in the columns because I'm desperate. When I think of you, I immediately picture a life raft. Thank you for always coming to my aid. You are my wordsmith Queen.

Kristen Roberts, my alpha reader and first book friend. How did I get so lucky? You were the first person to read *Hunterland* and tell me it was something special. Thank you for all your excitement. It made everything that followed my rough draft so much easier.

Everyone at CamCat Books! Thank you for your patience and enthusiasm for *Hunterland*. I am so excited that this book has such an amazing home and team behind it.

The Next Step PR firm! Thank you for always being in my corner, and for always keeping me and *Hunterland's* marketing strategy on track. I love you ladies like the soul sisters we are!

My author friends, especially Jennifer Shore, Eva Pohler, Wendy Higgins, Jane Washington, Lynn Rush, and Cameo Renae, who took the time to read *Hunterland* before it was polished and provide me with such superlative reviews. I'm beyond grateful you took a chance on me and dove into my story.

And lastly, my biggest thank yous go to my father and to my husband, my rocks.

My father was the first person to introduce me to the magical world of wonder through books, movies, TV, and characters. Throughout my formidable years, we would get lost in fantastical worlds together. And to this day, my father is my biggest cheerleader, handling both parental roles ever since my mother passed away. Without my father, I wouldn't believe in the impossible. And because of him, I'll never stop reaching for the stars.

To my husband, Jason. You are weaved into my soul. Thank you for playing *Call of Duty* next to me in our office so we can be together when I write. Thank you for ignoring the light from my kindle when I'm reading while you sleep. Thank you for loving me for exactly who I am and showing me the real-life version of romance. You and I will always be the best love story of all.

About the Author

Dana Claire is an award-winning author whose stories explore identity, fate, and destiny in the crossroads of romance and adventure. But her writing career didn't begin when she published her first book, *The Connection*, in 2020. It started as a young girl when her mother, an elementary school teacher, inspired her to create imaginary worlds between the pages. Dana's love of romantic tension, the supernatural, and non-stop action has elicited positive feedback from many readers, as their online reviews reveal her flair for spine-tingling action and unforgettable characters. But it's not just readers who love her; literary critics have also taken note, and Dana was given the Children's Moonbeam award for *The Connection* in 2021.

Dana is now sharing her stories through speaking events and book signings, introducing more readers to the worlds she created. Dana is living her dream as a published author: seeing her name on the spine of a book, creating worlds that combine love, science fiction, the paranormal, magic, and adventure, and fulfilling what her well-read, compassionate, patient, and selfless mother would have dreamed of doing with her: writing books, telling stories, and changing the world, one reader at a time.

If you enjoyed

Dana Claire's *Hunterland*,

you'll enjoy

Our Vengeful Souls by Kristi McManus.

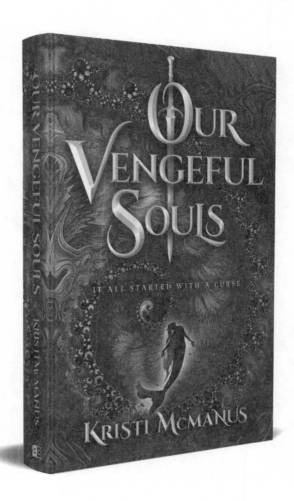

Chapter One

Our swords collide with a deafening crash, sparks sizzling and dying in the water as the blades strain against each other. The moment they touch, they break apart again like opposing magnets never able to resist each other, yet never able to truly connect.

I pivot quickly, narrowly missing Triton's next strike as the blade swings by my cheek. The disturbed water brushes softly against my skin like a caress, but warning sings in my veins of how close he came to spilling my blood.

Spinning to face him again, I clutch my weapon with both hands, fingers tightening along the hilt as I eye my prey. His tail is curved, coiled like an eel preparing to strike as he takes inventory of me just as I am of him. His cerulean blue eyes are narrowed, lips parted, muscles tense. His chest heaves, panting breath escaping through clenched teeth, evidence that he is winded. The longer we face off, the angrier he becomes. Not at me, necessarily, but at himself for taking so long to defeat me.

We've been at this for hours, barely allowed a moment to rest. Not that either of us would admit to needing one. To require rest would be to admit weakness, that the other is skilled enough to push us to our limits. Such a concession is unacceptable. Beyond our teachings of strength and focus, our endless hours in this ring, our pride is the strongest factor in our stamina.

We never back down from each other.

He surges forward through the water without warning, blade poised overhead in his iron grip, ready to hand out a match ending strike, but I am faster, lithe and swift, bringing my sword up to block the impact inches from my face.

Rather than retreat again, continuing our dance, he remains poised above me, his superior height blocking the few rays of light piercing through the water until he is little more than a silhouette before my eyes. His blade presses against my own, metal grinding in protest, neither of us relenting.

My muscles quiver at the effort it takes to keep him at bay. They burn with an exquisite pain, reminding me that I am alive, that I am powerful. My teeth grind, lips curling back as I stand my ground. I see a glint of light reflect off the steel in my hands, shaking as I resist the possibility of defeat.

His full lips curve into a grin, teeth grinding despite the playful, goading gesture. Golden hair spills from the tie at the nape of his neck, dancing around his face, catching the light from the surface. The sharp jaw and angular features that cause the other mermaids to swoon are tense with the effort of our fight.

"Tired, Sister?" he asks coolly. Despite his attempt to appear indifferent, the lines of his face are hard, his jaw tense. He is struggling. Weakening. The realization causes my lips to quirk into a smile to match his own.

"Not at all, dear Brother." Bringing my face closer to his, and in turn, closer to our connected blades, magic prickles beneath my skin. Strands of my white blonde hair wave around me like a crown under the influence of the sea, my green eyes burning into his. "I will endure as long as you require. I wouldn't want to bow down too soon, thus not giving our precious heir a suitable sparring partner."

My taunt does as I hope, his teeth snapping as a growl erupts deep in the back of his throat. The moment I feel the pressure of his sword weaken, I strike, swiping my tail outward and knocking him off balance. He collides to the sea floor with a thunderous impact, sand and stone billowing out from around his prone form. Pride sings through my muscles, burning away the exhaustion. Putting Triton to the ground never ceases to thrill me, no matter how many times I best him.

A gasp ripples from those around us, the select permitted to watch us train. A few of the maids present, hovering in the corner to gawk and swoon at my brother, cover their mouths in horror. His muscular frame lays sprawled across the floor, hair once smooth and controlled, now wild and loose in the gentle current. No longer does he look as pristine and perfect now that I have cracked his confidence.

This area of the palace is restricted for most. Beyond the coral halls and glistening stone floors of the living quarters, banquet halls and meeting rooms, rests the arena in which we barter our worth. Sand floors and towering stone walls breaking to an oculus ceiling high above, allowing the remaining reach of the days sun to breach to our depth. It is an expanse of weapons edging every wall, blades and staffs, all with the singular purpose of training the royals.

Casting a glance to the edge of the hall, I find my parents lingering in the shadows. Their scales glitter, catching the light like precious gems, brighter than those around them. Even without their crowns, they exude regal poise. Something I have yet to master.

Looking their way is a mistake, of course. A weakness I repeatedly chastise myself for, as it never provides the assurance I hope. And yet, every time I force Triton to his knees, I cannot help but look for a sign of approval.

My mother watches with keen green eyes, the kind of look that makes you feel as though she is cutting right through your soul. Her hair, the same white blonde as my own, plaited down her back, is contrasted against the deep greens of her sea lace top. Long sleeves adorned with pearls cling to her slender, envious frame, the neck high to her jaw. Her skin shimmers like diamonds are embedded in her skin, a symbol of our kind, luminous and beckoning. She is stunning, her mere presence demanding attention and respect. And her hypnotizing gaze is locked on me, a proud smile toying with the corner of her coral lips.

Against my better judgment, I allow myself a glance at my father. He is as I expect to find him; jaw tight and teeth clenched, his deep blue eyes locked on the shape of his eldest son and heir pushing up from the ground. Displeasure radiates off his form, causing the water around him to ripple against his power. When his eyes turn to me, I do not see pride. I see fury, barely concealed.

He isn't proud that his daughter is a skilled fighter. No more than he is proud that my magic exceeds that of my brother. He is angry that I dare embarrass him by putting Triton on his back.

My confidence wavers under his stare, grip weakening on the hilt of my sword.

The momentary distraction is all Triton needs. I feel the water move before I see him from the corner of my eye. By the time I tighten my hands around my sword, steady my stance, he collides with me, knocking the air from my lungs.

His massive weight knocks me back, forcing me to drop my blade rather than end up on the ground. I backflip out of the fall, landing coiled and ready to respond to his next attack, but he doesn't retreat or pause his pursuit, satisfied with disarming me. Instead, his large hand grips my throat, throwing my body to the floor painfully, his blade poised above my heart.

Breath knocks from my lungs at the impact of the ground at my back, bones aching in protest and muscles burning.

My hands grapple at his arm, body writhing against the weight pinning me, but it is no use. He has won.

A smile curves his lips as he loosens his hold on my neck. "Always so easily distracted," he taunts, running the blade along my cheek like a lover's touch. "Well done, baby sister."

I growl, unable to form words, as he pushes up and releases me. Soft applause fills the hall as he swims away, arms raised above his head, relishing his victory, the muscles of his back flexing with each flick of his tail. The maids in the corner of the arena titter as he comes their way, running their fingers through their hair, their tails swaying seductively.

I lay on the floor a moment longer, my eyes trained skyward, through the oculus to where the sun dances beyond the surface of the water. Its brightness is muted at this depth, battling against the power of the sea. The sand is soft at my back, like a gentle touch consoling my loss. From where I lay, I cannot see the walls of the arena for the open ceiling, the ombre blues of the ocean leading to a world beyond this one. From here, I can almost pretend I am somewhere else.

Rubbing my face with my hands, I exhale a long breath before pushing up and accepting my defeat.

I don't look their way, but in my peripheral vision I can see my father clapping Triton on the back, congratulating him for his win. My jaw clicks against the force of my teeth biting together. It doesn't matter that I had him on the ground, or that I could have ended the match in my favor more than once. All that matters is, in the end, Triton was victorious.

That is all that ever matters to him.

Swimming off the floor, I head towards the exit, desperate to make it back to my quarters. All I want now is quiet, solace, to collect myself and my pride. Fury ignites the spark within me, and I can feel my magic simmer under my skin. Flexing my fingers, it crackles as it comes alive, whispering consolation and reminders of where my true power lies.

Before I can escape, I am met by my mother at the edge of the hall.

"You did wonderfully, Sereia." Her hands reach out to tuck a lock of my hair behind my ear. She usually scolds me for allowing my hair to be loose, reminding me of the expectation that it be tied and tamed rather than left wild and free. Today it would seem she recognizes the dent to my pride, and holds her tongue.

"I lost, Mother." The words are bitter on my tongue. I run my fingers over the scales of my tail, feeling each ridge, watching the iridescent colors merge from blue to green to purple. I lose myself in the tactile sensation, grounding myself and my body.

I am powerful, I remind myself silently, a chanting prayer to sooth my honor. *I am strong. I have magic beyond his wildest dreams.*

"Only because you allowed yourself to be distracted," Mother says gently, pulling me from my thoughts. "You lost focus, allowing Triton to take advantage. If you had remained in the ring, both mind and body, I have no doubt-"

"No doubt that Father would have continued the match until I was weakened, exhausted and breathless, so Triton could use his strength to win."

Her lips curve downward, the green of her eyes darkening. "Never allow yourself to dwell, Sereia. Whether Triton is meant to be victorious is irrelevant. It does not diminish your skill, or your worth."

Looking up from under my lashes, I find my brother and father conversing with a member of the council. No doubt already deep in conversation about kingdom matters. Things that my sister and I are not privy to.

I cannot help but wonder what my father would have done if I had been the first born. If rather than a son born in his likeness, a daughter bright and powerful were his heir?

Would he still dismiss me? Think me nothing more than breeding stock to his line?

Following my gaze, my mother's lips purse.

"Your brother may be superior in strength, my daughter," her voice breaks me away from the sight. "But you harness the most potent magic of us all. While he excels in the ring, you strike fear and power through your gifts in a way no one else in our history ever has. Never doubt yourself, Sereia."

I nod in silent agreement, ready to change the subject as my eyes skim the room.

"Where is Asherah?" I ask, pulling my shoulders back to straighten my spine. I refuse to appear defeated, for others to see me cower, even if my soul wishes to escape and lick my wounds.

Mother's lips twitch. "Off on another adventure, I'm sure."

A single laugh escapes me. "If Triton or I ran off so frequently, we would have been dealt the whip," I remind her with a quirked brow.

Mother waves her hand dismissively. "You seem to forget all the trouble your brother and you got into when you were her age. Just because you are of age now, don't fool yourself to think you were never as tenacious as her. You were hardly obedient or cautious."

I snort in response, but don't bother arguing. It would be pointless. Memories of breaching the boundaries of the kingdom, venturing into the darkest depths of the sea were still fresh in my mind. With Triton at my side, I was fearless. Unshakeable.

Just as he stood taller knowing I had his back, that nothing could defeat us when together.

It felt like a century ago. When our childhood was still filled with freedom and possibility, and the expectations of our birthrights felt like a far-off dream. Before we were pitted against each other, the heir versus the girl who grudgingly held the position of spare.

"You let her run wild like a hellion," I point out gently, earning myself a soft look of warning from my mother. I smile innocently, but continue. "She's still a princess. Anything could happen—"

My words are cut off by a flurry of raised voices, the swishing of tails in the corner of the arena. Breaking my gaze from my mother, I watch as a group of guards approach my father, their faces hard. Their golden armour catches the dying rays of sun from the surface, the dark obsidian scales of their tails marking their rank imposing in contrast.

MORE YOUNG ADULT TITLES FROM CAMCAT PUBLISHING

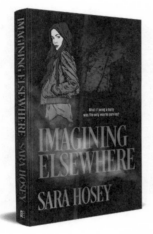

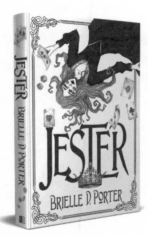

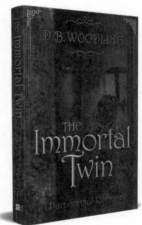

Available now, wherever books are sold.